# THE LOST EPISODES OF REVIE BRYSON

## BRYAN FURUNESS

Black Lawrence Press

Black Lawrence Press
www.blacklawrence.com

Executive Editor: Diane Goettel
Cover design: Rebecca Maslen
Book design: Pam Golafshar / Rebecca Maslen
Author photo: Miriam Berkley

Black Lawrence Press
326 Bigham Street
Pittsburgh, PA 15211

Published 2012 by Black Lawrence Books, an imprint of Dzanc Books
Printed in the United States

*For Shelly*

# Section 1
## Crucifixion

# Chapter 1

The year I turned twelve, I believed I was the second coming of Christ. I have a good guess about how I came up with this idea, but it's harder to say what sustained the belief beyond an initial *What if*? Nothing about me suggested divinity. Apart from my overdeveloped imagination, I was a pretty normal kid: skinny, buzz cut, prone to daydreams, but still a B student because my teachers preferred my occasional catatonia to the spastic violence (bloody knuckles, wet willies) displayed by my classmates.

The fact that I had lived for eleven years without so much as a hint of holiness did not dissuade me. After all, the first Jesus didn't find out his true identity until he was twelve.

According to my mother, anyway, who made up Bible stories.

Actually, she claimed that her stories were chapters of the original Bible that hadn't made the final cut, but even I could tell she'd made them up. Her "lost episodes" were mostly about the boyhood of Jesus, but they featured cars, steel mills, and transistor radios among other artifacts not generally associated with life at the outset of *Anno Domini*. Her Jesus watched *Cheers* while halfheartedly strumming his electric guitar. I might not have grown up in the church, but even I knew that Christ did not come of age in the mid-eighties in Paris, Indiana.

Still, her lost episodes were not easily dismissed. My mother's imagination was a swirling galaxy, and her stories were spirits moving over the face of the deep, calling forms out of the void. Wild as prophecy and seemingly just as coded, her stories told a truth deeper than reality.

She never actually told me I was the second coming—not in so many words—but nevertheless, this was the message I took from her stories. Her Jesus felt as real and recognizable as a lost twin. It never occurred to me that she might have modeled Jesus on me. I was certain I'd been modeled on him.

Summer evenings, while my mother watched videos and my father gave private golf lessons, I sat in my darkening bedroom and listened for the voice of God in the distant wail of trains. Headlights from passing cars streaked across my bedroom wall like comets, those old harbingers of fate. Laying my hand on an alphabet puzzle, I waited for Holyghost to guide me, like Ouija.

Whenever I considered my destiny as the second coming, my scalp prickled wildly. In fact, my whole body felt charged with electricity, individual hairs rising like antennae to receive the signal. In those moments that I understood as a foretaste of my divine power, I would be tempted to try out a miracle—just a small one, like turning bath water to cherry Kool-Aid—but I held back because I knew this tingling wasn't the real thing. Not yet. These little bursts of ecstasy were sent to gauge my readiness, like tests of the emergency broadcast system.

The feeling could come over me anytime: while I was tying action figures to bottle rockets before sending them to their glorious, fiery demise. *I am the Lord; feel my wrath.* Or caddying for my father. *I walked among you, and yea, you knew me not.* Or when my mother was telling me about the Adventures of Holyghost, a name she pronounced as one word, like Superman. *Anoint me, Holyghost.*

Did my mother know the effect her stories had on me? She'd grown up reading palms at county fairs and flea markets; she knew the human condition inclines toward faith. "You don't have to make people believe," she'd told me more than once. "You just have to let them."


The old part of Paris, where we lived, was a spread of sooty ranches for teachers and mill workers, though there were fewer of the latter every year. Each layoff at the mills in nearby Gary was said to be the last one—*now* they were efficient, *now* they could compete with that cheap Japanese shit—until the next last layoff a few months later.

But even as blight ate through Gary, new subdivisions sprang up around the larger Calumet Region featuring houses with three-car garages and in-ground swimming pools. Low taxes and depressed real estate values made the Region an idyllic bedroom community for Chicago, or so the new billboards claimed. A lot of regionnaires resented the growing population of FIPs (fucking Illinois people), but FIPs were good for my father's business, what with laid-off mill workers not exactly chasing him down for a private lesson to straighten out their slices.

But every real estate boom, no matter how successful, has its washouts. A few blocks south of my house was an aborted development that everyone called Napalm Alley, because it looked like scorched earth. The developer had barely managed to clearcut the parcel and pave a few roads before all his heavy equipment got repo'd.

Most adults called the site an eyesore, but for my friends and me, it was a soundstage for the movie that was our lives. The beauty of Napalm Alley was its blankness. *Terra rasa.* It could become anything. On the empty roads, my friend Woz and I mounted bicycles and jousted with giant Tinkertoy lances. We conducted experiments, such as belching into an empty tennis can, then sealing it up quick and tossing it in a shallow hole. "Ten years from now," said Woz, "we can dig it up and smell that very burp."

And Napalm Alley, with its paved roads and relative lack of obstacles, was the perfect location for my mother to teach me how to drive.

Apparently, giving your keys to an eleven-year-old was not unusual where she grew up, south of Paris in the ocean of corn that seemed to make up the rest of Indiana. "All the farm kids drove," she told me at the start of my first lesson. "Now give her a little gas."

I was not a farm kid. My only driving experience had been the bumper cars at Kiddieland, where I routinely got my car stuck in a corner for other children to ram with glee. Now I was behind the wheel of a two-ton station wagon. I was a little nervous.

"This is okay with Dad, right?" I said.

My mother snorted like I'd made a joke. Which meant he wasn't going to ask, and she wasn't going to volunteer anything.

My father enjoyed having a family, I'm pretty sure, but he didn't want to get bogged down in the day-to-day details. For her part, my mother cooperated by giving him only the broadest description of our home life. She might tell him, for instance, that we'd watched a movie that morning. Did he need to know that it was a home movie, one that we'd been shooting over the past month with her 8mm camera? Did he need to know that she played Nell Fenwick, while I played both Dudley Do-Right and Snidely Whiplash? Or that, earlier that week, the neighbor's Weimaraner had gotten so excited by my mock-assault that it jumped the fence to attack my mother's petticoats, and I ran inside the house as my mother got dragged across the backyard, all the while keeping her hand pressed to her forehead, mouthing in an exaggerated fashion, *Where, oh where, is my Dudley?*, even as her fellow actor was standing at the kitchen window, cracking his knuckles in terror and shame, more Snidely than Dudley, until at last the dog gave up and slunk away, looking embarrassed and confused?

No. That was more than my father could bear to know. We kept him from the knowledge as much as we kept it from him.

In the car, my mother reminded me that excess caution hurts as many people as recklessness. "Hit the gas," she said.

"It's not like this heap is going to accelerate out of control."

I fed the car a little gas. Very little. The needle nudged up to twenty. That was school-zone speed, right? Surely the police wouldn't allow you to go a killing speed around little kids. The needle still pointed at twenty when I initiated my first left turn.

The tires squealed. Panicking, I clung to the wheel of the station wagon like I was piloting a ship through a gale.

"Easy there, McQueen," said my mother. Her voice was so calm that it seemed to belong to a different situation, one that didn't involve our back tires painting an arc across the asphalt.

After the wagon came to a rocking halt, we got out and looked at the skid mark. My right heel bounced like the needle on a sewing machine. We almost died, I thought. I almost just killed us.

Not that my mother appreciated how close to flaming death we'd come. "That's called a fishhook," she said, in the same way that someone else might say, "Oh, look. A woodpecker."


A week or so before my twelfth birthday, I walked to the Lutheran church across the highway to see if I could get better reception on my prayers. The front doors were unlocked and the sanctuary was empty, but I thought I might get in trouble for walking into a church uninvited, so I hid by lying down flat on a pew.

We weren't churchgoers. Sunday mornings were a busy time for my father at the Broadmoor Country Club, and my mother took pride in never having set an alarm clock since dropping out of tenth grade. But even if she had been an early riser, it's hard to imagine my mother, as she was then, mouthing a creed along with the rest of the congregation, or sitting quietly while some guy told her what to think about God.

What little religious education I had was cobbled together from my mother's stories and a children's Bible from the bookshelf downstairs. What made it a Bible for children? Large type and grisly illustrations. The Old Testament was a real bloodbath, apparently, but what really caught my attention were the drawings of the Passion, from the whip dancing across Christ's back to the puckering spear wound in His side.

Good thing I wasn't the first Jesus, I'd think whenever I looked at the crucifixion scenes. Good thing the second coming looked like a whole different ball game. The illustrations in the Book of Revelation featured dragons! Buff angels with flaming swords! Some really sexy lady! And in the middle of all the action was New Jesus, broad-shouldered and fierce atop a white steed, wearing what appeared to be gold-plated cowboy boots: now *that* was a kick-ass vision of divinity a boy could get behind.

I didn't notice the contradictions between Revelation's vengeful scenes and the message of the Gospels. Or the notion that all this power was attached to the end of the world. I had tunnel-vision for glory.

The exposed beams of the church were washed with watery tones of violet and gold from the stained glass windows, like faint beams from a distant and broken movie projector. "Pick me," I whispered to God, and listened for my answer.

"Someone in here?"

My feet jerked out, kicking a stack of hymnals to the floor. A man walked up the aisle with his hands out as if to say *I come in peace*. His sandals made big smacking sounds against his soles. "I'm the pastor," he said. "Pastor Mike."

"Nothing," I said, though he hadn't asked me what I was doing.

Pastor Mike looked about my father's age, but his curly black hair was shot through with gray. A little paunch folded over the top of his tight, beltless jeans. "You're welcome here, you know," he said, but he also eyed the mud crumbles my shoes had left on the pew, so I brushed off the nubbly fabric before re-stacking the hymnals.

He asked a few questions—Could he sit? Did I live around here? Was this my first time in the church?—but my answers were short and soon he ran out of prompts. We ended up sitting quietly in the pew. I didn't mind this; it reminded me of being around my father. The silence seemed to make Pastor Mike nervous, though. He kept checking his hands, and saying Ah or Um before falling silent again. At last, when it seemed like he was about to make an excuse to slip away, I brought up The Subject. "So I hear Jesus is coming again."

He laughed. "So I hear."

I paused—was he making fun of me?—but decided to go on. If he kept laughing, I could always run out, leaving fresh mud crumbles all over his stupid church. "So it has to be someone, right?"

"Jesus?" He looked a little surprised. When he spoke again, it was in the guarded tone he'd used coming up the aisle. "I suppose, sure."

My mouth went dry. I looked at the empty cross as if it held a flashing VACANT sign. "What if it's me?"

Pastor Mike didn't answer right away. Outside, on the highway, cars swept past in traffic-light cycles, the surf of the suburbs.

"When I was a boy," he said, "I thought I might be a prophet. This was right after I'd read the Samuel story—you know, the one where the Lord calls to him in the night?"

I had no idea what he was talking about, but I nodded anyway. That story must not have made the final cut of my children's Bible.

"I stayed up nights," he said. "Must have been for a week, listening for my name to be called. Once, I even thought I heard it." He smiled at the memory, then shook his head. "But it was probably sleep deprivation. Or wanting something enough to fool myself."

I shook my head at the empty cross. "You said Jesus had to be someone."

"I'm not saying it's not you. I'm just saying… either way it goes, you should know you're not alone."

That wasn't what I wanted to hear. I wasn't looking for a band of like-minded idiots; what I wanted was to be exceptional, all-powerful, The One.

When he said, "You are not alone," I heard: "You ain't so special."

# Chapter 2

When my father met my mother, he was a twenty-two-year-old country club pro with a swing as strong and beautiful as the high note in the National Anthem. She was a palm reader at the Broadmoor's annual Arabian Nights Bazaar. According to my father, my mother had an unusual style. She tended to linger with her customers instead of booting them out of her tent after a couple of broad predictions, which, along with her attractiveness, led to a long line composed mostly of men. And her revelations were surprisingly specific, sometimes about herself, and occasionally true. That first night, for instance, she told my father a number of things, including that she was eighteen (a lie: she had just turned sixteen) and that he had high blood pressure (true: a doctor confirmed it a few days later).

The next week, when he found out that she was a counselor with the Broadmoor summer day camp, he sought her out with the excuse of telling her she'd been right about the hypertension. It seemed to flare up, he noticed, when he was around her—his heart going like a piston, his hands swelling, a flush crawling up his neck—which he turned into a running joke: Read my palm, tell me if I'm having The Big One. Is a quadruple bypass in my future?

In those early days, they liked to talk about the future. My father was saving up to go to California, where he was hoping to play his way onto the pro circuit. That's where my mother wanted to go, too. It was her Mecca, the birthplace of the movies she loved. Early on, California was what they had in common. A few months later, *I* was what they had in common and California was out of the picture.

Things must have looked pretty bleak. Forget losing their dreams—how were they going to make a living? A golf pro didn't make enough money to support a family, especially during the cold months, and a pregnant palm reader would earn even less. That's when my father, who was not known for inventiveness, hit upon the biggest idea of his life: the golfdome.

The business equation was sound: put up a giant inflatable dome, and when inclement weather came, so would the golfers. And it *worked*. The winter after the dome was built, memberships shot up, private lessons followed, and my father was transfigured into an earner, a dependable and steadfast provider.

I've heard the dome was something of a marvel when it was first inflated—a dewy white bubble struggling awkwardly from the ground like a boxer fighting a ten-count—but on the afternoon just before my birthday when I biked through the rain to see my father, the dome was paunchy, its skin the dingy shade of roadside snow. The inside was totally derelict. Steel beams were lined with dust as thick as felt, the air had a fungal smell like an old tent, and holes pocked the net that divided the dome down the middle.

When I arrived, my father broke away from his lesson with a little boy in a sweater vest and trotted over to me. He pointed at my wet clothes. "You biked down here in the rain?"

"It was a warm rain."

"You ask your mom to drive you?"

"It was like a shower. Want to have lunch?"

He looked at the roof of the dome. Behind him, the kid in the sweater vest stabbed his golf bag with his pitching wedge—"Die, die, die," he was chanting—but my father was too busy doing mental equations to notice. Most people think a golf pro leads a life of leisure, but the truth was that my father worked like a dog. Freeing up even a half hour in the middle of the day was tough. But who can say no to a wet child?

"Give me twenty minutes to finish up here, all right?" He tossed me his keys. "I've got a spare change of clothes in my locker. Meet me in the dining room."


All my early ideas about wealth were formed by the locker room of the Broadmoor. The green carpet so thick it ate sound, mahogany benches and lockers that shone darkly, a clock with Roman numerals, blue toilet water—it all seemed like the trappings of a life of trust funds and charity balls. Coming into the empty locker room on a rainy day, it was easy to imagine it as my private dressing room with a gold star on the door.

I took my time getting ready for lunch, first showering, then sampling the complimentary line of grooming products arranged by the long mirror. I gargled my way through half a bottle of mouthwash and shaved with a yellow safety razor, though I had nothing but downy fuzz on my cheeks. Thinking of my father waiting on me made me feel important.

Not that he actually waited. I arrived in the dining room to find him halfway through a Salisbury steak. He pointed his fork at a plate of cold chicken fingers. "I took the liberty of ordering for you."

From the kid's menu, evidently. Which explicitly said "Li'l Duffers: for children ten years old and under ONLY." And in case the patron couldn't read so well, there was a picture of a dorky cherub obviously ripped off from the *Love Is...* comic strip. The fact that I actually liked chicken fingers and could eat them all day long was beside the point. The point was that his order painted us both in an unflattering light: him as a tightass, and me as a little kid.

"Geez," he said through a mouthful of meat. "Those clothes actually fit you. You're getting huge. Do you tower over your classmates, or what?"

I didn't, in fact. According to the charts in the school nurse's office, I was only slightly taller than average. My father and I were the same height, though he had a few pounds on me, thanks to the doughy roll around his beltline. If he had shaved off his brush mustache and cut out the sweets that were his weakness, he might have passed for my brother. Still, I was pleased enough by his remark that I didn't complain about the chicken fingers. Besides, I had come to discuss a bigger piece of business. "About my birthday," I began.

He stopped sawing at his steak. "What do you want?"

"You don't have to buy me anything."

"What? No presents?"

"Presents are kind of a little kid thing, aren't they? I mean, you and Mom don't give each other presents for your birthdays, right?"

I didn't mention that I had no need for presents because soon I would be able to manifest whatever I wanted with a snap of my fingers. Or maybe a quick thrust of my hips. I wasn't sure; I was still working on my signature miracle move.

My father wasn't convinced. "Enough games," he said. "What do you want?"

I petted my smooth, smooth chin like I was thinking. The dining room was full. You had your old ladies playing cards, as usual, but now they were joined by tables full of restless golfers, drinking scotch and watching rain streak down the windows. My father noticed the golfers, I'm sure, and even then he was probably calculating how many of them might give up waiting on the weather to clear, and drift over to the golfdome, where he could snooker them into private lessons.

"Maybe you could take the day off," I said, as if the idea had just occurred to me. "We could all, I don't know, have a picnic at the Dunes."

The distant look of calculation left his eyes. He regarded me flatly. "You want me to take the whole day off."

I nodded. He kept looking at me. Thunder rolled like a marble across the floor.

Rarely have I met anyone as comfortable with conversational pauses as my father. This made him a good fit with my mother, who happily poured herself into every silence he opened up. But talking wouldn't help me now, I knew. If I opened my mouth, it would be to plead, or reduce my request, or offer some foolish explanation that would only weaken my case.

A waitress came by during my silent siege to re-fill his coffee cup. She sighed wistfully. "It must be real peaceful at your house."

After she walked away, he leaned in toward me. "This is the time of year I make my nut. The golfdome keeps us from starving in the winter, but the summer is... I mean, what's wrong with dinner?"

Dinner at the clubhouse was my birthday tradition. I was permitted to order anything I wanted, with the exception of surf-and-turf. On my ninth birthday, I'd scarfed down a filet, a lobster tail, and about a pound of buttery linguine before re-depositing it in the parking lot. My father said, "That's a thirty-four dollar puddle right there," as I sobbed, embarrassed. My mother attempted to lighten the mood—"Oh, Revie. You're not supposed to put the surf *on* the turf"—but my father was too busy kicking gravel over the mess to laugh. Then, as he did every year, he sent us home and returned to work.

"This birthday feels like kind of a big deal to me," I said. "I'd just like you to be there if you could."

"Lunch *and* dinner," my father countered, glancing at a group of golfers who were standing and hitching up their pants. "With surf and turf back on the table."

Not good enough. I needed him there when the big voice came from the sky, declaring me His son, with whom he was really excited to be working. I knew if my father came home to hear my mother raving about her son the savior, he wouldn't believe her. The whole deal hinged on him. Look at the first Jesus. Why did the angel appear to Joseph, too? Why hadn't God trusted him to take Mary at her word? Because so much depended on a father's faith.

At last he nodded. "Fine. The whole day. You drive a hard bargain, you know that?"

There was a touch of admiration in his voice for my restraint. But my silence was different than my father's, then and always. I spaced out. I took commuter flights of daydream. My father's silence was full of calculation.

"Hold up, guys," he called to the golfers who were ambling out of the dining room. Glancing back at me, he said, "Tell your mother I'm probably going to be two, maybe two-and-a-half hours late tonight."

The next day I was at Woz's house, throwing paring knives at the birch tree in his backyard. Or trying, anyhow. I'd seen a man throwing knives on TV and it had looked as easy as pointing. But these knives just fluttered through the air like maple-seed copters before falling harmlessly to the ground.

I frowned at Woz. "Something's wrong with your knives."

"Great, let's put them away," he said. When I'd taken the knives from his kitchen, he'd moaned that we were going to bend them and his mother would get mad, but as usual I helped him overcome his fears by calling him a pussy.

Woz was a big softy, in every sense. He was pudgy, with loose curls of light hair, and long eyelashes that half the girls at school would have killed for. And he could always be persuaded to go along with my ideas, even the dumb ones. He might protest at first, but eventually he'd give in because he needed me: I was his only real friend, so he heard my requests as ultimatums. His neediness made him the perfect confidant.

"Can you keep a secret?" I said, touching a flimsy blade to the approximate area of his heart.

"Don't," he whined. "You're gonna bend the knife."

I prodded his fleshy chest. "Swear you'll cut out your own heart if you ever tell anyone what I'm about to tell you. Swear it."

"My shirt—you're gonna make a hole."

Close enough. I revealed my news. After a moment of skepticism—"*The* Jesus?"—Woz began nodding vigorously. "Let's do it," he said, though I hadn't asked him to partner with me. "I'll be your disciple. Disciple number one. Sir Woz."

I tried not to show my irritation that he had confused the apostles with the Knights of the Round Table. After all, I didn't want to alienate my first believer. But I had to tell him: no disciples. "It's going to be more of a fan-club situation."

"Why?"

Mostly because I wanted more of the spotlight for myself. But also because I didn't want anyone close enough to betray me, and this is what I told him.

Woz's mouth hung open. "You think I would betray you?" He spread his arms wide. "Test me."

For the next hour, after tying Woz to a birch tree with an extension cord, I interrogated him for information on "his precious Jesus." He shouted back at me, but stayed in character and after a while I realized he was enjoying it, which disgusted me. I redoubled my efforts, even letting a little spit fly into his face, but the more I yelled and whacked his thighs with a garden spade, the brighter his eyes gleamed, and the heavier he breathed. Bringing out the hose, in fact, was his idea.

I sprayed his midsection halfheartedly. Through his shirt, I could see his big sad nipples. Turning off the hose, I said, "This is stupid."

"Keep going," Woz gasped, his eyes closed in—ecstasy? "Spray my face."

"What?"

"Spray my *face*. That's what would happen in real life."

I turned the hose on full-force, almost before he finished speaking, aiming it right at his mouth to teach him never to overrule me again. I couldn't have been more than three feet away. Woz was snapping and twisting, trying to catch a breath, and I kept spraying—just until he begs for mercy, I told myself—but he wouldn't beg for mercy. Because I was scared that he might drown, and pissed that he was being so stubborn, I turned off the hose and picked up a knife.

I put it to his chest with enough pressure to dimple the skin. "Give."

"Never," he gasped, still excited from the hose.

I had a knife to his heart and still he wasn't taking me seriously? "Idiot," I grunted. "*Give*." Then I noticed a dark bloom on his shirtfront, spreading fast.

Woz followed my eyes down to his chest. "Hey," he said in a distant way, then his knees buckled and he sagged forward against the extension cord.

It took me a couple of minutes to untie him because my hands were shaking so badly. "Take off your shirt," I said, glancing around, hoping none of the neighbors were watching.

Woz slumped against the birch, taking shallow breaths that made his gut rolls quiver. "I didn't give," he said. "I could have, like a million times, but I didn't."

When I imagined my life as Jesus, I saw skeptics, hecklers, head-shakers and stone-throwers. I saw men twisted in prayer, women kissing my feet, entire crowds prostrate before me— but I hadn't counted on anything like this. I pressed his balled-up shirt as hard as I could to the slit in his chest, which looked like nothing more than a paper cut, though it must have been fairly deep because blood welled up every time I took the shirt away. I grabbed his jowls with my free hand. "Stop *bleeding*, you pussy!"

If Woz's mother saw the blood, she'd find out about the knife. And then she'd find out about the binding. And the hose—it would all come out and there would be no way to explain it away without sounding like a lunatic or a liar: *Your son asked me to torture him, Mrs. Wozniewski.* Squatting in the wet grass, cramming a t-shirt to my friend's chest, I was suddenly furious—at myself, but at Woz, too, as though he'd tricked me into all this trouble. After checking the wound again—still bleeding, shit—I started praying. *God, get me out of this mess.*

"You should heal me," said Woz.

*Maybe turn back time? Let me find a first-aid kit buried in the mulch?*

"Your first miracle," said Woz. "Do it." Then he closed his eyes, just as he had when he told me to spray him.

I hesitated, then put my palm over his wound. All I felt was cold, wet skin and the light knocking of his heart. What did I have to lose by trying? Maybe everything. Could I blow this whole Jesus deal by calling on my powers too early, or in a cover-up? If I tried to heal Woz and failed, what would that mean? And what if it *worked*? I was surprised to find that I wasn't ready for either outcome. Yet.

But looking at Woz, his eyes still closed, I saw the power I did have.

"The time's not right," I told him, pulling off my own dark T-shirt. "Put this on. It'll hide your cut until you can get to the Band-Aids in your house."

Woz looked disappointed, but he took my shirt. I had to help him yank it down, it was so tight. "So am I in?" he asked.

No chance. I couldn't have disciples who dwarfed my own faith; I couldn't be surrounded by followers who were better and stronger than me. But now was probably the wrong time to reject Woz, so I helped him up, then raised my hand the way I'd seen Jesus pose in my children's Bible while admonishing his followers. Woz followed suit, like he was about to take an oath. A wet spot appeared on his chest, but the shirt was dark enough that it looked like nothing more than sweat.

"Go forth," I said, "and never say a word about this shit."

Woz mouthed *Amen*, and just like that he had his own Lost Episode.

# Chapter 3

The morning of my birthday, the sky was piled high with thunderheads. Squinting out the kitchen window, my father blew into his coffee. "So much for the Dunes," he said without offering a contingency plan. Neither of us was good with contingency plans, but then, as long as we had my mother, we didn't have to be.

She was still in bed. She'd stayed up late the night before, watching movies in the front room with the lights off. The low light of the television cast everything in black and white, including my mother. Moments like this, she looked like a starlet from the old movies she liked to watch. She wasn't a classically beautiful woman—her nose had a small crook; "Dogleg left," my father liked to joke—but she was lithe and blonde, with large, urgent eyes, all of which went a long way toward suggesting glamour.

I'd stayed up late, too, waiting for Holyghost to show up on my porch like Ed McMahon and the Prize Patrol. In the morning, when I'd heard someone knocking around the kitchen, I rushed out of my room, expecting—what? An archangel poking through the cabinets? Instead I saw my father swaying before the coffee maker. "Happy birthday," he said in a froggy voice.

"Well, it *will* be."

Around nine my mother came out of her bedroom full of energy. After a quick look out the window, she said, "Plan B. And C and D and E."

The way she could come up with games and activities, you'd think she spent her days exchanging ideas with other housewives and clipping out magazine articles with titles like "Family Day Out? Family Day In!" or "Turn Blahs into Hurrahs!"—but the truth was that her ideas, like her stories, were struck on the anvil of the moment. "Ideas are born, not made," she often said with scorn for those of us, including me, who needed the crutch of preparation.

That morning, she hauled her costume trunk down from the attic and we played Fantasy Island. I ran around, shouting "De plane! De plane!" as my father awkwardly looped a plastic lei around my mother's neck. We improvised entire episodes, taking turns playing the guest. My father was mostly confused, but this only added to the hilarity. "What a doofus," my mother said, pinching his cheek when he forgot his fantasy for the umpteenth time.

Around mid-morning, she laid strips of masking tape on the concrete floor of the basement and we played shuffleboard with brooms and tuna cans. My father disappeared a few times to "make a couple of calls," encouraging me to take his turns. Then we played Platters, a game where my mother played a song on her record player and we made up stories about what happened next to the characters in the song. The game allowed my mother to ask her trademark question, the one she was forever asking at the end of stories and jokes: "Then what happened?" She didn't trust endings. She poked at them like a detective who taps a wall until he finds the hollow spot that will reveal a safe, a tunnel, some further adventure. My father, on the other hand, wasn't interested in further adventures.

"Everyone died, the end," he declared when it was his turn to provide a postscript to "The Wreck of the Edmund Fitzgerald," despite the fact that my mother allowed that the ghosts of the characters could come back to visit their families. Then my father asked his own version of my mother's trademark question: "So do we have anything planned for after lunch?"

"Well," she said, "I guess it depends on the weather. I don't know if those clouds are going to open up, or blow over, or just threaten us all—"

"That's the good thing about the dome," said my father. "No weather."

I saw, then, what he was planning. Call it prophecy, or call it knowing someone well enough to anticipate their moves: Soon he would say he was sorry we couldn't go to the beach, but since we were just sitting around the house with no apparent plans for the afternoon, why doesn't he run over to the dome to see if he can scare up a few private lessons?

"Hey," I said as my father pushed back his chair, "you want to see me drive?"

The first raindrops fell as my mother turned into Napalm Alley. "Really, you're sure this is all right?" my father said.

"Not, say, totally illegal?"

He'd required a lot of assurance to get into the passenger seat, and in the end, I had to press my birthday advantage, claiming that driving would make up for missing out on the Dunes. My mother talked me up like I was a prizefighter and she was my promoter.

"Just wait until you see him drive," she said. "He's a natural. Gas in his veins. One with the road."

She must have been embarrassed, then, when I slid into the driver's seat, took a deep breath, and pressed the gas pedal. The engine revved, but the car did not move. Sweat pricked my forehead. I floored the pedal. Over the roar of the engine, a high whine emerged like a soprano descant, but still, no movement.

"Might want to put the car in gear, there, Revie," said my father from the passenger seat, staring rigidly ahead.

"Leave the boy alone," she said. "He knows what he's doing."

"What is he doing, exactly?"

"Flushing out the fuel injectors."

I popped the car in gear and rolled forward. For a moment, no one said anything. I think they were both surprised that I had successfully pulled away from the curb. Then my father started back in.

"Wipers," he said.

"Tim," my mother said.

"Lights."

"*Tim.*"

"Check your mirrors."

"There's no one on this road. Would you stop? You're making him nervous."

"It's called coaching," he snapped. "And I happen to know a little about it. Good Lord, woman. Did you teach him anything, or did you just put him behind the wheel and say, Have at it?" Pointing at my hooking skid mark down the road, he said, "That's what happens when you let kids run wild." He shook his head, muttering about crazy teenagers.

I'd never heard him snap at her like that before. But for some reason, his anxiety had a calming effect on me. We were going twenty miles an hour, for God's sake. On empty roads. In a station wagon. It wasn't like I was piloting a helicopter over treetops.

"Relax," I said, putting my arm over the back of his seat. I goosed the gas pedal and watched the needle on the speedometer nose up to thirty. "Enjoy."

He eased back in his seat, looking at me warily. He might have done better to watch the road, though, because then he might have cautioned me to slow down for the upcoming corner.

The road curved. The tires turned. We didn't.

"Fishhook," said my mother as the tires panted across the slick pavement.

"I *knew* it," said my father. I turned the wheel this way and that, but none of my efforts seemed to make the slightest difference, so I just let go and watched Napalm Alley whirl in front of us like a spun globe. We made about two or three screaming revolutions before hitting a stump with a soft, crumpling noise. The car rocked up on its side, then settled back down with a squeak.

I put my hands back on the wheel so no one would see how badly I was shaking. My father was muttering, too softly for me to make out any words. I took my foot off the brake and touched it to the gas. Once again, the engine revved, but the car didn't move. I'd busted the axle.

Then I saw my father yanking at his leg. The stump had crimped in the door, pinning his foot to the floor. He pulled and pulled, letting loose a daisy chain of curses. My mother craned over the front seat, looking as dumb and frozen as I felt.

"Now what?" I prompted her.

She said, "Um—"

I said, "Ambulance?"

She said, "Okay."

But she just sat there, watching my father haul away at his leg, until at last I had to say, "*You.* You call an ambulance."

She sprang out of the car and ran through the rain. I don't think I'd ever seen my mother run flat-out before. She looked birdlike, the way her head jutted around, her legs all stiff and springy. Running was not her most glamorous activity. By the time I turned back to my father, he had pulled his foot free, but was still holding his leg like a spare part for a marionette. "Does it hurt?" I asked.

He gave me a dark look. "It hurts."

Lightning veined the sky. Tears backfilled my eyes, but I didn't let them go. The only thing worse than crushing my father's foot would be forcing him to console me. In a loud voice I hoped would disguise any shakiness, I said, "I AM SO SORRY."

"Not your fault," he grunted toward his window.

"YES," I said. "YES IT IS."

"You've been getting bad advice," he said, which was probably a phrase he used a lot in his private lessons. "We need to break it all down and start over."

Tears fell out of my eyes. I cuffed them from my cheeks, then squeezed my eyes shut as hard as I could, furious at myself—for crying, for screwing everything up—and when I opened my eyes again, everything looked new, vibrant, washed clean. The car was filled with the soapy smell that follows lightning. My limbs tingled with electricity.

"I can fix it," I said, as much to myself as to my father.

"The car? I don't think so."

"Your foot."

My voice was calm, self-possessed, like someone you could believe in. I hardly recognized it as my own. My father gave me the dark look again. "This is hardly the time."

I looked him in the eye, longer and more directly than I ever had before. He was wrong. This was the time, time in all its fullness. Every cell in my body sang with electricity as I grabbed his knee. When he twitched and grunted, I took this to mean that he felt the current, too.

"Fear not, father," I said. "For I am the Lord."

"Oh, my God," he said, but he wasn't being worshipful.


I didn't heal his foot, of course. What had botched the healing, I decided, was my father's lack of faith, not a short-out of my divine power.

By the time my mother returned to the car, I'd already confessed how I'd come up with the idea that I was Jesus. My father sent me to the very back of the wagon so he could have a "private conversation" with my mother up front. He wanted to know what else was going on at home. "I know we're not just talking about crazy stories and driving. Poor judgment is like cancer. It spreads. Tell me *everything.*"

The sudden yelp of a siren made us all jump. We were so sunk in our own misery we hadn't even noticed the ambulance pulling up behind us.

My mother and I sat on the back bumper of the station wagon while the EMTs extracted my father through the driver's side. The rain had slowed to a drizzle. A policeman with a shower cap over his hat walked up and pulled out a notebook. "So what happened?"

My mother sat up straight, rubbed her hands briskly along her thighs. "My husband," she said, "was teaching me to parallel park."

My mouth opened with a tiny smack. She gave me a cautionary look: *not a word.*

Such a small lie, but something about it sent a shock through me. Seeing her summon her old composure was like watching someone putting on a mask. And her tone was familiar; it was the off-handed confidence of her storytelling voice.

The EMTs tried to get my father to lie down on the gurney, but he refused. As they rolled him past us, he was sitting up like a deposed king being evicted from his castle on a sedan chair. He shook his head vaguely, perhaps going over all the overlooked signs and wonders that had pointed toward this holy mess. And just before the EMTs lifted him into the ambulance, he looked at me.

He was not angry or in pain. His face was full of something more permanent and terrible. We might have harbored different illusions before that afternoon, but in that moment our vision was burned clean, and we were the same.

Our faith was gone.

# Chapter 4

When I was in fifth grade, a gonzo scientist came to my school to put on a demonstration. After a half-hour of dipping various objects into liquid nitrogen—racquetballs, bananas, a textbook—and shattering them against the gym walls, he went into his big finale. After making a big deal about how dangerous this part was, after putting on a welder's mask and gloves because mere contact with air would cause this next substance to burst into flame, he pulled out a comically small bottle with a few amber chunks floating around in water. A nervous chuckle went through the crowd. We thought he was messing with us. It looked like bouillon cubes. But he wasn't laughing like he had been when he was pitching frozen fruit against the basketball backboards. Now he was in full dramatic mode.

"Phosphorus," he called out, his voice made distant and hollow by the welder's mask, "is Greek for 'bringer of light.'" He placed a tiny chunk on a metal base at mid-court. "Or Latin," he said, backing away, "for 'Lucifer.'"

He raised his hands, shouted, "Behold!" and the waxy chunk burst into the brightest flame I have ever seen. It was like watching a filmstrip burn up on the screen, only the film was life and the screen was my world. How bright was it? Ten minutes later, when we filed out of the gym onto the playground, the sun looked dim.

Likewise, some events seem harmless when they happen. Innocent. A lark. But tell somebody about it and the moment the event hits air, it becomes Something Terrible.

After coming home from the hospital with a cast up to mid-calf that looked like the White Sox logo, my father launched into a full audit of my mother's parenting. In his own variation on *Then what happened?*, he kept asking her, "What else?" and she told him everything. Even about the spring afternoon she had dressed me up in a wig and ball-gown, and had applied the tiniest bit of rouge and eye-shadow to my sunburned face.

At the time, it had seemed like no big deal. I had liked the close attention from my mother, and for a strange moment I'd even felt beautiful. When we were done, we laughed, put the gown away, and I don't think either of us felt the slightest embarrassment.

But hearing that episode reported in detail—my parent's voices coming through the cold-air return in my room, as tinny and echoey as an old-time radio show—it sounded bizarre at best, and at worst, horrifying.

"My God," my father said after a long pause. "Does he still like girls?"

I pressed my hands over my face, feeling like I might burst into flame. *Behold!*

"I'm sorry." My mother couldn't have sounded more stunned if she'd just learned of the incident, too. "I didn't realize… well, I just didn't realize."

Nights, he bled confessions out of her. During the day, he went to work and she holed up in her room, turning up the television loud enough for me to hear it through her door. Every now and again she ventured out, still in her flannel housecoat despite the killing heat of August outside, to reheat a cup of coffee in the microwave that, more often than not, she forgot and wandered away from. Whenever I tried to talk to her, she ducked her head and held up her hand. *Not now.*

"You need to get her out of that room," I told my father over the phone.

"No way," he said. "This is called remorse. I know you're not used to seeing it, but it might be the first appropriate thing your mother has done in twelve years."

Her confessions had shaken him. After so many years of carefully coordinated ignorance, coming into all that truth at once must have been a soul-jarring experience. I could almost forgive his callousness—"She's got a lot of thinking to do," he said. "We both do"—but all the same, I felt that *someone* had to get her out of that room.

One afternoon I went to her door, rapped once as a kind of warning shot, then turned the knob without waiting for a reply. The smell of lilac and spoiled milk washed over me like a warm sea—and then I saw the mess. The *squalor.* The riot of videotapes and shoes and perfume samples torn out from magazines. Coffee cups and cereal bowls stacked in a frog palace on the nightstand. And in the midst of it all, sitting cross-legged on the bed like a yogi on top of a trash heap, was my mother.

I pulled the collar of my t-shirt up over my nose. "You mind if I open the window?"

"No, I'm watching this," she said without looking away from the TV. The glaze in her eyes told me she hadn't just turned it on.

I cranked open the window. The day was hot as sin, but at least the air was breathable. As I pressed my nose to the screen to get a clean breath, I could practically see a purple cloud rolling out of the room.

I waded back through the mess and snapped off the TV. "Clean up your room, little lady," I said in a big, jokey voice, "and then maybe you can watch a little TV."

She stared at me blankly.

I made a silly face, hoping she would smile. Roll her eyes. Maybe grab me and tickle my ribs. But then clean this room, definitely.

Her eyes squinched up in a way that meant tears were coming. "Look, I'll help!" I said, pulling up the corner of the fitted sheet, but it snapped out of my hand. Cereal bits flew through the air like flak. She closed her eyes before they strafed her face, and that did it, that broke the dam, tears came running down her cheeks.

"I'm sorry," I said. "I didn't mean—"

She raised her hands, like *Come here.* I hesitated only a second before crawling into the bed. She pulled my head onto her lap and ran her fingers through my hair. It felt good— wonderful, really—but it wasn't enough to block out the magazine pages crinkling under me, or the Lucky Charms sticking to my legs like gravel. "It probably looks worse than it is," I said, meaning the room. "If we both worked on it, I bet—"

"Hush," she said, plowing her fingers through my hair again. "It's no use. Just leave it be."

It was a hazy August morning, about a week after the accident, when I found out where all this thinking and confessing had led.

I remember coming into the kitchen, surprised to find my father still home. He was sitting next to my mother in a wash of pale light, coffee steaming on the table in front of them. The scene was all mist and light and quiet voices until my mother noticed me.

She touched my father's arm. He stopped talking. We all looked at each other.

"Have a seat," he said. She looked at her hands. I shuddered, hard, like a fish on a stringer.

A cooling-off period. That's what they were calling it. My mother would go down to Florida to stay with Madame, her mother, until my parents could "figure everything out."

In the kitchen, they took turns speaking to me in a slow and careful way, as though talking me down from a ledge. She was leaving on the weekend, which gave me a couple of days to say goodbye. School started on Monday, which, according to my father, would be "a welcome distraction."

He wasn't trying to be an asshole. He was just the kind

of guy who saw work as a balm for grief or other personal problems. In that way, he was no different than most men of his generation.

"Any questions?" he said. I didn't know what to say. My head was a hundred alarms, all going off at once. "Yes," I said, then walked stiffly back to my room, lay down on my bed, and stared at the ceiling for the next couple of hours.


By that night, I was composed enough to ambush my father in the garage when he came home from work. "Send me," I said, the moment he stepped out of his car.

"Jesus." He clutched his chest. "I didn't expect you there. What are you doing up? It's almost midnight. Didn't your mother—ah, never mind."

I said, "I could go live with Woz for a while. I'm sure his folks wouldn't care."

My father stumped over to me, leaning on the car for support. He hated the cane the doctor had given him, and found other ways to prop himself up, pushing off from countertops or chair backs, propelling himself forward like an infirm Tarzan. When he reached the steps, he pulled me down next to him, blowing out a beery sigh. Sometimes he stopped off at Al's Tap on the way home, though he usually didn't stay out this late.

"Why would I send you, too?" he said.

"Not *too*. Instead."

If anyone should be sent away, I argued, it was me. After all, I was the one who'd caused the accident; I was the one who'd begged for stories, then totally misinterpreted them. Military school, an exchange program—it hardly mattered where he sent me, as long as it was away.

He listened to my whole spiel, his eyes sagging with beer and sympathy, but in the end it didn't make any difference.

"You're staying," he said. "She's going. End of story."

He put his hand on my shoulder in what seemed like a comforting gesture. But then he pushed down to help himself up, and hobbled into the house.

Over the next couple of days, I badgered my mother to back out of the deal. I told her I'd caught my father weeping in the bathroom. I threatened to chain myself to her bumper. She only shook her head, murmured, "No, no, no," and continued packing. It wasn't until I tried to side with her against my father that she finally snapped.

"*We* decided," she said. "Together."

It was the day she was supposed to leave. We'd spent the morning packing the used station wagon my father had recently bought for her, and we'd just finished eating pizza from paper plates so we wouldn't have to wash dishes again. Now she was telling me that they had worked together. To separate. Well, that was just perfect.

"You really don't get it, do you?" she said. "We're doing this for you."

"Well, don't," I said. "This is me, asking you to do something else."

"In case you haven't noticed, Revie, I've done a lot of

damage here. I've been damaging *you*."

"Did *he* tell you that? Who died and made him the expert on—"

"The cooling-off period wasn't his idea."

All the wind went out of me. I felt like I'd been gut-punched. Not his idea?

"I was the one who…" Her voice wobbled. Her gaze drifted up, above my head. This was how she looked when she told me stories, like she heard something in the distance, or was channeling signals from Holyghost. Normally I loved it, but not just then. *Look at me!* I wanted to shout. She cleared her throat and went on. "I am not a good mother."

"Well, *that*," I said when I could find my voice, "that is just bullshit."

"Exhibit A," she said, lifting her hand. "You learned that word from me. What kind of mother talks like that around her son? What kind of mother dresses her boy up in a wig and make-up?" She shook her head at the ceiling, as if addressing these questions to God. "What kind of mother puts her boy in harm's way?"

I said, "You are too a good—"

"Don't," she said softly, looking at me at last. "Never bullshit a bullshitter."

Then she glanced at the clock and told me we only had a few hours left. "Last call," she said. "We'll do whatever you want, as long as it doesn't involve arguing."

I had been about to make one last suggestion—*what if we sent HIM away?*—but I dropped it. At last I saw the limits to a child's power: you got just enough to screw things up, but not enough to fix anything.

"A story," I said. "A Holyghost story."

I didn't know that's what I wanted until I heard myself say it. But I'm glad I asked, because it turned out to be the last story she ever told me.

As the original third wheel, Holyghost had my sympathies. In my imagination, he was always left out of the action by the Other Two, who called out promises of next time, don't worry, your time is coming, come on now, don't be like that, Ghost, of course you're important to us, we didn't forget about you, we said next time, didn't we?

In my mind, God and Jesus were overworked and stressed-out, while Holyghost sat by his phone, trying to look busy.

"Oh great," sighs Jesus. "Here comes another batch of Lord's prayers. Haven't heard *that* one before. Delete, delete, delete. When I told them that one, I just meant, like, this is one example. I wish they didn't take me so literally."

God looks up from his messy desk and rolls his eyes. "Tell me about it."

Holyghost lysols his phone.

Since I'd discovered that I wasn't the second coming, I wasn't sure what to believe anymore. Some days Jesus seemed like a story that didn't make a whole lot of sense. God was simply too big and intimidating to wrap my mind around. But Holyghost felt small and intimate, and I wanted to keep him around. I didn't know what to do with him, but that was okay. He and I were both used to that.

"So, Juke is working late," my mother began. "He's copying a proposal for the boss when the copier jams."

My mother and I were in the backyard, under the canopy of the willow tree. The end of August usually pressed down like a hot iron, but this year Indian summer had come early. A light breeze blew in from the south, carrying the sweet smell of hay and green apples instead of mill smoke.

Juke was Al Djukic, beleaguered salesman. I knew this character the way other kids knew Pinocchio, or the Big Bad Wolf. Juke had good intentions, bad luck, and chronic hopefulness. He was the Sisyphus of salesmen.

"The jam's a bad one," she said, "deep in the machine. Juke sticks his hand inside, deeper and deeper, searching for whatever's stuck, until he's in up to his armpit. Just as he's about to pull out and reassess the situation, he feels something flutter against his fingertips, so he gives one last big shove. There's a groan of bending metal. The machine whirs, and something clamps onto his hand."

My mother sat on the ground, hugging her knees. I reclined on the chaise lounge with the spongy cushion that smelled like a locker-room. Sunlight atomized in the yellow leaves of the willow that my father had planted the week I was born. The shallow, hungry roots had already caused minor upheavals in the concrete patio, and my father worried aloud about the foundation of the house. But the sound the willow made in a soft wind was holy and beautiful, and switches cut from the branches made the best whips.

"Juke tries to wrench his hand free, but that sucker is *in* there. 'A little help?' he calls, but his co-workers went home hours ago. He chuckles to keep himself from panicking, then makes a fist and rattles the machine. His hand doesn't budge. He tries to make it small and sneak it out. No dice. He coaxes his hand, talking to the copier in a sweet voice. When that doesn't work, he kicks the machine, but not real hard: he's in enough trouble at work without breaking the copier.

"The copy room's hot as hell, and by now Juke's sweating pretty good. With his free hand, he drags over a footstool so he can sit down and think. He remembers reading about a guy in Ottawa who got his arm stuck in a vending machine, but he can't remember how the guy got himself free. Or if he got free. Now that he thinks about it, the vending machine might have fallen over and crushed him. Not that Juke's worried about getting crushed by the copier. He's a little worried about his hand, and what he's going to do if he has to go to the bathroom, but mostly he's worried about his job. His sales numbers are in the toilet."

"Again," I muttered. Why this poor man didn't try another line of work was beyond me. Change seemed like the easiest thing in the world, but only as it applied to other people.

"Juke looks up to the ceiling where he sees a water stain that looks like the profile of Abraham Lincoln. He says, 'I could use a little help here, Lord. Or Abe. Whoever's available.'

"Since he can't fold his hands in prayer, Juke puts one hand over his heart, like the pledge. He says, 'A miracle would be nice, but I'll take a sign, whatever you got.' He sprinkles in some of the language that God likes. 'Showest thine mercy upon mine hand, and upon mine job. Amen.' Then, feeling a little foolish, he closes his eyes to give the miracle a chance to work in private."

She was quiet for a second, tugging on the grass with her toes. Feeling a little foolish myself, I touched my fingers together in a secret prayer for Juke's miracle.

"When Juke hears the fluorescent bulb flicker and buzz, he opens his eyes—but nothing's changed. His hand is still stuck, and now it's numb. He moans a little—" My mother moaned, an oddly comforting sound, "—and leans his forehead against the machine. That's when the copier starts up again."

A car came around the corner. My mother held up a finger. If it was my father, the story would be over.

"Keep going," I said. "It's not him."

She gave me a funny look. "How do you know?"

There was no way my father could come home in the middle of this story. I believed this as surely as I had ever believed anything. Was I placing my faith in God or Holyghost? Possibly. But it's more likely my faith was in her story. Like Scheherazade, I knew a story could stretch out time like taffy, until, at last, minds changed and skins were saved. All we needed was a little time and a little help to put things right, the same as Juke.

"I just know," I said.

As if on cue, the car accelerated down the street. My mother smiled at me gauzily until I got the sense that she was trying to lock in her image of me, the way she'd remember me during the cooling-off period.

"The copier," I prompted her. "It starts up, and…"

"Ah. Right. The copier starts up and Juke feels a sudden, crushing pain, and then he feels nothing. He jerks on his arm to see if anything's been severed, but it's still stuck. Copies drop onto his lap. Juke picks one up. It's a picture of his hand.

"Well, this is perfect. Just freaking perfect. Over the machine is a sign that says NO PERSONAL COPIES. He has to laugh. Copies of his hand keep dropping into his lap until Juke gets the sense that he's waving himself goodbye.

"By this point," she said, "his hand isn't looking so hot. On the copies, it looks squished pretty good. *Great*, he says to the box of Tax Documents 1982. *Shit on me*, he says to the microwave rimmed with exploded ravioli. By now Juke is pretty sure he's going to come out of this room jobless and handless and probably responsible for the cost of a new copier. It's only a matter of time before he becomes a humiliating paragraph in newspapers around the world, the man who needed the Jaws of Life to rescue him from a Xerox machine.

"But then," she said, turning on her side and propping herself up on one elbow, the pose that meant she was getting to the good part, "miracle of miracles, he sees the copies of his hand taking on different shapes. On one copy, Juke sees a thumbs-up. On the next one, it's the okay sign. Then he's giving himself the bird. Pretty soon he's laughing his weary ass off in there, until he relaxes so much that his hand falls right out of the machine.

"Oh!" he shouts. His hand's swollen and floppy, but he manages to complete the boss's proposal with his good hand before dropping all of his personal copies into the dumpster and driving himself to the emergency room, thanking God for automatic transmission."

She stopped for a moment, as if that were the end of the

story, but I knew better. This was just her way of teasing me, to make me ask *Then what happened?* For once, though, I didn't ask right away. Because when I asked that question, I'd be asking for the end.

My mother didn't seem especially eager to press on, either.

I said, "Since it was your idea to leave, I bet Dad would listen if you told him that you've changed—"

"So. The doctor's holding the x-rays up to the light while Juke's telling him the story, but the doctor stops him. He says, 'Son, why don't you tell me what really happened?' Juke's like, 'What do you mean?' The doctor says, 'Your hand is pulverized. Your bones are gravel. There's simply no way you could have made those hand-signs.'"

She paused to let it hit me.

"Ohhhhhh," I said. "Holyghost."

"*Holyghost*, that's right. Holyghost made those signs. And the kicker? The next day, when Juke went into work and opened his desk drawer? He found a single copy of the hand, giving him the thumbs-up."

She smiled and I was flooded with belief. Belief in divine intervention, in miracles, in *deus ex copier machina!* Belief in my family, which wasn't the confederation of three people, but one nation under God, indivisible, my mother and myself of one being with the father, forever and ever. Belief in the cosmic inevitability of rescue because nothing truly bad could ever happen to the stars of the picture, who were, clearly, us.

My heart soaring, I sat up in the chaise longue to fling my arms around my mother's neck.

That's when I heard my father's car pull into the driveway.

My father and I stood on the front lawn, squinting into the setting sun. He held his arm up in a stiff wave that shaded his eyes. She nodded at us and started the wagon. If anyone was watching, they'd have thought my mother was going on a little trip. My mother might have been dramatic, but we didn't broadcast our problems to the neighbors. We weren't white trash, after all.

The final goodbyes had happened very quickly—a hard clinch, a few pats, and promises that turned to lead as soon as they hit the air—and she had closed the door to the station wagon before I realized that she wasn't going to change her mind, and he wasn't going to ask her to reconsider.

Now she was backing down the driveway.

I couldn't believe it. Or maybe my problem was too much belief.

"*Do* something," I said to my father.

Still holding up his hand, he said, "We are."

I touched my fingers together, praying for something to stop her. "Holyghost," I whispered.

Her car stopped.

My idiot heart swelled as a line of cars came around the corner. The traffic was no coincidence. I knew that as surely as I'd known that my father couldn't come home during her story.

As if I were pulling cosmic strings, I whispered, "Now pull back in."

My father's hand fell on my shoulder, a comfort and caution both.

My mother turned her head and lowered her visor. A weak stream of mascara appeared on her cheek. The ragged sun illuminated the car and I could see that her chin wasn't trembling like mine; it was set and fierce and beautiful in a way I'd never noticed before.

The cars kept coming and the moment stretched on until it seemed like time had slipped into neutral, the way it had under the willow, when I could imagine that story going on forever, or at least long enough to save us from ourselves. It was a rare, suspended moment, one that might be possible only in the womb of a story, but even then, only until the story ends, or there's a break in traffic, and then it's gone.

# Section 2
## Burial

*Portrait of Lucifer as a Young Man*
*-a Rosalyn Bryson story-*

*Lucifer's father was a portrait painter for hire. If you mailed him a photograph and a check for four hundred dollars, he would paint your likeness in dark, smoky oils. Not a bad deal for a classic ego trip and the surest way to make new money look old. It was the nineteen-eighties. His business boomed.*

*He wasn't the world's greatest portrait painter, truth be told, but his clients didn't complain, and he loved the work. Loved it so much, in fact, that when he was finished with paying jobs for the day, he liked to paint Hoosiers of guttering fame—men like Hoagy Carmichael or Booth Tarkington, men whose names rang a faint bell, but you weren't sure why, though you thought they might have pitched for the Cubs or served in your grandfather's platoon.*

*The idea behind these unpaid portraits was to revive some of the subjects' former fame, but since no museum or gallery had commissioned them (or would accept them, even as donations), they ended up lining the living room wall in rows, a jury box of befuddled uncles.*

*Growing up, Lucifer thought portraits were ridiculous, and that his father's clients were shallow idiots. But around the time of his twelfth birthday, curiosity began to gnaw at him. If his father could make a grain dealer look like a university president, how dignified would Lucifer look in oil?*

*"Oh, you'll find out soon enough," his father said. "But it won't be from one of my portraits. You'll be so famous you won't need a shlub like me to boost your image."*

*This wasn't your standard case of a doting father with high hopes for his boy. Lucifer was lousy with talent, and lousy at hiding it. Plenty of people thought he was going to make it big. Some even hoped for it. What was he good at? Everything. By the time he was ten, he could whip his father in the Jeopardy Play-at-Home game. At his fifth-grade graduation ceremony, Lucifer gave such a stirring delivery of Tennyson's "Ulysses" that the entire crowd stood up in the bleachers; no one could say why. In gymnastics, he could whirl his body around the pommel horse so fast that his legs blurred into a propeller, but the real marvel was that none of the other boys in school made fun of him for it. Lucifer was electromagnetic, and fame seemed to be flying toward him.*

*What he didn't know—what his father didn't know, either—was just how famous he would become, and for what. But they were about to get a hint.*

*His father tried to tell him no, but Lucifer wheedled. He cajoled. He reasoned, issued mild and veiled threats, promised rewards, and posed leading questions to draw his father into a minefield of rhetorical traps and trip wires of guilt. The boy did not (ever) beg, but he employed every other form of verbal persuasion known to man, and a few new ones besides. His approach wasn't smooth yet, but he was persistent. Finally, when he sensed that his father would agree to anything to stop the noise, Lucifer closed the deal.*

*"Look," he said, stroking his bare lip. "No mustache."*

*Mustaches were the bane of his father's work. His portraits usually looked okay until he could no longer put off the mustache, and then the subject would look like he'd trapped a caterpillar between lip and nose, and was waiting, slightly cross-eyed with fear, for animal control to arrive.*

*"Oh, for Christ's sake, sit down," his father said. "Let's get this*

*over with."*

*Lucifer arranged himself on a chair while his father set up the easel in the living room. Usually his father whistled* Peter and the Wolf *as he painted, but today his whistle came out thin and shrill, and after a few minutes he fell silent. Now and then he made a brushstroke, but mostly he frowned at the canvas and tapped the end of the brush against his chin. "Hold still," he said several times, though he was the only one fidgeting.*

*After a few agonizing hours, he plucked the canvas off the easel. "Forget it," he said. "If you want a portrait so bad, we'll call Peter Muntz. He does kids."*

*"Show me what you got," said Lucifer.*

*His father looked at it again. "Nah, I'm just going to get rid of it."*

*Lucifer stepped toward him. "Show me."*

*"I'm not used to working with live models. Too many... dimensions."*

*But when Lucifer took hold of the portrait, his father let it go with a sigh. The boy was going to get his way eventually, so why fight him?*

*At first glance, Lucifer didn't see the problem. It looked like him, all right. Maybe he looked a little older than eleven, but that might have been because of the brown suit he'd put on for the painting.*

*But his face—it was a little long. And the way his head tilted down while his eyes looked up expectantly... the boy in the painting looked as though he had been amused a moment earlier, but was not any longer. He looked like he was about to say:* Where's the money? *Or:* I'm waiting.

*Lucifer began to understand why his father had kept squirming. The portrait put the viewer on the spot. Looking at it, you felt like a laugh had started up your throat and swelled into a lump.*

*Lucifer put it back on the easel, tried a joke. "Put a mustache on it."*

*His father dabbed his brush in the blackest paint and drew a thin cartoonish mustache, complete with big swirling curls. Lucifer laughed, so his father added a sharp little goatee in four rough lines. "Horns," said Lucifer, and watched a pair of goat horns appear on his forehead.*

*They took turns then, adding wicked black eyebrows and a weird serpent tail and a forked tongue, each of them forcing out a laugh at every embellishment, so the other would know that this was hilarious, a mere mistake, some fun, not something that scared the hell out of them both.*

# Chapter 5

We were near Chattanooga when the Dramamine took hold. I remember saying something like, "Maybe I shouldn't read so much in the car…" and suddenly gravity lost its grip on me, and I had to grab onto the dashboard to keep from floating around the car, which was going eighty with the windows wide open.

Then it was quiet again. The windows had closed. "Too much?" said my father. "I thought fresh air would help."

We'd driven all night and still we had more than seven hundred miles to go to Florida. They would be tough miles. Somewhere around the Kentucky border, I'd taken a double dose of Dramamine, and my father, who claimed to love driving at night because there was no traffic, had downed a packet of something called SUPER TRUCKER BUZZZ *(We take the ZZZ's so you don't have to)*. As the miles went by and the pills kicked in, he leaned over further and further until at last he was bent over the wheel of the Impala like he was racing a motorcycle.

The drive from Paris, Indiana, to Fort Carsen, Florida is twelve hundred and seventy-one miles. If you drive straight through, setting your cruise control at seventy, you can make it there in about eighteen hours.

Or, if you stop at every rest station along the way, eat leisurely meals at truck stops, and take in a scenic vista or two, the trip could stretch out to twenty-seven hours.

Such were the calculations my father had made the day after my mother left. We'd started calling Madame on Sunday afternoon—about the nineteen hour mark—to make sure that my mother had arrived safely, only to be told, no, she hadn't shown up yet.

With the car windows closed, my father started talking about Madame. He was sure that she knew more about my mother's whereabouts than she was letting on. But how would we ferret out her secrets? Apparently by giving up our own. "We'll start by telling her everything about our situation," he said, something they had apparently neglected to do when my mother arranged to stay with her.

This strategy sounded like a waste of time to me. After all, Madame was a psychic—wouldn't she already know all of this?

"No such thing as a psychic there, Revie. No such thing as palm-reading, fortune-telling, voodoo, hoodoo, juju, gris-gris, or mojo. No lines of communication with spirits of this world or any other. What Madame does—and this is her real gift, oh boy—is sniff out weakness. Your doubts, your fears. Once she finds out what you're trying to hide—" He smacked his hands together, then blinked, as if startled by the noise. "You're dead meat, pal. Best to be honest and forthright. Give her everything up front."

This from the man who had been less than forthright, not

only with Madame, but also with my mother's friends, when he'd started calling them around the twenty-eight hour mark. He asked broad questions, volunteering nothing. *Have you talked to Rosalyn lately? Did she mention any plans? Oh, no reason.* When he started getting busy signals, I knew it was because these people had started calling each other, and rumors were mushrooming.

I hung up the downstairs extension quietly, and sent up a short prayer. *To Whom It May Concern*, I thought, *Keep her safe. Make her call. Let them both figure out how retarded they're acting.*

That night, my father had come downstairs, looking awful. His ear was red from pressing against the phone, his mustache bristling from hours of tugging on it. "I called the police," he said, his voice crackling like tires rolling over gravel. "Reported her as a missing person."

When I could find my voice, I asked, "What happens now?" And for the first time in my life, my father had to come up with the answer to that question.

"Pack a bag," he said. "We're leaving in ten minutes."

In the car, I rolled my window back down for some fresh air. My father gave an exaggerated shudder, and his teeth started chattering. What was in that stuff he took?

"Hey!" he said. "Who's hungry? I bet there's a Waffle House around here. What do you say? You want waffles?"

I managed to stick my head out the window before vomiting, but the wind whipped the mess back against the rear door of the Impala. My father got real quiet.

Around dawn we stopped at a gas station. My father scrubbed at the orange flame of bile with a windshield squeegee, with little success. "It's eating the paint," he said through locked teeth. When he got back into the car, he sat all the way back in his seat for the first time in hours.

He looked grim, but recognizable. I felt better.

# Chapter 6

I expected a trailer. In a sad little park with a green pond from which an alligator would periodically emerge to snap up a Pomeranian. I expected wooden spool tables, oxygen tanks on dollies, and satellite dishes big enough to beam in signals from heaven.

So when my father pulled up to a white house with a wraparound porch that looked like it had been lifted from the set of *Gone with the Wind*, I naturally assumed that Madame had been reduced to working as a servant.

My father gave a low whistle. "I guess they made out all right when they sold their farm."

Better than all right, apparently. Their old home had been small and dark and covered with multi-colored curls from several generations of sloppy paint jobs. Once, my father had offered to scrape it all down. My grandfather declined, saying, "Any day now, I'm expecting a sandstorm."

Sometimes it was hard to tell if my grandfather was joking or batshit crazy.

My father clutched my arm as we went up the walk. "No weakness," he said. "Whatever you tell her she'll use against you. Or against me. She turns people against one another. It's what she does."

"I thought we were supposed to be honest. Tell her everything up front."

He stopped me on the porch to stare into my eyes. Eighteen hours of driving under the influence of dubious amphetamines had wizened him. "Not *that* honest," he said. "Geez, why not just hand Jack the Ripper a knife?"

He gripped my shoulders. His eyeballs looked like they were trying to get away from him. I couldn't blame them; I wanted to do the same thing myself. "Let go," I said. "You're scaring me."

"Then you're in the right frame of mind," he whispered, his breath smelling like superheated tin.

Just then Madame's voice came out of everywhere and nowhere all at once, like the voice of God from the burning bush. Although it was at least ninety degrees outside, chilblains rose on my arms.

"Timothy and son," the voice said. "I was wondering when you'd get here."


Growing up, my mother would go into town on Saturdays with her father. She sat with him at a diner through the long hours of the afternoon, watching traffic wind around the town square as his coffee cooled. He bartered with other men in the diner, mainly to bring something home to validate his trip into town.

Over the years, the same junk circulated among these men:

tetchy lawnmowers, various Coke machines frozen with rust, a motorcycle sidecar (sans motorcycle) reputed to be former Nazi property, and an Oscar statuette that her father swore was authentic though he couldn't explain why a button on its base caused a flame to appear from the top of its golden head.

Saturday nights, her father took her to the movies. In the summer it was the drive-in with clouds of gnats passing through the filmlight like bad thoughts. In the winter they went to the old Crown Theater with the big yellow bulbs around the marquee. "It didn't matter what was playing," my mother told me. "Seeing that marquee filled my soul with helium."

At the Crown, her father fell asleep right after the house lights went down. He must have looked forward to Saturday nights almost as much as my mother did. My grandmother, who billed herself as *Madame Zygovia*, ran her business from the front room of their house. Customers came when distraught, or assailed by hope, or compelled by drink—none of which tends to happen during normal business hours. My grandfather, who had a hard enough time falling asleep with strangers in his house, was occasionally awakened by the sound of loud knocking. *Do you hear that?* Madame would bellow at a customer. *The footman of fate is calling for you!*

The knocking came from Madame herself, rapping her knuckles under a table; it was never a customer at the front door. Madame installed herself more or less permanently in the front room so she could watch the walkway and dramatically open the door a moment before a visitor could ring the bell, as if to say *I knew you'd be here.*

For some reason, my grandfather slept soundly in the crowded movie house. Maybe his sleeping problem at home had nothing to do with noise or strangers, and everything to do with intrusion. In any case, my mother would let her old man sleep through two screenings of the same movie before waking him to take her home.

Sunday mornings, Madame would hang up her hand-lettered sign—"Temporally Indisposed"—so she could watch my mother perform the movie. Solo. Line for line. Every character. With improvised narration to make up for the lack of scenery and special effects.

I would be tempted to call this story one of my mother's exaggerations if I hadn't seen her do it myself. When I was sick in bed at nine years old, she performed "The Graduate" for me by memory. The woman wasn't able to remember her own anniversary date, but if she saw a movie twice, it was burned into her mind.

This was how my mother grew up, watching and re-enacting movies from the time she was a little girl until she was sixteen years old. What happened then? She met my father and had me. The end.

Stepping into Madame's house from the sun-blasted porch was like coming into a cave. A single lamp was on, but heavy drapes covered the windows, and it took a moment for my eyes to adjust. At first, I could just make out the blocky shapes of furniture—a loveseat, a piano, the fuzzy star of the lamp—and then the loveseat stirred.

"Tough drive?" it said.

Madame filled the loveseat as though it were a chair.

Her hair, limp with sweat, curled about her face in loose tendrils. My father put one hand on my shoulder, as though afraid she might snatch me away. In a cracked voice, he asked, "Where is she?"

Madame held up her finger—*one moment*—then picked up what appeared to be a slender microphone with a little keyboard at its base. She pressed one of the keys and spoke into the mike. "Roger, they're here. Will you kindly help them with their bags?"

My father and I looked at each other. She had the whole place wired. That explained the voice of God on the porch. The next thing I heard was my grandfather's voice. "What, are their legs bro—"

She released the key. "Roger will be up in a moment." Then she looked at me and smiled broadly. "Oh, Timothy. Your boy is handsome as a nickel."

My father would not be sidetracked. "I want to know," he said, "what you know."

She nodded. "And I, you."

He cocked his head, confused, but before he could speak, Madame held up her hand, looking pained. "But there is time for all of that. After we greet each other like civilized people." She beckoned to me, and her muumuu billowed, flag-like. "Send me my grandson."

My father pushed me forward. I was surprised, but now I think he might have seen me as the *tit* for her *tat* of knowledge. I stumbled forward into the living room, but pulled up when

I heard her sharp little wheezes. What did he want me to do, hug her? It would be like embracing an inflatable pool.

"You're nervous," she said.

I shook my head. Then, remembering what my father had said about honesty, I shifted into a nod. Behind me, he groaned.

"Take a minute to look around," Madame said. "Acclimate. I'm not going anywhere."

Maybe that was her attempt at a joke; maybe it wasn't. All I knew was that when I'd visited her as a child, Madame had been about as mobile as a glacier, and she didn't look like she'd spent the last seven years getting more agile.

I scanned the room, feigning interest in the bookshelves that lined the walls. Madame picked up a short metal wand from a basket next to her loveseat. It was probably just a broken television antenna, but when she telescoped it out, I assumed it was a special tool for seat-bound psychics. "Science fiction," she said, pointing the tool at one wall, then sweeping it around the room. "Philosophy. Religion. The occult. Self-help."

I nodded and she chuckled, a deep sound. "That was a joke, son. Any of these books could fit into any of those categories. What you call them says more about you than it says about the book. No finer mirror than a book." She swirled the antenna like a wand. "Go ahead and take one."

My father cleared his throat. "Oh, you don't have to give him a book, Madame." His voice had a strained, polite tone, but I could tell he really meant *DON'T give him a book*. "Maybe later," I said, and she gave me a long look. Beads of sweat sat atop her lip like diamond seeds. Before I knew what was happening, she had taken my hand.

"No-ho-oh," said my father, thunking across the room.

"No palm-reading for us today, thank you." Prying my hand from her grip, he smiled hard, which made him look demented.

Madame winced and pulled her hands in toward her chest. Against the dune of her body, her hands were small things, almost dainty, as pale and harmless as gulls. "Oh, forgive me. What was I thinking? No sooner do you walk in the door than a fat lady grabs your hand. I *am* sorry," she said to me. "I don't get many palms in here any more." She made a sour face and shook her head at my father. "Worst move I ever made, coming down here. Rich people don't want to know their fortunes. Too much to lose, I guess. Every once in a while I'll get a gardener or a cleaning woman, but that's about it. I'm learning Spanish from audio tapes." She looked at me, folding her hands prayerfully. "*Lo siento, niño* of my *corazo.*"

My father watched her warily. Then he jerked his head at me and started for the door, telling me to give him a hand with the bags. Before I could follow him, though, she grabbed my hand again, and her voice came low and quick: "Do you think your father tells you the truth?"

I looked back and was caught by her eyes, green with flecks of amber, just like my mother's. For a strange moment I got the sense that my mother was trapped inside of Madame, peering out from underneath all that flesh, and it made me feel motion sick all over again. Then my father was yanking on my arm, telling me to go, *get*, the adults were going to have a little conversation, but I sank my hips and pulled against him, all the while keeping my eyes on Madame. Whatever she was going to tell me, I had to hear.

Maybe Madame was really psychic, or maybe she was not. One thing was certain, though: she had no shortage of powers. Suspense was her juju. Her gris-gris bag was full of questions shaped like hooks.

Our struggle was short-lived. My father got his arm around my waist and towed me, kicking air, out the door, but not before I heard her say, quietly, as though two males weren't battling in her living room, having turned on each other within ten minutes of arrival—I heard her say: *you were no accident.*

# Chapter 7

In the backyard, I found my grandfather in a fraying lawn chair next to the mini-barn. After grunting a greeting, he returned to tinkering with the small motor in his lap. He looked like he didn't want to be bothered, with bags or relatives. Fine with me. I was bothered enough for both of us.

My father was still in the house. He'd pushed me out the door with orders to help my grandfather with the bags, then stepped back inside with a wild look in his eyes, apparently ready for round two with Madame.

I plunked myself down on the ground and stared into the setting sun. It hurt, and I liked it. What had Madame meant, *not an accident*? Of *course* I was an accident. I'd figured that out as soon as I could do basic subtraction, and my mother—never one for holding anything back for my benefit—had essentially confirmed it. At the same time, she told me it didn't mean she didn't love me, or even that she hadn't wanted me: the accident was merely in the timing. "You know me, Revie," she said with a shrug. "I never could schedule for shit."

Was Madame suggesting that she had gotten pregnant on purpose, maybe to trap my father? That didn't make any sense. Both my parents had wanted to go to California. Why would my mother sabotage their plans?

And if Madame had meant her words to be a lie of comfort—*You were wanted, after all*—she had missed the mark. Being an accident hadn't bothered me for years. What bothered me was having the story of my origin called into question.

The other thing bothering me just then was how my grandfather was letting me look into the sun. Was he just going to sit there and let it happen? Didn't he know that I could burn out my vision?

I said, "Everything is white. Pure white."

"I bet it is."

Now I knew where my mother had gotten her reckless streak. When I heard a car engine turn over, I looked around, but my vision was filled with big white holes, like melting celluloid. "What's that?" I said.

"Your father, pulling away. Madame, going with him."

"What are they doing?"

"What am I, the narrator?" A moment later, he relented. "Looks like they were arguing. Will wonders never cease…"

They were looking for my mother, I decided. After all, if all they wanted was to argue, they could have stayed in the house. I was about to suggest this to my grandfather, but he had already returned to working on the small motor. He obviously didn't care about what was going on with his family or my eyeballs, so I dropped both subjects and got up to poke through the barn.

The mini-barn was the proverbial twenty pounds of shit in a ten pound bag. Maybe thirty pounds of shit. There was a lot of shit in there, is what I'm saying. Rusted tools hung over flywheels and mower blades and extracted van seats. Along the wall was a palisade of rakes and hoes and weed pickers. Everything reeked of two-cycle gas. With all the metal points shining in the afternoon sun, the barn looked like the devil's yawn.

I stepped into the narrow aisle that ran down the middle of this mess, looked toward the back of the building—and that's when I saw it.

It was up against the wall, serving as a hitching post for broken weedeaters. The tank was midnight blue. Chrome extended in every direction like a crazy Christmas star. Unlike the effeminate *Spree* and *Razz* scooters that were starting to appear on the streets of Paris, this one looked like an actual motorcycle, only smaller.

"Hey," I called out. "Does this bike work?"

"Works enough to get you killed."

"So, would a person need a license to ride it?"

My grandfather appeared in the barn door. He sucked his teeth. "I'm getting ready to sell it."

"Yeah?" Looking at the leathery tassles hanging off the handlebars made me feel lovesick.

"So don't wreck it."


The road into town was nine miles of flat ribbon, a straight shot lined with ditches and tomato farms. The scooter topped out at fifty miles an hour, which, if you're on a bike for the first time without a helmet, feels like the speed of sound.

After helping me maneuver the bike out of the barn—no mean feat, navigating through all that crap—my grandfather had shown me how to twist the handlebars to accelerate, and squeeze the hand-brake to slow down. "Automatic," he said. "It's idiot-proof." Then he looked at me and seemed to doubt his own words.

The road was so smooth I felt like I was floating, which may not be a necessary condition for ecstasy, but it helps. I hadn't exactly forgotten about what Madame had said, but it was tumbled under a rapturous feeling of escape.

Had my mother felt something like this when she'd pulled away from our house? I thought she only felt terrible, as terrible as I'd felt at that moment, but maybe there was a second chord in her heart, a major chord of freedom and speed, the same one playing in my heart as I twisted the throttle and felt the bike *leap*.

My God, this was the best thing I had ever done. I decided right then that I would never buy a car. I would get a bike and follow two-lane roads around the world, stopping only for gas and adulation from small crowds. This feeling was better than the old electric feeling; it might have been better, even, than *being* Jesus.

I bent over the handlebars. The headlight came out of my mouth like a sword of light.


By the time I reached town, the sun had set. Insects hung in shaggy crowns around the yellow streetlamps on the town square. Older boys lounged on benches beside the sidewalk, smoking and lobbing hockers onto the courthouse lawn. They struck poses of bored rebellion for the benefit of the few girls who flitted by on the sidewalks, all of them checking each other out while pretending not to look or care.

It might have been an old game, but it was new to me. I parked the bike on the square so I could watch how the game was played, so that one day, hopefully not too far off, when I—

"Nice ride."

I turned to see a girl slouching on a bench. She was tall and lanky, or maybe she just seemed that way because her old jeans and tank top looked like one long stripe. Next to her were two rawboned boys, sitting back like boxers between rounds of a fight. All of them were older than me by at least two years, maybe three.

"Thanks," I called back, trying to sound bored, though I had a panicky feeling like my stomach was looking for the emergency exit. "I'm saving up for a bigger one."

"How big?" called one of the boys, smoothing his feathery mustache. The other boy didn't speak, but his amused sneer seemed to indicate that he would be glad to kick in my ribs for me.

I held out my arms. *About yea big.*

Mustache boy snorted. "Like, how many cc's?"

Shit: what was a cc? Carbon copy? "About twelve thousand," I said.

Oh, they enjoyed that one. The boys punched each other and flopped around the bench in hilarity. The girl turned her head and said *leave him alone*, and my heart fell through a trapdoor, because the only thing worse than getting my ass kicked was having a girl stand up for me.

Then she started walking toward me, and I felt better.

"Lissy," cried one of the boys. "We were just messing. Come on, now."

Biting her lip, she flipped them off without even turning around. Wow. Sexy. Was this happening in real life? Was this girl really walking toward *me*? And would those boys, who were now giving me a whole semaphore display of threats—throat-slicing, fist-pounding, mouthing of *dead meat*—actually kill me for it? Anything seemed possible, and that was as terrifying as it was thrilling.

"Don't judge our town by those dillholes," she said, shaking her head. Her blonde hair, held back by a banana clip, tossed like a soft mane. Easy for her to dismiss the dillholes. It wasn't *her* heart they were pretending to yank out and eat raw. Apparently my heart was delicious. Apparently my heart-juices would run down their chins and drive them mad with pleasure.

Forcing myself to look at her instead of the dillholes, I said, "How'd you know I'm not from around here?"

She grinned. "That's the second dumb thing you've said tonight." She crossed her eyes and made buck-teeth. *"About 12,000 cc's, durrrrrr."*

For the next twenty minutes, as the boys ran out of pantomimed threats and eventually slumped back onto the bench, she proceeded to burn me down to the ground with ridicule. She started with my hair—"It's amazing what a Flowbee can do nowadays, isn't it?"—and worked her way down, insulting my Adam's apple, my skinny arms, and my dark jeans, before shifting from observation to conjecture. "I bet you dance like a goon," she said. "Show me your best move."

I laughed and laughed. Her insults were little darts of pleasure. When she lifted her tank top to scratch lazily at her tan belly, I clutched my hands together, half-afraid I might stick a finger in her belly button. Good Lord, this girl was a tease, in every sense of the word.

Gradually, her insults slowed down, and she began to give me expectant glances I didn't understand. Was it my turn? Was I supposed to make fun of her back, or make fun of myself so she wouldn't have to do all the work? This would have been hard enough to figure out if I'd been thinking straight, which I wasn't, either because she was too quick for me, or because a glimpse of her navel had me flustered, or because half of my mind was still occupied with my damn family.

"Something bothering you?" she said, stepping closer. I *was* bothered. In every way. And then, because I didn't know what to say, and because she was standing close enough for me to feel heat radiating from her skin, and because she was obviously waiting for something, I rose up on my toes and tried to kiss her.

It's amazing how fast a girl can turn her head.

"I'm not trash," she said when I fell back on my heels. "I'm a lady, all right? I don't move that fast."

I pulled a strand of hair from my lips, then asked what seemed to be the only logical question. "How fast do you move?"

She slapped my arm, though she also seemed impressed by

my nerve. "You don't ask a girl *that*."

I rubbed my arm. "What the hell am I supposed to say? I don't know how any of this works."

"That's obvious. Say: when can I see you again?"

"When can I see you again?"

"Who said I *want* to see you again?"

I scuffed a toe against the street, sending a spray of gravel against the curb. Goddammit, why did everything have to be so hard?

"I'm just playing," she said softly, searching out my eyes. "You can play back, you know."

"I know," I said, except I didn't.

"Come back some other night," she told me, then held up her hand in a dainty way for me to kiss—and I actually balked. A kiss on the hand shouldn't have been a big deal, even to someone who had never kissed a girl, but I was so stirred up that I was afraid of what I might do with that hand. Lick it, maybe. Stuff it in my pants. Grab her and scream, *You don't know what you're doing to some people!* or *I want to chain you up and bring you presents for a hundred years!*

Somehow I managed a simple, dry kiss to the back of her hand. I managed not to scream when the small hairs tickled my lips, or when she walked down the sidewalk without looking back, or when the dillholes grinned and waved *bye-bye*, their cruelest gesture of the night.

# Chapter 8

The next afternoon, I awoke with my father's foot prodding my ribs, and my first thought was, *I'm busted.* He had been asleep when I got back to Madame's the night before, but I did not think for a minute that I'd gotten away with anything. He knew about the scooter. He had to know. Punishment was coming, I knew—but still, what he said next made me worry.

"Get up," he said. "We're going for a little drive."

"Where?"

"Out. Around. To the country."

To the *country*? A chill went through me. That's what gangsters said in movies, right before someone got gakked. Two guys drive out, only one comes back. I knew my father wasn't going to murder me, but still, the fact that he wanted to take me out where no one could hear me scream—this couldn't be a good sign.

"Move it," he said, giving the mattress another pop with his foot. I scrambled out of bed. The last thing I wanted was to make him angrier.

No sooner was I in the car than I began to have second

thoughts. I should have made a run for it when I stepped into daylight. But where would I have gone? What would I have done next? I had no idea; my imagination wasn't as powerful as my mother's. All I knew was that when my father closed his door and started the car, I felt like I had lost my last chance at escaping real harm.

If my father noticed that I was still wearing the same clothes from the night before, he didn't mention it. At first, he didn't say much of anything. He had the look on his face like he was working out algorithms, but the calculations kept coming out wrong.

After about an hour of driving, during which I hung my head out of my open window, ready to shout for help or clamber out if things got ugly, he pulled over at a gas station. "Stay in the car," he said, before going over to the pay phone. I couldn't hear his conversation, but I watched him go through the entire emotional spectrum of head-shaking, from angry denial, to disappointment, and finally to disgust. When he got back to the car, he started talking.

"Nobody knows nothing," he said, starting the engine. "Not the police, not Madame. If you believe her." He pulled out onto the country road, then gave me a low look. "Which I do not."

I was confused. The police? Is that who he was calling back there?

He turned on the radio, then snapped it off again. "She is totally unreliable. Take the stuff she was saying the other day, for example. That business about you not being an accident? Total horsecrap."

"Huh," I said. I was surprised he was bringing this up now—*this* was what he had been thinking about all morning?—but also more than a little relieved that I might escape an ass-beating.

He said, "Madame's problem is that she holds a grudge. She's still mad at me for taking away her meal ticket."

He paused, apparently hoping I'd ask *What do you mean?*, but I did not. Not only because he was a clumsier tease than the women in my family, but because I was willing to take him at his word. If he said I was an accident and Madame was a bullshitter—well, that was good enough for me. Questions are crowbars, and I was more than happy to keep this particular box nailed shut.

"Understood," I said, but he went on anyway.

"Madame used to trot your mother out to every county fair, craft show, and Greek fest within a hundred miles of Paris. This all started when your mother was your age, Revie. By the time she met me, she'd been reading the palms of lonely men for four years."

I looked out the window, seeing tall weeds and broad ditches and little else. My stomach was sinking, though I didn't know why.

"I didn't plant any ideas in her head," he insisted. "I didn't turn her against her family. She *wanted* out. That's what Madame refuses to understand."

"*I* understand," I assured him. Why wouldn't he stop?

"The other thing she refuses to acknowledge is that a lot of factors are involved in conception. Chance, timing, luck, unconscious desires... a *lot* of factors. So for her to imply that it was all my fault is just, well, it's ridiculous."

I felt something catch inside of me. "Your fault?"

"Like I could snap my fingers and say, bam, you're pregnant."

"*Your* fault?"

"It takes two to tango, is what I'm saying. And while one party might have had certain responsibilities, the other party could have easily provided a back-up option. Or said no. No tango. If she really didn't want to get pregnant."

"I rode the scooter last night," I blurted. "I didn't even wear a helmet."

"Risks are involved," he said. "No matter how safe you try to be. You *could* say, I guess, if you wanted to get real technical about it, that I increased some of those risks. You could say that the odds were changed when I damaged certain things, don't make me say what. But you cannot say—" He shook his head at the ridiculousness of Madame's charge. "—that I got her pregnant *on purpose*. That would make me God!"

I said, "I could have gotten killed. Hit a semi. Run off a bridge. It was the stupidest thing I've ever done."

He sighed, but it had nothing to do with scooters or semis. I'm not even sure he heard me. Even if he did, I stood no chance of derailing his story. No army is as powerful as a confession whose time has come.

"We were going to run away to California," he said. "Well, she was running away. I was just, you know, moving. But then I started wondering, what if we both flopped out there? Or worse, what if I flopped, and she didn't?"

He shook his head. At some point he'd taken his foot off

the gas and we were now coasting down the empty road. For a second, I entertained the thought of opening my door and flinging myself into the ditch.

"I kept thinking," he said, "that she might turn to me, once we got out there, and say, *Thanks for springing me from my family, Tim, and it's been real nice getting to know you, but actually I'd like to be completely free for once.* Scenes like that kept knocking around my head, wouldn't let me sleep. I just kept thinking, what if she leaves me?"

I let my head fall back against the headrest. Motion sickness was coming on again, and I felt like I was floating. Or maybe like I was in free-fall. It can be hard to tell the difference until you hit the ground.

He said, "Then one day I had another thought. I thought, well, she won't leave me if she's pregnant." He snapped his fingers. "Just like that, all the questions went away. And I slept like a baby."

# Chapter 9

In the old days, I'm told, crazy folks would go live on the outskirts of town. Conventional wisdom says they were cast out by the townspeople, but I'm not so sure. It seems just as likely that they'd experienced more than they could bear, and, stunned, limped away to be alone.

When we got back to Madame's, I retreated to the mini-barn.

Some children might have heard a note of good news in my father's confession—*I wasn't an accident after all!*—but not me. I'd been living inside a lie. My whole life was a story. I was worse than an accident: I was an ambush.

As the sun slid down the sky, I remembered how my mother had left, how she hadn't protested at all, and I felt like an idiot. No wonder she didn't beg to stay—she'd probably seen it as a pardon, not an exile. What prisoner doesn't dream of escape?

"Ah, this is horseshit," my father said.

Startled, I looked around, but my father was nowhere to be seen. When his voice came again—"You just want to put a curse on me"—I noticed, near the door of the mini-barn, a white speaker with a tiny red light.

My father's voice was small, as though he were a long way from the microphone, but when Madame answered, her voice was clear and loud. "I thought you didn't believe in any of that nonsense, Timothy."

I walked over to the intercom. What was going on? And why did Madame want me to hear it?

"I'll make you a deal," my father said. "Tell me what you know—all of it—and then you can do whatever you want to me."

"Sweet Jesus," she snapped. "Use your head. Do you really think I'm obstructing the search for my daughter to *spite you*? God on high, you have the biggest ego I have ever—" Her voice broke off, and the intercom was silent for a moment. When she spoke again, it was in the calm, theatrically enunciated tones of her Madame Zygovia character. "If I knew anything, Timothy, I might not tell you—"

"I knew it."

"—but I certainly would tell the police. Whatever else you think of me, I am a mother. *Her* mother. I'm just as worried as you are, even if I don't express it in such vulgar and harried ways."

A long, quiet moment followed. I squinted at the white box, as though, if I focused hard enough, I might see what was happening in the room. Was my father calculating? The longer his silence went on, the less likely that seemed. More likely he was changing his mind, a process that was like the Queen Mary making a U-turn: it took a long time, and it was best to give him a lot of space.

"Ah, hell," he said at last. "I'm wasting my time here."

"Untrue."

"You don't know shit. You just admitted it."

"I don't," she said. "But you might."

"What the hell?" I could practically see him bristling.

"Haven't you ever had *déjà vu*, Timothy? That's your brain telling you, *You knew this was going to happen. Déjà vu* occurs when just a little of your natural foreknowledge leaks out. Imagine if you could tap into the source. Wouldn't you want to know what's going to happen? Right now, wouldn't you like to know how all of this is going to turn out?"

I did. But then, I was a sucker, a boy with zero immunity to bullshit, so is it really a surprise that I fell for Madame's ploy? My father, on the other hand, had warned me specifically about her trickery. No way would he—

"Natural foreknowledge?" he said.

"Come closer," she said. "Let me tap it."

"You need a knife to do that? Can't you just, you know, read my palm?"

I looked at the house. "Oh, no."

Madame said, "Get on your knees over that bowl."

Oh, my God. She was going to cut his throat, and she wanted me to hear it. She was broadcasting the death of my father. I mashed every button on the face of the intercom, shouting *Stop it* and *I'm out here* and *Let's think about this for a minute* until I realized that she must have blocked me out. I was about to run into the house when I heard her say, "Give me your finger. No, that one."

I turned back to the intercom. "His finger?"

"Now suck on it," she said. "Don't get any blood on my furniture."

A pinprick. I laughed out loud in sheer relief. I closed my eyes and dropped my head against the intercom—and just then, as if I'd closed a psychic circuit, I could see Madame's front room as clearly as though I was looking in the window. Call it extra-sensory ability, my inheritance of imagination, or pure delusion: what you call it may say more about you than about the picture in my mind.

The only light in the room came from an old-fashioned candelabra on top of the piano, three candles branching out of a brass trunk like the Father, Son, and Holyghost. Little tongues of flame reflected on the spines of Madame's books. On the floor was a white cereal bowl, filled with tap water. And there was my father, on his knees before the bowl, sucking on his ring finger as his blood caught the currents in the water and made them visible.

In her loveseat, Madame leaned over the bowl, wheezing sharply. From her hand dangled a letter opener, shaped like a little sword.

"What do you see?" my father said.

In the barn, I opened my eyes, but I did not lose the picture. I was in both places at once. Out here, the sun was nearly down, and the small path through the center of the barn was a column of flame.

"What's going to happen to us?" my father said. This was why we had come here, for Madame's counsel and prophecy, even if my father hadn't known it when we left Paris.

All over my body, goosebumps rose to sharp points. I

held my breath, the better to hear her vague and rambling pronouncement, filled with warnings and cryptic promises, portents that might only make sense in retrospect. I did not expect a single sentence, as quick and painful as a knifing.

"You're going to lose her," Madame said, and the speaker went dead.

# Chapter 10

The sound of the wind in your ears when you're riding without a helmet on a scooter at fifty miles an hour—you might think it would be loud enough to drown out thought, but you'd be wrong.

I bent over the handlebars for more speed and sound. When I came to a stop sign at a blind corner, I blew through it without easing off the throttle. I took ninety-degree turns too fast, leaning hard, waiting for the slip that would lay me out on the asphalt.

Risks were involved. You could say, if you wanted to get technical about it, that I was increasing some of those risks. You could say that I changed the odds when, on one long stretch of road, I closed my eyes for a ten-count. But you could not say I was trying to kill myself on purpose.

I was pushing fate in the chest to see if it would hit me back. I was throwing my life at God, saying *Heads up!*

At an intersection ahead of me, the traffic light turned red. I gunned the bike and bent down until my forehead touched the speedometer. Wind drilled the crown of my skull. My stomach floated like a soap bubble. Never in my life have I felt speed so purely.

A horn sounded in my ear. I felt like I was in free-fall, this time so strongly that I thought I'd actually taken off, flying through the air like a human spear, or was maybe already dead, killed so quickly by a truck that I hadn't even felt the impact, an overloaded semi striking me like a cosmic mallet, knocking my soul out to heaven, or to space, or to—well, I didn't know, but I was ready to find out.

Luckily, I didn't get what I wanted.

Eventually, the falling sensation faded and I looked up to find myself still in the world, attached to the bike, with nothing in front of me but an empty road. A station wagon swung out to pass me, and the driver glanced over with a look of amazement and annoyance. *What the hell is wrong with you?*

I wished I knew.

"I didn't think you'd come back," said Lissy. "You seemed so frustrated when you left the other night."

The town square was dark except for the soft yellow lamps around the courthouse. The dillholes were nowhere to be seen, and I allowed myself to think that Lissy had come here specifically to see me. Her french braid? Her bright white undershirt, which was maybe even new? For me. All for me.

"I didn't have anything else to do," I told her. I meant that to sound casual, like seeing her was only slightly preferable to watching re-runs on TV, but my voice wobbled with emotion, which made the line sound desperate. I tried to explain. "My mom left."

Her eyes widened. "Left, as in *left?*"

Without thinking, I nodded.

"Just now?" she said. "Like, today?"

My head kept nodding. Why, I didn't know.

"Are you sure she's gone, then? I mean, if she just left today, maybe she's just, like—"

Now I shook my head, as if there was no hope. What was I doing? I wasn't sure she was gone. In fact, I wasn't sure of *anything*, so why was I acting like I'd never see her again?

"Oh," said Lissy, and the next thing I knew, her arms were tangled around me and I could smell the bleach from her shirt and feel the padded firmness of her bra against my chest. "I'm sorry," she whispered, her mouth moist against my ear like this little sea creature. Every hair on my body stood on end, just like when I used to think about becoming Jesus.

"Take me for a ride," she murmured. "I want to show you something."

Her naked body: that's what I thought she was going to show me. And then I would be naked, too. And then she would teach me how to play another game.

*My body, given for you.* Whether her offering would have been to soothe me, or merely to distract me, I didn't know. The logic wasn't clear, but the idea was no less persuasive for it.

But even as my mind fast-forwarded to the naked scenes, I felt the drag of reluctance. I might not have been sure about God anymore, but cruising along dark country roads with a girl clinging to my back, I discovered that I still believed in hell.

That's where I would end up, I was sure, if I had sex with Lissy under false pretenses—a phrase that had always prompted my mother to say, *What other kind of pretenses are there, dear?*— and perhaps even immediately. I'd heard of men dying in the act (*I thought he'd just passed out*, the women always said later). It didn't escape my notice that these deaths never seemed to happen when a man slept with his wife. No coincidence, to my mind, but instant damnation.

The fact that I had no wife and Lissy was no hooker made no difference to my mind. I didn't know much about girls but one rule was pretty obvious: you don't use pity to get into a girl's pants. That much was common sense, as my father might have said.

Of course, he'd had his own pretenses with my mother. And he'd used *me* to make her his wife. Was he going to hell? Well, at least I'd know someone there.

Her chest was flush against my back like a warm cape; her hands were laced around my waist. Already it felt too good to stop.

"Pull over up here," she shouted over the wind, pointing to a dark meadow. I swung the bike over to the side of the road. Lissy hopped off before I came to a full stop. By the time my shaky foot found the kickstand, she was already slipping through a split-rail fence.

*Honesty*, I told myself. *Forthrightness. Best to give her everything up front.*

Her legs were long, and I had to run to catch her on a grassy hill. She smelled like sweat and apples, and I almost faltered, but I thought again of hell, and I said, "I am not a good person."

She kept walking. "Hush with that."

"I'm a liar. An awful liar."

Her braid danced as she shook her head. "I don't know what made your mother leave, and neither do you, but you cannot blame yourself. That is one thing you cannot do."

"But she's not gone," I said. "I mean, not all the way. Not yet. The truth is, we don't actually know—"

She stopped so abruptly that I nearly plowed into her. "Oh, Revie," she said, turning and taking my hand. "You need this worse than I thought."

*Well*, I thought. *I tried.*

Milkweed scratched my shins as I walked with her up the hill. My heartbeat was a series of explosions. My legs got heavier and heavier until they felt like concrete footers, which made no sense to me. I was acting like something terrifying was over that hill, instead of sex.

Just then, we crested the hill and I saw a junkyard of farm equipment, or appliances stacked in weird ways, stovepipes and kettle-curves under the moony sky—and then one of the appliances began snuffling.

"What the hell kind of cows are those?" I said.

"Not cows," she said. "Camels."

"Like, for tourists?" I pictured camels slouching around a dirty ring while children stuck lollipops to their humps.

A few years ago, she told me, archeologists had discovered camel fossils around here. Shortly thereafter, this old rancher got the idea to bring camels back to "their native land."

"Okay," I said hesitantly, still trying to understand what these camels had to do with all the sex we were going to have. A few of the beasts stood up, complaining loudly, and began to lumber up the hill in our direction. I took a step back, but Lissy tightened her grip on my hand. "Hold still. This is why I brought you here."

My heart fell down, disappointed and relieved all at once. But as soon as Lissy plucked a handful of grass, saying, "You better feed them so they don't get pissed," any relief I'd felt was gone.

"Are you *crazy*?" I said. "What if they chew off my arms?"

"They definitely will if you don't feed them some grass."

I couldn't tell if she was serious, but I didn't want to take a chance on being eaten by camels or worse, looking like a sissy in front of a girl. So I pulled up a clump, closed my eyes, and stretched out my hand.

What reached me first was the camel's breath. It smelled like an old purse left out in the rain. A large, leathery mouth brushed my knuckles. The feeling was strange but good, somewhere between a tickle and a shiver.

Opening my eyes, I saw a weird, muppet face, with slitted nostrils opening and closing, and comically long eyelashes under the shelf of a brow.

"Pet his nose," Lissy said.

Taking care to avoid the whiskers, which were as thick as broom straws, I smoothed the camel's nose with my palm. It sighed, a strangely delicate sound. I was bending over to pull up another hank of grass when Lissy said, "Okay, for this next part, you're going to want to go down by the fence."

I'd like to think that if I'd known she was going to do something dangerous, I wouldn't have shrugged and trotted down the hill, relieved to be in possession of all my limbs. In other words, I'd like to think I didn't just abandon her.

The first scream came before I reached the fence. A high, night-splitting sound.

I froze. *The camels got her,* I thought. But did I run back to save her? Did I even look around? I did not. I sprinted to the fence and vaulted over it. Only when I was safely on the other side did I turn around, and that's when I saw Lissy running across the ridge of the hill, screaming her head off, only now her scream didn't sound like an expression of pain or fear, but like awkward joy, and it seemed to be scrambling the camels' brain waves.

The camels ran after her, spazzing out. Legs flailed—to the sides, up in the air, every which way. Their necks whipped around like dropped fire hoses. The best rodeo rider in the world couldn't have stayed atop one of those beasts for three seconds, that's how crazy they were going. The whole scene might have been funny if Lissy hadn't been up there with them, or if the creatures weren't so damn big, or if they weren't closing in on her.

At the far end of the ridge, the camels caught up to her. All their shapes blended together and sank into the earth and the screaming stopped.

I gripped the rail. "Lissy?"

I waited for her to come sauntering over the hilltop, laughing at me. *You were so scared!* I would laugh, too. Whew! You really had me going there for a second. Very funny.

Verrrrrrrry funny. And then I could grab the straps of her undershirt and pretend to shake her—*Arrrrgh!*—which would turn into an embrace, and a soft kiss, and at the top of the hill, a bull camel would appear in the moonlight to bray hoarsely in a salute to our love—

She wasn't sauntering over. The hill was silent.

"Hey!" I shouted. "I'm worried here! Quit screwing around!"

I should hop over the fence, I knew. I should already be racing over that hilltop. And yet I clung to the top rail as shame and fear warmed my body. This was just how I'd felt when my mother had been attacked by the neighbor's Weimaraner. Paralyzed, and hoping it would end quickly without a huge loss of blood.

To God and the night sky, I screamed, "THIS IS NOT FUNNY!"

Then I thought: what if Lissy wasn't coming back? What if she was trampled on the other side of the hill, where she could hear my shouting just fine, but was unable to call back because her windpipe had been crushed by a camel hoof? What was I supposed to do about that—take her to a hospital? I had a *scooter*, for God's sake. I couldn't haul her trampled body to a hospital, even if I did know where one was, which I did not. Should I find the rancher and ask for help? Only if I wanted to get arrested for trespassing, and also contributing to the trampling of a minor.

Maybe, I thought, I shouldn't do anything.

After all, no one had seen us together that night. Had she mentioned to her parents or friends the possibility that she might see me? Ha. Doubtful. Clearly, the reasonable thing to do was to save the only ass I could—my own—by getting the hell out of here.

I spit in the weeds in fury. "Goddammit," I said, and pitched myself over the fence. That's when I heard her voice behind me.

"Three minutes. Not bad. I've seen better, but at least you didn't try to take off."

Lissy sat on the scooter, tapping her watch. I glared at her, feeling hot in about seven different ways. "What was this, a test?"

She grinned and shrugged. In a taunting voice, she sang, "You came to save me."

"Under false pretenses." My mother's voice echoed in my mind: *What other kind of pretenses are there, dear?*

Lissy's eyes danced until I began to wonder if this whole excursion was some kind of payback. Did she know that I'd lied about my mother? And what I was hoping she would do to me in this meadow? Or maybe that mocking look was her natural expression. Lissy might have only been fourteen or fifteen years old, but she knew how to wield silence like a grown woman.

I walked over and put my hands on the straps of her undershirt, but the *Arrrrrgh* got stuck in my throat. She looked at her watch. "Would you look at the time," she said, though not unkindly. "I really should be getting home."


We left Fort Carsen that night. My father was waiting on the porch when I got back to Madame's house. He dragged his cast across the wet lawn, looking even more exhausted than when we'd arrived. How long had he been out here waiting for me?

A step or two away from me, he opened his arms, and I thought he was going to wrestle me off the bike, or maybe collapse onto me, but instead he pulled me to his chest in a tight embrace.

He didn't say a word, and neither did I. If my father had ever hugged me before, I couldn't remember it. This was as close to an apology or a confession of love as he would ever come. Was it good enough? It would have to be. He was all I had.

I clutched my hands around his back. I nestled my face into his shoulder.

When I think back on this day, one of the longest of my life, what I remember first aren't the confessions or lies or predictions. Not the motorbike, or even the camels, backlit by the moon, running across the hilltop. It's this moment. And for some reason it's mixed up in my memory with Lissy's first embrace. I smell my father's cologne, but I also smell bleach and apples. I feel moist heat against my ear, but I don't know whose it is.

It's a hell of a thing to mix up, my father with a teenage girl, but those two moments might have been the only good ones in the whole trip. Both times, I felt electricity running smoothly between us. Two bodies, closing a loop, returning current to one another.

# Chapter 11

The morning after we came home, my father and I sat at the kitchen table, drinking coffee and staring at the *Post-Tribune*. He should have been at work, and I was supposed to be at school, but by mid-morning it was starting to look as though neither of us would make it out of the house that day. We hadn't dressed or showered or spoken a single word. Not that we were having some kind of stand-off. I think we both felt awful and tender.

The house was so quiet that when the phone rang, it sounded like the air was tearing apart.

My father picked up the phone, and braced himself for bad news. "Hello," he said, and then, after an excruciating pause, "I see."

*Cops?* I mouthed. *Mom?* He swatted the air in my direction, but I couldn't tell if this meant *no*, or *go away*. He said, "I guess I don't know how to feel about that."

"Feel about *what*?" I said.

He turned his back on me. I shouldn't have been surprised. He had a hard time handling distraction on a good day, and these days were far from good. For his part, he shouldn't have been surprised when I slipped down to his bedroom to pick up the extension in time to hear him say, "—that checking the machine wasn't exactly my top priority. Besides, we've only been home a few hours. I haven't had time to do anything yet."

"Well, I did call. Several times."

At the sound of my mother's voice, my heart fired off bursts like a roman candle. Squeezing my eyes shut, I mouthed, *thank you.*

She said, "As soon as I got out here, I started calling. Let the record show. When you guys didn't answer... well, I started to freak out."

When I got out here? Where was *here*? I didn't interrupt. If I could keep my mouth shut long enough, my mother would spill everything. . . Unless my father pissed her off.

"Oh," he said. "*You* started to freak out. Well, I *am* sorry about—"

She said, "I didn't mean for anyone to worry."

"You never do."

Her voice turned prickly. "What does it matter, Tim? If I'm away from you guys, who cares if I'm with my mother down in Florida or if I'm out in California?"

"You're in *California*?" I said.

I couldn't help myself. It just came out. I winced, expecting my father to yell at me to hang up the phone, but he didn't say a word to me. Maybe he'd expected me to eavesdrop, after all.

"Tell us, Rosalyn," he said. "Where are you, exactly?"

"First," she said, "You have to promise—"

"No," said my father. He didn't follow this with reasons or

recriminations; he just waited. Silence is the universal solvent. But did he ever wonder what years of silence and absence had done to his marriage?

For a moment, my mother matched his silence, but she wasn't built for this kind of game, and at last she answered.

"Hollywood," she breathed.

My knees buckled and I sat down heavily on their bed. The roman candle moved to my brain. My voice sounded about a hundred yards away when I said, "Oh, man."

"I'm going to be an actress," she said in the same voice that sounded half like confession, and half like worship.

I fell back on the bed, feeling sick. "Oh, man."

If my father was stunned, he didn't let on. In the same calm, business-like tone, he asked if she had a phone number. She didn't, not yet. She was calling from a pay phone outside her motel, but she had a lead on an efficiency apartment, and once she got that, she could—

"Give us a call when you get a number," my father said. "After that, we'll call you."

He was done with this conversation. But my mother, as usual, tried to push past the ending. "Actually," she said, "I was thinking—"

"Lots of luck, Rosalyn," my father muttered. Then came the small crunch that meant he'd hung up. I waited for her to hang up in retaliation, or for my father to yell at me to get off the phone, but there was only silence in both of my ears, and after a moment I realized I could talk to her all I wanted; no one was going to stop me.

"Hello?" she said.

What could I say? *Come back?* Or: *I want to see you on the big screen?*

I wanted both, but even then I knew it wasn't possible. Everything in my life had been broken in half, it seemed, and each half was incompatible with the other. I felt like I had to choose, but that was the last thing in the world I wanted to do.

"Revie?"

I reached out my hand.

She said, "I want you to know that I still—"

As gently as squeezing a trigger, I pressed the switch hook, hanging up on my mother.

Thus ended the cooling-off period.

# Chapter 12

Al's Tap was like a big, dim, loud ark: everything was made of wood and coated with sticky lacquer, and the only sources of light were the beer signs that gave off a flickering glow suggestive of a firefly in the end stages of ass disease. When my father and I walked in at four o'clock in the afternoon, the bar wasn't even half full, but it sounded packed. Everyone seemed to be shouting at once, not in anger or with any other clear purpose, but shouting apparently for the joy of shouting, like Pentecostals set loose on the floor of the stock exchange.

"The happy hour crowd," my father murmured into my ear as he steered me toward the end of the bar, where a battered television was bolted to the corner of the ceiling.

That morning, after my father had phoned the school to ask them to excuse my previous absences because I was getting over mono—"A bad case," he said, overcooking the lie in his inexperience. "The doctors are thinking about including him in a study of real bad cases, mono-wise"—he'd asked me what my plans were after school. When I shrugged, he told me to walk down to Al's. "We'll have dinner."

"School gets out at 3:30."

"I know that," he said, but his hesitation told me he didn't. "Just come down there."

What was this about? It seemed like the kind of thing my friends with divorced parents had to endure: *bonding time*. Now, though, I think the reason he invited me to Al's Tap was because he already knew me. Enough, anyway, to worry about what might happen if I spent too much time alone in the house.

As I settled onto my stool, my father grabbed a couple of menus from the end of the bar. "How was school?" he asked. "Everything go all right?"

"Sure," I said. "Fine."

The truth was that I'd spent most of the day inside my own head. When I wasn't wondering what my mother was doing in Hollywood, I was daydreaming about Lissy in the field of camels, imagining that scene with a sexy alternate ending, then mentally auditioning other girls from school in the role of Lissy. Some of these girls had really developed over the summer. It was amazing: you'd have thought ten years had gone by, the way some of them had shot up and out in thrilling directions. Woz, sitting at my lab table in science class, sketched their figures in his notebook, labeling the exaggerated bust lines with words like *Juggernauts* and *Boobzookas*. In the background he drew a surprisingly pretty field of *fleur-de-lis*, which, upon closer inspection, turned out to be a hail of penises.

At the bar, a hefty woman leaned on her forearms across from me. "Your father," she said, looking me in the eye, "is a tightass and a fussbudget."

"Hello, Shirley," said my father without looking up from

his menu. "Bloody beer, please."

"In ten years," she said, holding her gray eyes on me, "I've only had one customer send back a drink." She tipped her head toward my father. "I'll give you two guesses who it was."

"And two stoshburgers," he said, pushing his menu across the bar. "Hold the onions."

Shirley leaned close, taking me into her confidence. She was built like a buffalo, but there was something soft about her, as well. Sweat tracked down her downy cheeks, and she gave off the scent of baby powder. "You know how much he tips? Ten percent. To the *penny*. It's true. I did the math. He gets out his little coin purse, and—"

"Now, hold on," said my father. "I sit at the bar so you don't have to walk the food all the way out—"

But she was already lumbering away with our menus, and my father's words were lost in the din. Before I could figure out if she was angry or just fooling around, I felt a hand clap onto my shoulder. It was a man wearing dark glasses, which I assumed were prescription, because no one in his right mind would think that glasses that big and clunky were cool. "Ah, hell." The man grinned. "I forgot it was Take Your Son to the Bar day."

*Heh heh*, I said and tried to shrug him off, but he started rolfing my shoulder, like he was trying to impress me with his hand strength.

"Revie," my father said. "This is Mr. Mishniewicz."

"Call me Mish." The man slapped me on the back, but thankfully knocked off the hard massage. "Columnist for the *Post*. You recognize this mug from my picture in the paper?"

I did not, but I nodded anyway out of politeness. That night I would go home and dig through the stack of old papers in our garage to find Mish's picture above his column, in which he was wearing the same dark glasses.

Shirley brought over my father's bloody beer, and a 7 Up with a splash of grenadine for me. "It's not a Shirley Temple in this bar, Tim's kid, so don't even ask."

After she walked away, my father excused himself to make his rounds. "Back in a minute," he grunted, looping his arm around Mish to hobble back to the booths, where most of the happy hour crowd had congregated. A few minutes later, the stoshburgers arrived under a slippery heap of caramelized onions, a pile so high that their presence couldn't be a mere mistake, but were clearly the culinary version of the middle finger at my father's fussiness. Normally, I would have scraped them off, but I didn't want to look picky or rude, so I tried them, and—Oh. *Oh*—they were good. These were onions? My only prior experience with onions had been the harsh scallions on the vegetable tray that was the cornerstone of nearly every dinner my mother had set out in my life. For years, dinner at our house had consisted of a veggie tray and cold cuts. Or a veggie tray and peanut M&M's. Veggie tray and a frozen pizza burned half to carbon.

My mother was a terrible cook—she freely admitted this—but this was not the reason my father cited for taking his dinners at Al's Tap. Convenience was his only claim. Smack in the middle of downtown Paris, the bar was just a few minutes away from the Broadmoor. He often gave private lessons in the evenings, and he didn't want to come "alllll" the way home, only to drive "alllll" the way back.

He never said that he didn't want to spend time at home, either, though the evidence on that count was pretty convincing, too.

"Doing all right, Tim's kid?" Shirley asked when she came back to re-fill my drink.

I gave her a thumbs-up, golden oil sliding down my wrist. Next to me, my father's stoshburger congealed on his plate as he stumped between booths, listening to jokes and stories. At every pause, two or three men would shout over one another. "That's nothing! Get this, Tim—"

My father, the born audience. Everyone wanted to be blessed by his attention.

And me? Was I jealous that everyone was getting this blessing except for me? Hell, no. I was just happy to be here. Here, where there were stoshburgers and free refills and TV and grown men bitching at the tops of their joyous lungs about taxes, the weather, Japanese automobiles, prostate enlargement, the price of gas, Jesse Jackson, and what passed for a good movie these days. No *wonder* my father ate dinner here all these years. I didn't blame him for one instant. My only question was why he didn't bring us, too? My mother would have loved this scene. Though there weren't a lot of women in the bar. Besides Shirley, who didn't really seem like a woman, there were only a couple of ladies in the entire place, and they scared me a little, with their rattly coughs and freeze-dried hair and slick jackets that read *Pipefitters Local 201*. Is that why my father hadn't brought my mother here? Because she would have felt out of place?

Not a chance. She never felt out of place. Wherever she went, she was the center of attention. When she entered a room, you could practically feel the oxygen suck away—and that, of course, is why he hadn't brought her here. She could have the rest of the world; Al's was his place.

And now he was sharing it with me.

By the time he came back to his plate, I was buzzing with sugar and gratitude. I wanted to throw my arms around him, nuzzle his neck and say *I love you*, and I might have done it, too, if I hadn't known it would scuttle my chances for a return visit. Instead, I pointed to his plate and said, "I'll eat your onions if you want me to." I was almost choking up. "I'll eat them all. I will, Dad. I will."

He smiled at me. His eyes danced around. He put his hand on the side of my neck and gave it a little pop in what was, for him and other men of that time, as close as they could come to an public embrace.

"Okay," he said, which meant *I love you, too*, and also *that's enough*.

# Chapter 13

"I don't know how to start," I said into the phone.

"How about 'Hello?'"

"Hello," I said, then asked my mother how she was doing and she said fine, and I said I was fine, too, because that's what you say in Indiana even if your arms have been torn off by a threshing machine. After a pause, I said, "Now what?"

My mother laughed like this was the funniest thing she'd heard in months.

I was in an old wooden phone booth at the back of Al's Tap. The only light in that corner came from the neon gold rim around the jukebox. Ten days had passed since my mother had first called to announce that she was in California; now, at last, she'd gotten an apartment—"It's called an 'efficiency,' because if you call it a rat hole, you can't charge as much"—and, more importantly, a phone number.

Ten days, but it may as well have been ten weeks for as much as my day-to-day life had changed. Already I was becoming a regular at Al's Tap. Some nights Shirley let me slice citrus while my father made his rounds. I liked that job, because it kept my hands busy and my head down, which was a good cover for eavesdropping. In this way, I learned that Mish, the columnist, couldn't keep his mouth shut about off-the-record comments once he got a few drinks in him. Momo, a hulking Serb who was occasionally pressed into duty as an unofficial bouncer, showed me how to pick up a man by his skull. Shirley taught me the poetic possibilities of cursing. Her favorite epithet might have been *precious babyshit*. One night she made me an omelet as "big as elephant pussy." It's a marvel that I managed to take so much as a single bite after that description, but I actually finished that omelet, every speck and flake, still afraid that the slightest misstep might queer my welcome here.

Ten days after my mother called to tell us she was in California, my father handed me a roll of quarters and a golf scorecard with a phone number scrawled on it. I could call her as much as I wanted, he said, as long as it was from the phone booth. The quarters were for the week; if I wanted to talk more, I could foot the bill myself.

I don't think his limits were about control or vindictiveness. Back then, "long distance" was a term that inspired terror in the hearts of the middle-class. It conjured up images of a meter spinning crazily while dollar bills went up in flames. I'm sure my father worried that if he let me call from home, I'd sigh into the mouthpiece until the bill hit four figures.

He wasn't the only one who felt the pressure of long distance: pressing the phone to my ear, I felt like I had to say something important to my mother, and say it right away.

"The house is a wreck," I told her.

"It was clean when I left it."

"Clothes all over the floor. The mail's in a big heap on the table. Dad hasn't done the dishes *once*."

"How is he doing, by the way? Is he getting enough sleep? Is he eating?"

I looked over to the bar, where he was running his finger along the edge of his plate to get the last crumbs of cake. I'd offered to let him talk to her first, but he declined, even when I tried to give him some of my quarters. Now he signaled to Shirley and pointed down at his empty glass and plate with both index fingers: *Fill 'em up, please.* When Shirley turned away, he reached down quickly to let his belt out a notch.

I said, "I don't think you have to worry about that."

We breathed into the receiver. On the jukebox, little bubbles streamed through the gold piping, making me think of divers with the bends. I said, "So how's it going out there?" praying she would say *awful.*

"Pretty good. I mean, I'm totally confused—it's not like anyone handed me a pamphlet on how to break into the movie business when I came into town—so I'm trying to figure everything out without *seeming* like I'm trying to figure everything out. Like, I've got a phone number for an improv group that I'm going to call tonight—"

Great. I wasn't even her biggest call of the night.

"—and I'm nervous about calling them. I'm actually sweating. Do I tell them that I don't have any actual acting experience, *per se*, or do I, you know, fudge it a little?"

My heart sank and sank. She didn't sound awful; in fact, she sounded nearly giddy, as though she expected me to share in her enthusiasm.

"Real sweat," she said. "Here's a drop right here. Geez, I'm practically dripping. *Whew.* I'm just going to go over here and turn up the air conditioner... oh, there we go. *That* feels good. Goo-oo-ood."

Something about this sounded off. "Are you doing improv right now?"

A pause. "How did I do? Did you believe I was sweating?"

This was the moment when I could have crushed her. I could have told her that if a twelve-year old could see through her act, she didn't stand a chance with professionals. But here she was with all her hope exposed, wanting stardom so nakedly... and I couldn't do it. I wanted her to feel awful, but I couldn't be the triggerman. Not so directly, anyway.

I said, "I was starting to get a little sweaty myself."

"*No,*" she said. "Really?"

"You're very persuasive," I told her, wishing that I was, too.

# Chapter 14

One day near the end of September, Mrs. Jankovic, the science teacher, took ill. She tried to make it through the period, teaching from a stool, then propping her head up with both hands, and finally laying her cheek against the lab table. "It's all right," she assured us. "I just need to cool down."

"If you have to barf, I can supervise the class," said Bettina Raymer.

"No," said Mrs. Jankovic, and that was the last word we heard from her for six months.

The next day, a stranger showed up in class. Slouched over, her dark hair pulled back into a sloppy ponytail, she looked like someone's dropout sister come to deliver a forgotten lunch. I don't think any of us guessed she was a sub until she wrote her name on the board: *Miss Dupay.*

"They're hiring bag ladies now?" murmured Woz. I shrugged, distracted. I was re-running the Lissy daydream, which grew more distant from reality with each viewing. The camels were out of the picture (too smelly, and I didn't like them watching) and now Lissy looked like Farrah Fawcett. In the newest version of the daydream, she jogged toward me in slow-motion from the far end of the meadow, her clothes falling off along the way.

The sub turned from the board and wiped chalk dust onto her hips. Her black, stretched-out sweater hung over baggy leggings, making her look like a sooty mushroom. "Who in here," she said, "is exerting gravitational force?"

No hands went up. In my mind, Farrah-Lissy unzipped her jeans and ran out of them without breaking stride. Woz drummed his pencils on the edge of our lab table, whispering, "Hot for teach-ah." Finally Bettina raised her hand. "Um, isn't gravity for planets?"

Miss Dupay started down an aisle. "Planets, stars, black holes—yes, little girl, all of these have serious pull, but anything that has mass exerts a gravitational force. You have mass, right?"

She addressed this to Ray Morley, a kid with slick hair and a pager. Ray smirked at the class before saying, "I'm a Presbyterian."

No one laughed, including Miss Dupay. But she didn't look exasperated, either, which was how most teachers reacted to Ray Morley. "You exert gravity," she said softly, holding his eyes until his smirk faltered. "You are a tiny planet."

Another teacher might have paused to let us absorb the momentous fact that we were all tiny planets, but not Miss Dupay. "Consider clouds," she said, moving down the aisle. "You see a cloud floating through the sky—what keeps it from breaking apart into millions of individual molecules? Why does it stay together?"

"For the sake of the child molecules?" said Ray, but he

no longer seemed sure of himself, and everyone ignored him. "Gravity?" guessed Carly Vellucci.

"No one knows!" said Miss Dupay, and threw up her hands in what looked closer to joy than frustration. "The answer probably has something to do with the total gravity of the cloud, but something else is going on, too. It could be *like aggregation*, which simply means that like objects attract. In the middle of the Pacific is a giant reef of condoms. Two miles long! Sixty feet deep! How did this reef form? Does it have a specific kind of gravity, some kind of homing signal that calls lone condoms through miles of open sea to the mother reef?"

Woz turned to me, eyes wide. *Condoms?* he mouthed.

Miss Dupay brushed past our table, smelling like a rain barrel. I felt the tug of her gravity, or imagined I did. In any case, I was no longer daydreaming about Lissy.

"Chinatown!" She passed the frog tank, the pencil sharpener, the ramshackle spider plants. "Bridge clubs! Red tide, senior living communities, the way cat fur clumps together on your carpet—whoever figures out this phenomenon, whoever connects the dots between gravity and like aggregation will see the living heart of all existence. That person, blessed soul, will understand the unifying theory of the universe."

She stopped at the front of the classroom, scanning the rows of desks as if she might recognize the lucky soul by sight. I sat up taller. Woz held his drumming pencils rigidly in front of him. In that moment—I believe this as strongly as I believe anything—every student in that room, boy and girl alike, prayed the same prayer, the same one I had prayed to Holyghost only a few months earlier when I wanted to be the next Jesus: *Pick me.*

The bell rang.

"Oh my God," said Woz. "I hope Mrs. Jankovic is out forever. I hope she's dead."


Mrs. Jankovic was not dead, as it turned out, or even ill. She was pregnant, suffering from morning sickness that lasted all day. Miss Dupay told us this, along with the fact that Mrs. Jankovic's doctor had ordered her on bed rest "for the duration."

Miss Dupay went on to offer a critique of bed rest. "On a basic physical level, a pregnancy is no different than an organ transplant or a giant cyst: a foreign body is lodged inside your own. But instead of applying modern scientific methods to pregnancy, we pretend we're in the stone age. *Bed rest*, for God's sake. If you had a tumor the size of a cantaloupe, would a doctor tell you to go lie down?"

Miss Dupay liked to draw connections between seemingly unrelated subjects. "There is no such thing as a *non sequitur,*" she was fond of saying, though she not only refused to define the term for us, but also discouraged us from looking it up, because why should we learn about a false concept?

By itself, science was boring and unreliable, she let us know, as was philosophy, or sociology, or folklore. But where these subjects intersected—*that* was the area she wanted to explore. "The unifying theory," she said again and again. "That's the Holy Grail."

I could have listened to her wild synapses of logic all day.

The fact that I had no idea what she was talking about half the time did not keep me from getting tremendously excited by her little speeches. Woz and I tossed around our own unifying theories on the way to school, though none of them were remotely as satisfying as Miss Dupay's.

In October, evenings came on with a sweet coolness, and soon, morning lawns were surprised with frost. The trees at the Broadmoor ignited into color, meeting their demise with good humor. At Al's Tap, men trotted out their winter arguments: the best practices of coolant replacement, where to find a good deal on rock salt, and whether it was worth it to buy that plastic film to insulate the windows of your house. "I don't care if it saves a few pennies or not," said Mish. "I'd feel like an idiot, standing in front of my windows, blow-drying a piece of plastic."

"You have a blow-dryer?" said Shirley. "*No*," said Mish, but his face flushed when Momo remarked on how much *body* Mish's hair had, could he tell us his secret?

Every night I called my mother from the bar, though our conversations were fairly short and shallow. This was all right, I told myself: we were keeping the lines warm for the moment that one of us figured out what to say.

One evening, my father asked to talk to my mother. Handing me a fresh roll of quarters, he said, "Let me have a few minutes when you chatty Cathies are done."

I couldn't have said more than five words to my mother that night before passing the phone over to my father. After more than a month of silence, whatever he had to say to her promised to be infinitely more interesting than a blow-by-blow account of my school day, so I moved to a table on the edge of earshot.

It started off as a calm discussion, mostly about practical stuff. When Revie was due for an eye exam. The mechanic had told her the station wagon was due for a new fuel pump; was that really necessary? How he'd gotten his cast off, and now the calf was all white and shriveled. "Like a baby's leg," he said.

After a few minutes, though, they ran into some kind of disagreement.

"I don't know," my father said. "That's a lot of grapefruit." A moment later he said, "Then you have those trash-bag suits where you can, you know, liquefy the fat." Apparently my mother didn't agree with this theory. "Sure you can," he protested. "Happens on a grill all the time."

Afterward, at the bar, my father chewed his thumb while his bloody beer grew warm. Their disagreement may not have been major, but it hadn't been resolved either—which gave them a reason to talk again.

Maybe they hadn't cooled off entirely, I thought. Maybe there was still an ember that could be fanned into a flame.

The neighborhood around the school was filled with rental houses, small ranches with porches like hooded eyes. As I walked to school one cold morning, I spotted Miss Dupay sitting on a porch, wearing wraparound sunglasses while smoking a cigarette and drinking coffee. I ducked my head, embarrassed to encounter a teacher outside of her natural habitat. Then I surprised myself by looking up and waving.

Across the street, she lifted her mug in a salute.

"You walk?" I called, because I had stopped and didn't know what else to say. Like an idiot, I added, "To school?"

Then I pointed to the school.

Miss Dupay rose, coffee and cigarette still in hand, and waded into the street without checking for traffic. In her long, quilted parka, she looked as though she were floating. She unwound her scarf, sprinkling herself with cigarette ash in the process. "Wrap this around your head," she said, handing me the scarf. It was red and crusted with some kind of whitish spill. Milkshake? "Like a swami, that's right. Seventy percent of body heat is lost through your chimney."

As I wound it around my head I felt ridiculous, but also like I'd been crowned. "What are you going to wear?"

She pointed to her hair, which was down this morning. It was longer than I would have guessed, and though I knew it was brown, it looked gray in the morning light. "Better than a hat." She tipped her head toward the school. "Shall we?"

I hesitated. On the far side of the school, Woz was waiting for me on his porch.

Miss Dupay raised her eyebrows. "Or, you know, I could just walk by my—"

"No," I said, a little too forcefully. Putting on a bad British accent, I said, "We shall!"

Woz could walk himself to school for one day, the big baby. It might even be good for him, I thought. Help him grow up a little.

My father made a crockpot full of cabbage soup and ate from it, morning, noon, and night. At home, he put it in a mug and drank it like tea. He carried it to work in Tupperware I didn't even know we had. At first I thought it was a cost-saving measure, but then I caught him standing sideways before the mirror, sucking in his stomach.

"You're on a diet," said Shirley with an air of accusation. It was Saturday night, All-You-Can-Eat Chili Night at the Tap, but my father was eating his own soup from stained Tupperware, acting as though each spoonful were an ecstasy.

"I'm cleaning out my system," he said. "Think of all the toxins that build up inside your body. Nitrites. Sulfites." He paused to think. "Crud."

"Love handles," added Shirley.

"We replace the coolant in our cars every winter, so why shouldn't we do the same thing for our bodies?"

"Oh, God," groaned Mish. "Not the coolant argument again."

Momo looked over at us with big, pleading eyes. "Antifreeze has no expiration date. It doesn't need to be replaced. It's good *for life*."

This link between auto care and the human body was just the kind of association that Miss Dupay would have enjoyed. I made a mental note to mention it on our walk to school the next morning, which had quickly become a regular occurrence. But apparently not everyone could appreciate such a connection, or get distracted by a dumb argument about coolant. Shirley bent down to give my father's bowl a quick sniff. "Oh, who are you crapping, Tim? That's diet soup."

My father denied it again, but the way he hunched forward told me her charge was true. My face warmed with shame.

This was the nineteen-eighties. Men did not diet. Not in Paris, Indiana. Oh, they might jog a little, or do a few bench presses or bicep curls if their doctors told them their hearts were about to explode, but if they couldn't eat a rib eye with twice-baked potatoes afterward, what was the point of living? Diets were for women. If you didn't know this, all you had to do was look at a magazine rack. If the cover featured a woman, chances were that she was inside a pair of jeans so huge they looked like waders, the headline proclaiming something like *Don't I Look A-Peeling?*, and inside, you'd find out that she'd lost seventy-five pounds eating the peelings of anything she wanted, which meant that this cover-lady had to carry a potato peeler wherever she went, which she tried to play off as the ultimate convenience—*No more wondering which utensil to use!*—like all of her weight problems had been caused by utensil overload.

"That diet works because it's tough to peel lasagna," said my mother. "But you're wrong about men. Men can too diet."

"Maybe in California," I said.

"Anywhere. Why not?"

"He's *married*. He doesn't need to diet."

I admit it: I was trying to kindle an argument. Ideally an argument between them, but I'd have settled for one between us. I might not have been willing to crush her dreams directly, but I wasn't above irritating her. Even then, I sensed that fighting could be an intimate act, even a hopeful act. If nothing else, a fight debrides.

My mother wouldn't take the bait. Her voice was smooth as cold-rolled steel when she answered. "Asparagus is a natural diuretic, did you know that? Tell your father to try that in his soup."

She was on a diet, too, as it turned out. Our family was the toxin my parents were trying to flush from their systems.

One night late in October, my father came home with several bags of clothing.

"Pro shop was having a clearance," he told me as though it were a sign from God: he needed new clothes, and lo, cheap clothes appeared. He dumped the bags onto the kitchen table with the kind of pride you might expect from a hero returning home from a long journey to show off his spoils. He beamed at me. "Colorful, huh?"

You could say that, yes. In fact, if you looked at them long enough, the colors actually seemed to pulse. Something else was strange about these clothes, too... "This says large," I said, holding up a paisley shirt.

He picked up a pair of tan slacks and bit off a tag that said *Slim Fit*. "I tried them on."

"You're not a large."

"Different clothes fit different."

I held the shirt up to my chest. I could have squeezed into it, but barely. Then it hit me. "These are boys' clothes."

He hesitated, then slowly folded the tan slacks. "Who cares? They fit."

"Show me."

He could have refused. He could have said that what he wore was none of my business, and he would have been well within his rights. The fact that he took a striped shirt into his bedroom without any further protest tells me, without a doubt, that he thought he looked bitching.

A minute later he called my name.

When I opened his door, I saw a strange sight. He'd managed to get the shirt over his head and shoulders before getting stuck. Now the shirt covered his face like a sack, and his arms were sticking straight up in the air.

The shirt-sack turned to me. "Little help."

His potbelly was heaving. He must have really struggled before calling me in. But did I take sympathy?

"Well, what do you know?" I said. "It's the Headless Horseman."

"Just pull it down. Give it a yank."

"Do you promise to stop haunting this neck of the woods?"

The shirt sagged. "Revie, this is hurting my shoulders."

Tugging the shirt down was like pulling a twin-sized sheet onto a queen-sized bed. It was even harder and grosser than when I'd put my shirt on Woz back in the summer. That little episode had been in service of a cover-up. What was this one about? Who was my father trying to fool?

Together, we got the shirt on, and my father stepped up to the mirror. The stripes warped across his shoulder blades like latitudinal lines. Chest hairs poked through the meshy fabric.

God, he looked ridiculous. Surely he would see that.

But as he tensed his arms and looked himself up and down, his eyes seemed to say, *Not bad.*

"Too tight," I said, wishing I didn't have to say these words to my father.

"Gives me a goal. Something to shoot for."

"To be the size of a boy?"

"I'm trying to get back down to my fighting weight."

"I thought you weren't on a diet."

He swiveled around, checking himself out from different angles. Then he glanced over at me, as though he'd forgotten I was there. "Hm?"


"Sugar is the purest fuel there is," said Miss Dupay, contemplating the Necco wafer in her hand. "It tastes great, digests quickly, and you don't need all that much to keep your motors humming. It's like high-octane gasoline for the body."

We were eating lunch in her classroom. I'd come in for homework help, but then I'd asked for her opinion, as a woman of science, about my father's diet. The room was dark except for the ambient glow from the frog tank, and in this light Miss Dupay looked different to me. Her neck, which before had seemed gangly, looked long and elegant. Instead of noticing her crooked ponytail, I saw the high curve of her forehead. She looked like a queen from an old painting.

Once she started talking, my homework was forgotten. She managed to stay in her seat, but her knees bounced and she tapped the fingernails of her Necco-free hand on the lab table.

The best way to lose weight, she told me, was not to exercise more, but to sleep more, because you couldn't eat while you slept. "Rip van Winkle wasn't fat, was he?" The mitochondria burned fat; it was the powerhouse of the cell. Certain animals, like bears, had a lot of body fat, but you never heard of a bear having a heart attack, and why was that? She meant to look into that topic one of these days, but that would have to wait until after she'd unpacked the last of her boxes. She'd recently moved up here from Georgia with Daddy and was not so sure about Indiana, though she was trying to keep an open mind.

"Daddy?" I said.

"That's what all the girls down south call their fathers."

"But you don't have a southern accent."

"I didn't say *I* was from the south." She looked triumphant, like she'd really put one over on me. "I take a little something from every place I live. A little personality souvenir."

I looked at her closely. The low light was really playing tricks on my eyes. "How old are you?"

She bit neatly into another wafer with her front teeth—as far as I could tell, her entire lunch consisted of wafers and juice boxes—and said, "Old enough to know better. That's what Daddy always says."


My father's weight dropped quickly. On the kitchen wall next to the calendar, he tacked up a chart. From his notations, I could tell that he was checking his weight daily, sometimes multiple times a day. Within a couple of weeks his clothes no longer stretched over him like sausage casing, but I still couldn't get over the fact that he was wearing boys' clothing.

I tried to lure him away from the cabbage soup by eating his favorite foods in front of him, like fried perch, and gyros, and every kind of pie, but my father only shook his head at me. "That's just more toxin you'll be flushing from your system later on." Then he clutched his stomach and glanced toward the bathroom. "Speaking of which."

By November, the days had grown short and brisk. The sun was almost down by the time I walked to Al's Tap after school. My father still met me there, but sometimes not until dinnertime. I don't know if this was his way of showing his trust, or if he'd just gotten busier at work, but in any case, I was on my own more.

Afternoons, Shirley put me to work polishing glasses. The law wouldn't let her pay me, she said with what sounded like honest regret, but no law said she couldn't make me a snack. She'd retreat to the kitchen, humming in a husky baritone, then emerge with stewed apples, or an enormous wedge of carrot cake, and give the back of my head a quick stroke after setting down the plate.

One day, instead of going straight to Al's Tap, I went over to Woz's house. Woz had an impressive collection of Star Wars action figures. His carrying case—a huge Darth Vader head that opened up, like a sarcophagus, to reveal hundreds of cells—was packed. In fact, his Vader spilleth over. Years of collecting had brought him more figures than the case could hold, a lot of which were either duplicates, or just dumb—who wanted Prune Face with Blaster Rifle anyway?—and these were the ones we decided to sacrifice in his garage.

My job was to set a figurine on top of an overturned garbage can lid and spray the little body liberally with WD-40. Woz got to be the executioner because it was his house and his figurines. He wedged a matchstick under the armpit of Boba Fett, his favorite figure, said, "Mr. Fett? Care to do the honors?" and torqued the figure to strike the match. I didn't care much about lighting stuff on fire, but I'd gone along with the idea because it had been a while since I'd played a game of any kind.

Recently, Michael Jackson's hair had caught on fire during the filming of a Pepsi commercial, so while each figure bubbled and melted inside a clear blue flame, we entertained each other by singing *Just beat it, beat it, no one wants to be defeat—OH MY GOD MY HEAD IS ON FIRE.*

When the lubricant burned off, we were left with melty black lumps of plastic that were soft and warm to the touch. Once they cooled, they were impossible to pry off the lid, a problem we discovered too late. "Is your mom going to be pissed?" I said, yanking unsuccessfully at one of the figures.

"Probably." Woz took a break from polishing Boba's helmet with his shirtsleeve to roll his eyes. This was a new gesture for him, and it was slow and jerky, like he was tracking a fly across the ceiling.

A few months ago, he'd been terrified that we might bend one of his mother's paring knives—and now he was indifferent about arson damage. Sure, it was just a garbage can lid, but still, something about him had changed.

He must have sensed my confusion, because he stopped shining Boba and gave me a flat look. "Look," he said, "she's going to bitch no matter *what* I do, so it's like, who cares?"

As if on cue, the door to the garage cracked open. "Alvin!" yelled his mother. "Is your homework done?"

He raised his eyebrows at me. *See what I mean?*

"And before you lie to me," she went on, "I know that it's not. You've been in that garage since you got home, and don't tell me you're studying out there—"

Woz opened and closed his hand several times. *Yak yak yak.*

"You've got ten minutes," she said, "and then you're coming inside, and you're sitting at your desk until your homework is FINISHED and CHECKED BY ME." The door closed, then opened right back up. "WITHOUT your Walkman."

When the door shut again, Woz gave another jerky roll of his eyes. "See what you're missing?"

"What?"

"You probably never have to do homework, or clean your room, or any of that crap anymore, do you? I mean, it's not like your dad rides your ass every single second of the day, right?"

I looked down at the garbage can lid, all those immolated pillars. It looked like Stonehenge made of dog shit.

"Life at the bachelor pad," he said wistfully, as though I lived at the Playboy mansion. A shrill sound came through the walls. It sounded like *Five minutes!*

Woz shook his head. "I hate her. I do." He set another Prune Face on the lid, and I knew I was supposed to spray it, but I no longer wanted to. This whole game seemed dumb, childish, pointless.

"Come on, man," he said. "Fett demands a sacrifice."

I gave Prune Face a couple of perfunctory squirts, and Woz flicked the match. *Oh, Alvin*, he said in falsetto as he touched fire to the figure, *stop having fun.*

A pain went through my neck and I realized I was clenching my molars.

*Come inside and do your stupid homework, or you'll never—OH MY GOD MY HEAD IS ON FIRE.*

I grabbed Boba Fett out of Woz's hand and tossed him onto the can lid. Woz screamed, sounding more like his mother than he probably realized. He tried to snatch Boba out of the flames, but I sprayed WD-40 over the whole lid and up came a hairy ball of flame, and when he yanked back his arm, I saw the little hairs crackling with fire, exploding like tiny trees, each one a blue pinburst.

I kept spraying and spraying, even though the figure was already a featureless lump, even though Woz was weeping with rage, even though the ball of fire was crawling back toward the can like the slowest comet. I didn't care. Woz had to learn. Sacrifice only mattered if you lost what you wanted.

# Chapter 15

In the region, autumn has a trap door. For a long time you bask in the warmth of Indian summer, the days full of golden light and a breeze that is ripe with the sweet mustiness of rotting apples and leaf piles, and then one day—it seems that sudden—the trees are skeletons, the wind is full of knives, and you're plunging into winter.

By the middle of November I walked to school in the dark and came home at dusk, the sun like a flat tire on the horizon as I trudged down sidewalks slick with wet leaves. It was often blustery, which made for a bitter walk to Al's Tap, so I began to stay home. My mother's ghost was heavy about the place in the afternoon—maybe because that's when I used to come home to her—and I found that I liked wallowing in nostalgia. I couldn't switch on the television without thinking of how she used to sit on the couch with a typewriter on her lap, transcribing movies for the two of us to perform as dinner theater. My role had been to work the VCR remote. "Pause," she'd say, clacking away on the typewriter, then, "Unpause."

I thought my father would crack down on my unsupervised state, but he didn't seem to mind. In all likelihood, what he really didn't mind was paying Shirley for only one dinner (his), and racing back to the golfdome to scare up a few extra private lessons. When he brought home a grocery sack full of Chef Boyardee, I took it as his endorsement of my gesture toward self-reliance.

One afternoon, I was at home, messing around with my mother's old record player when the doorbell rang.

I wasn't actually playing any records, just opening and closing the box to hear the springs squeak. That sound—and the memories it stirred up—was somehow more satisfying than actually talking to my mother on the phone. When I heard the doorbell, I closed the record player—hanging open, it seemed vaguely incriminating—before going to the door.

I can't say who I thought I would find on my front porch—a kid selling M&M's, Jehovah's Witnesses, my repentant mother—but I can say that the last person I expected to see was Miss Dupay. Holding, of all things, a casserole dish.

My mind locked up, a ten thought pile-up during rush hour. That road's shut down, I don't care where you need to go, nobody's getting through there for a while.

Miss Dupay lifted the saran-wrapped dish. "It's chicken chip bake."

I said, "Hm."

She waited one more beat, then pushed the casserole into my hands, bulled past me into the house, and called over her shoulder, "You're in for a treat." Still, I continued to stand, dumbfounded, in the doorway until I realized that—Oh, God—she was headed for the kitchen.

My gestures toward independence did not include

cleaning. Neither did my father's. We'd run out of regular dishes weeks ago, but instead of doing something so sensible as washing them, we called up the reserves—platters, pans, crockery—to press into duty as plates. One morning we ran out of cereal, and we found ourselves eating canned chili from pot lids. "It's like a bowl with a handle," my father said with no small amount of admiration for our ingenuity. "This would be great for picnics."

The kitchen was a dump. No, more than a dump: a domestic Superfund site. It was the kind of kitchen you would see on the show "Cops," with officers playing a flashlight over the mess and saying, "My God," and "What did you do in here, lady?" while a woman sobs in the background, "I just cleaned the day before yesterday, I swear." They were wrong, both the cops and the lady. This kind of mess took men, and it took time.

"Wait," I cried, but it was too late. She was already standing, wide-eyed, at the entrance to the kitchen. "Wowsers," she breathed. "This is worse than I thought."

Over the sink, fruit flies swirled like ash coming up from a fire. The smell of mildew came from somewhere, maybe everywhere. On the table, dishes were piled in petrified mounds, mortared with food. Two pot lids, coated with dried chili, crowned the heap, looking like shields crusted with gore.

"I was going to do some cleaning tonight," I said lamely.

Miss Dupay shuddered, then forced a smile. "It's okay. It's not like I'm the neatest person in the world, either." She plucked out her shirt to show me an amoeba-shaped coffee stain, and I caught a glimpse of her tan bra strap. Then she was on the move, just like in the classroom, only now, instead of pacing the aisles, she was flicking the oven on to preheat, emptying the sink, and filling it up with hot, soapy water. "I'll wash and you dry," she said.

At last I realized she had come over to help (*For a smart kid,* my father sometimes marveled, *you're awful slow on the uptake*). I hadn't told her I was struggling, but she probably noticed that my lunches had gotten increasingly strange. Once, the previous week, I'd taken plain spaghetti in a sandwich baggie. And even though my father and I went to the Laundromat on Saturday nights, most of my clothes had gotten lost in the ruins of my room, so I was down to a small rotation of a couple of jeans and about three sweatshirts.

I was now officially a charity case. That didn't exactly make me proud, but as long as no one found out, I guessed it would be all right. Better than dying of dysentery, anyway.

When the dishes were done, Miss Dupay asked me if we had any light bulbs to replace the ones that were missing. The bulbs weren't missing, *per se*; my mother routinely left a bulb or two out of a fixture because she thought everything looked better in low light. But I felt weird about explaining this, so I fetched a carton of bulbs from the hall closet, and held her chair while she screwed them in. "There," she said, smiling down at me. "Isn't that better?"

The kitchen had never looked so clean and bright, had never been filled with the creamy smell of a casserole, but admitting this would have amounted to cheating on my mother.

On the other hand, if I said no, Miss Dupay might not

come back.

"It's okay," I allowed.

The oven timer dinged, and my mouth flooded with saliva. I was going to have a harder time showing restraint once the chicken chip bake came out of the oven, I knew. Luckily, I didn't have to hold back. Miss Dupay set the casserole on the stovetop, and started toward the door, pulling off her oven mitts and handing them to me on the way. "Hate to cook and run," she said, "but I've got to get home to make dinner for Daddy." She told me to let the casserole set for about ten minutes before digging in, then she winked at me with both eyes and slipped out the door.

I might have waited a full minute before attacking the casserole with a serving spoon. Eating straight from the pan, I burned my mouth with hot ooze, but did I stop? Did I even slow down? I did not. I ate furiously until my stomach was as hard as a basketball. By the time I stepped back from the stovetop, the casserole looked like it had been violated by a backhoe.

A couple of hours later, I went at it again. That casserole was probably supposed to last me two or three days, but it never saw the light of morning.

The strange thing was, I wasn't even that hungry, especially on round two. I'm not sure what came over me. Appetite, I guess.

# Chapter 16

The next day, I found that I didn't want to go home after school. The idea of messing around with my mother's record player now seemed dreary and childish. Al's Tap would be empty for a while, so I went out walking. I didn't exactly plan to go to the Lutheran church, but that's where I found myself.

As in the summer, the doors were open, and nobody was inside the sanctuary. But something was different about the church. Instead of long, stately banners in the sanctuary, a huge movie screen hung next to the cross. Speakers were drilled into the crown molding, and a drum kit crowded the pulpit.

"Hey, man."

I turned to see Pastor Mike at the back of the church. His hair was so black it looked wet, the kind of color that only comes from a bottle. I started to tell him my name, but he waved me off as he came up the aisle. "I remembered you as soon as I spotted you on the security cam. You like our new set-up? We're going with the youth movement. Attendance is through the roof. You should come by sometime."

In the summer, he'd been crouched and hesitant, as if even he wasn't convinced by what he was saying. Now he seemed breezy and confident. We sat down and he spread his arms across the back of the pew. "So how's it going with the second coming?"

"Not so good."

I told him about the car accident and my father's leg, and, to my surprise, I didn't stop there. Some levee crumbled inside of me, and I heard myself talking about how my mother left, my father's diet, and Miss Dupay's casserole. A wave of embarrassment washed over me—why was I telling him all my private business?—but I couldn't stop. Apparently I couldn't talk to Pastor Mike without spilling my guts. He was like kryptonite for bullshitters.

"Can I tell you a story?" he said when I finished.

I hesitated. His last story about listening for God's voice had made me doubt myself. What terrible gift was he offering this time? But he'd sat through my drawn-out confession without yawning once, so what was I supposed to say: *Thanks, anyway*?

"So there's this boy," he said, "who gets sick of life on the family farm. *Wouldn't it be great*, he thinks, *if I could go live in the big city*? Problem is, he doesn't have any money. Then, one day, it hits him: he could ask his father for his inheritance."

The story sounded vaguely familiar. I guessed it was from the Bible, but I couldn't remember any illustrations in my children's Bible about a boy wandering around a big city, so I wasn't entirely sure.

"The father says okay, gives the boy his inheritance, and the boy heads off to party in the city. Well, you can probably guess how that worked out. Just a few months later, the money that was supposed to last a lifetime is gone, and the boy finds himself alone and hungry, slopping pigs for a living.

"It's a pretty miserable life, and one morning the boy catches himself eyeing the pig slop, thinking he might just scoop up a bowlful for himself. *What am I doing?* he thinks, and right then he decides to go back home. Maybe if he begs and begs, the old man will hire him as a servant."

I said, "Or maybe the old man will say, *Tough.*"

"Maybe. I mean, the boy didn't know what would happen, right? But he set off for home anyway, because he figured that nothing was worse than sleeping with pigs." Pastor Mike raised his finger to indicate that he was quoting. "But while he was still a long way off, his father saw him and was filled with compassion for him; he ran to his son, threw his arms around him and kissed him."

I waited for him to go on. When he didn't, I said, "That's it? That story makes no sense."

Pastor Mike hunched over, resembling the hesitant man I remembered from the summer. "Here's what I'm driving at," he said. "God builds the universe on circular tracks. The bad part of this deal is that what we love goes away—our faith slips, we turn our backs on God's grace, we lose the ones we love."

He paused, looking at the drum kit so long it seemed like he'd lost the thread of his thought. Then he leaned back and draped his arm over the pew again. "But the good news is that the track bends. Sometimes so gently that we start coming around without even realizing it. Seasons change. The runner turns onto the homestretch. The son comes home and the father runs out to welcome him."

I nodded because it seemed like the polite thing to do, all the while thinking *well, this was a big waste of time.* But then, like a coin dropping into a jukebox, I understood why he was telling me this story.

"Wait," I said. "Are you saying that my mother—"

He raised his hand, like *Whoa*, as though he could already see where I was going, which only increased my confidence in his powers of foresight.

"—are you saying that she is *coming back*?"

"Hold on," he said. "That's not—I can't say that."

And he wouldn't, no matter how much I pressed him. It was just a parable, he claimed, something to illustrate the "nature of things," not a specific promise or prediction. "Last time I robbed you of hope," he said, "which is something a pastor should never do, especially with young people. I just wanted to give you some of that hope back." He searched my eyes. "Understand?"

I understood that I wasn't going to get a pastor's promise to cancel out Madame's prediction. I understood, too, that I would never get what I was looking for when I talked to Pastor Mike.

"You should stick with God," I said, getting up to leave. "Leave that universe business to the scientists. You obviously don't know what you're talking about."

I walked toward the big swinging doors, leaving him, I hoped, dumbstruck. And maybe he was. But not long enough for me to make it out of the sanctuary.

"Hey," he called. "Why'd you come here today?"

I glanced back, tossed up my hands. Even if I'd known, I wasn't about to confess anything else to him.

"Everything orbits," he said, turning his back on me. "Including you."

# Chapter 17

A few days passed—probably the length of time Miss Dupay had expected the casserole to last—before she showed up again at my door, this time with a sack of groceries in each arm. When she thrust the bags at me, I caught a whiff of her musty cardigan.

"Time to teach a man to fish," she said, plopping down in the entryway to take off her shoes like a little kid: cross-legged, prying off one at a time without bothering to unlace them. "Your dad around?"

I had to laugh. As little as he'd been around the house before my mother left, he was even scarcer now. The house must have been a booby trap of memory for him, too, but he didn't take a morbid enjoyment in it like I did. He spent nearly all his waking hours at the golfdome. If he'd have thought of dragging a cot into the locker room at the Broadmoor, he might have taken to sleeping there.

"As little as possible," I told her.

"Lucky." She frowned at the broken plastic tips of her shoelaces. Then she glanced at the bags in my arms and seemed to remember why she had come over. "Well, what are you waiting for?" She popped up and forced a grin. "Those bags aren't going to put themselves away!"

Miss Dupay banged around the cabinets, looking for a big saucepan while I unloaded the groceries. *It's Taco Night!* she'd told me as she led me into the kitchen. But some of these groceries confused me. When I pulled out a package of Land O' Lakes, I said, "You use butter in tacos?"

"Butter's a staple."

When I just stared at her, she explained. "Like milk, eggs, cooking oil, sugar, flour… stuff that's good to have around no matter what you're making."

I peered into the bags. All the items she'd named were in there. It struck me as both generous, but strangely old-fashioned. Who cooked from scratch anymore?

Certainly not Miss Dupay, who wasn't above taking a shortcut or two. While the ground beef sizzled in the saucepan, filling the kitchen with the smell of hot blood, she showed me how to pour the packet labeled TACO into the hot pan along with a quarter cup of water. But she cut no corners with place setting. She made me set the table with the whole deal, plates, forks, trivets, serving spoons, napkins—"Hey, you've got company, pal"—offering me guidance and praise the whole time, saying "Good, good," as if putting napkins on the left side of a plate was a real accomplishment.

Knowing you're being patronized doesn't suck all the pleasure out of it. And between her close attention and the hot food, the night had no shortage of pleasure—for either of us, apparently. "Mmm," she kept saying once we sat down to eat. "I like the way you made these tacos."

The next Saturday, my father called me at home to ask if I wanted to run down to the golfdome. "Got some easy work if you want to earn some shake."

The money didn't mean much to me, but I said yes, anyway, because how else was I going to fill a whole day? That had never been a concern when my mother was around, but now, weekends were great sinkholes of time, especially since I couldn't go over to Woz's house anymore. In science class, he'd built a little partition out of microscopes down the middle of our table. When I apologized and offered to buy him a new Boba Fett, he acted like he didn't hear me, so I "accidentally" knocked one of the microscopes onto his crotch.

What did I do with my weekends now? Before my father had called, I'd been watching *Soul Train* with the curtains closed so no one would see me practice my dance moves. I was trying to learn how to breakdance, alternating between moonwalking across the berber carpeting and doing "The Worm," a move I approximated by flopping around wildly on my belly, trying unsuccessfully to imitate the smooth undulation of the dancers on the screen. By the time the phone rang, I was covered with sweat and carpet burns.

"Give me a half-hour," I told him. "I'll be right down."


When I got to the golfdome, I saw a gaggle of six or seven ladies standing around a tee box, talking and laughing loudly. The few men strung out across the other tee boxes exchanged dark looks, like they wished the ladies would pipe down, but none of them dared to say anything.

"There he is," my father said, coming up behind me to clap me on the shoulder. He was wearing the meshy shirt he'd gotten stuck over his head several weeks before, but no longer did his flesh squeeze through the tiny holes like garlic through a press. In fact, the shirt may have even been a little loose. Looking at him, I felt something like heartbreak.

"Ready?" he said, and I caught a whiff of minty chemicals. Had he just gargled?

"I thought you didn't teach group lessons," I said.

"Wasn't my idea." He pulled me close and marched us forward.

Something about these ladies put me on edge. They wore Capri pants and little polo shirts in tropical colors as though it was June, or like they were in a movie about golfers. Surely they hadn't gone outside like that. I'd worn a coat and ski cap on my walk down, and still I'd been cold. Were these special outfits just for the golfdome?

Twenty feet away, they started calling my father's name—*Tim! Timmy! Tim-a-roo!*—making little yips and cat-growls and other animal cries. My knees locked up, and he practically had to drag me the last few steps.

"Is this the one you've been telling us about?" said one lady with an improbable tan. She tilted her head. "What a little gentleman."

"Key-yoot," said another. "Cute, cute, cute."

I tried to laugh, but it came out as a moan. My father's hand tightened on my shoulder. I think he was afraid I might bolt for the exit. "Revie's here to caddy," said my father. Then he explained that caddies could carry more than bags. That, in fact, if you used your imagination, caddies could carry just about *anything.* "Drinks, for example."

Oh, the ladies thought this was clever. It didn't seem all that funny to me, but they were laughing and winking and elbowing each other like it was the most devilishly clever thing they had ever heard.

The first drink order came in right away, and I was grateful because it meant I could get away from them, at least for a minute. But I wanted to hurry back, too, because I didn't want to leave my father alone with them for long.

I skidded to the clubhouse through leaf muck the consistency of soggy raisin bran. For some reason, Rick from the Pro Shop was behind the bar. "Oh, hi," I said, keeping my eyes up high so I wouldn't look at his hand. "What are you doing here?"

"Bartender's sick," Rick said. "The boss told me to cover all the bases."

Rick used to be a club pro until he'd flipped over a golf cart while riding drunk under the moonlight. By dawn, when the first foursome stumbled across him, he'd sustained enough nerve damage and loss of circulation that the doctors wanted to amputate his arm below the elbow. Rick refused, believing the arm was just asleep and would come back to life, tingling with pins and needles, any minute.

Four years later, he was still waiting, and his forearm had wasted away so badly that it looked like the skinny end of an overcooked drumstick. Because he wore a child's golf glove, no one knew what his hand looked like, but he was forever calling attention to it.

I gave Rick the drink order, then trained my eyes on the television in the corner, hoping that he would, for once, just do his job and skip the—

"Check it out," Rick said, flopping his hand on top of a stack of cocktail napkins. Woody Woodpecker was on the screen, but try as I might, I couldn't keep my eyes off the hand, as wilted and crumply in its tiny glove as a deadhead on a pansy. "I call this one 'the paperweight.'"

"Ha," I said, because what else could I do? Say, *Your dead hand makes bad jokes, Rick? When you do that, I kind of want to scream?* If his hand wasn't funny, then it was terrifying, so I made myself smile.

"Check it out," said Rick, holding his dead hand above the wrist and dragging it back and forth across the bar. "String mop."

I had to get back, I told him. The ladies were waiting on their drinks. *Aye-aye*, he said, and I managed to avert my eyes before he could flail the hand against his brow in a terrible salute. "Fine," he said, and picked up the soda gun, but only blinked at it.

"What are you *doing*?" I said.

"Is that all you know how to ask?" He ran his thumb over the grid of buttons on the back of the gun. "Jesus, this thing is worse than a calculator."

Groaning in disgust, I moved behind the bar. By that point I'd watched Shirley enough that I knew how to build a drink. "Ice, alcohol, *then* soda," I said, pouring a gin and tonic. Handling liquor as a minor was illegal, of course— even I knew that—but in the region, this particular law was considered to be in the same class as removing mattress tags or making illegal photocopies. As long as I didn't actually take a drink, no one cared.

"Ohhhh," said Rick. He made himself a gin and tonic. "Like this?"

I gave him a look. He grinned and raised his glass. "*Salud.*"

The ladies kept me running between the golfdome and the bar. Every time I came back in with another tray of drinks, they were whooping and teasing each other, braying about God knows what, and some other guy would be on his way out, tearing off his golf glove with an angry rip of velcro, muttering something about the integrity of the game. On one trip out of the dome, I heard a lady say, "Look at him walk. Just like his dad. He's going to be a *killer.*" My ears burned. Rick got slowly bombed, but at least he stayed out of my way, sitting on the edge of the bar to practice fancy handshakes between his good hand and his dead hand. High-five, low-five, soul shake, tip tap, "what it be, what it is, give me some skin, broth-ah…"

I scooped the ice; I made the drinks; I did my best to ignore all these idiots. What was so goddamn funny to these ladies? And why did white guys always do that soul brother shit when they got drunk? God, I hoped I didn't act so retarded when I got old.

In the afternoon, coming back to the dome with my arms full of screwdrivers and a single styrofoam cup of peanuts, I heard the group squealing. "Go ahead," my father was saying. "Try to pinch an inch. You can't, can you?"

The ladies were in a loose circle around him. Their hands

darted at him like snakes. He recoiled at each pinch, but he didn't lower his arms or tell them to stop—until he saw me standing there, holding all those cups. He stepped behind his golf bag. "Ladies, your drinks have arrived."

After the lesson, we drove to Al's Tap. He was silent on the way over, but once he parked on the street, he put his hand on my arm before I could open my door. "I know how that probably looked," he said. "But it wasn't like that."

Looking straight ahead, I said, "I don't know what you're talking about."

"Those ladies, they're just crazy gals. All bark, no bite. Understand?"

Sure, I said, no problem. I understood just fine. I felt him looking at me for a long moment, probably trying to figure out if I was being sincere, and eventually he sighed, got out of the car, and didn't say another word about it. Neither did I, until I called my mother that night.

"Your father's an attractive man," she said with a sigh, like it was some birth defect that had only made his life harder. She was not nearly as worked up as I'd hoped. In fact, she seemed to be affecting a *c'est la vie* attitude. I could picture her slumped in a windowsill, smoking a cigarette through an ebony stem. Or at least pretending to do so: I could hear the little smooching sounds, the sharp intake of breath, the decadent exhalations. "And some of those women are married to real ogres, so it's hard to blame them."

"But aren't you afraid that... something might happen?"

"No," she said. "I'm not afraid anymore."

That last word struck me. "You used to be?"

She laughed. "Oh, I used to be *so* jealous." She painted a picture for me of a young wife, stuck at home with a baby, feeling *uck*, while her trim husband gave private lessons to lonely wives. "At least this is a group class. If anything, it's safer."

"So you're not afraid he'll do something?"

"I'm not afraid," she repeated.

Which is different from *He won't do anything*. But all I understood was that she didn't care what he did, and that sucked the hope out of me. I couldn't even respond. I looked at the mirror behind the bar, which was almost completely papered over with old poster boards for betting pools—NCAA tournament brackets, esoteric Superbowl bets, the date the Cubs would be eliminated from playoff contention—all of them expired. Then there were the Polaroids of banned customers, most of the pictures taken in the act of expulsion, the light of terror in each drunk's eyes, probably because the giant hands of Momo were wrapped around his skull. Layer upon sad layer of history. The only current item on the mirror was a kitten calendar. Shirley *X*'d out each date as it passed, which lent a penal feeling to the establishment. November was almost gone, I realized as I saw that Shirley had also *X*'d out the eyes of the kitten.

"I have to get out of here," I said.

"You get like this every winter. You'll be fine in the spring."

Spring was five months away. I said, "I'm serious, I—"

Just then I had an idea. An idea so simple, so clear that I actually clasped my forehead. I said, "Don't come home."

"Don't," she said. "Don't?"

Pastor Mike was right: the universe was built on a circular track. But for the first time I realized that my father and I didn't have to sit still. We could go into orbit, too.

"No!" I said. "*We* are going to come out *there*."

I almost cackled in my Eureka joy. I felt fantastic. I felt *transfigured*. I wouldn't have been surprised to look down and find beams of light coming out of my body like golden two-by-fours. I—I, alone—had figured out the answer to our problems. I, alone, would save us.

She said, "We?"

"Me and Dad, silly." Why was she having such trouble catching on? For once, I was the one who had to slow down and explain something to her. Now *that* was funny. It really was. I barked out a laugh. At the bar, Shirley glanced over with a worried look. I said, "California is where you guys were headed before, like, I happened, right? You were going to be an actress, and he was going to join the circuit—"

"People don't always get where they're headed."

"*You* did."

Silence on the line. The smoking sounds had stopped. The next thing I heard was the music of ice cubes tumbling into a glass. She said, "Revie, I've learned a lot about myself in the past couple of months. One thing—"

"I'll handle Dad, if that's what you're worried about. Shouldn't be too hard. He hates the winter, anyway."

"—one thing I've learned is that I am not a mother."

That threw me, but only for a second. I lowered my voice. "Just me, then. Dad doesn't even have to know. I'll take a taxi to O'Hare, and—"

"I never got you ready for school because I stayed up late, watching movies. I fed you *hors d'oeuvres* for dinner. When you were sick, did I ever know what to do?"

"I'm still alive, aren't I?"

"And that's all the evidence of grace you'll ever need. Revie, I'm a woman who had a child," she said, and my mind added *forced on her.* "Not a mother. You may not see that right now—and I can't blame you if you don't—but one day you will. One of these days—" A tremor went through her voice. She paused, and I heard the chime of ice cubes again. When she spoke again, her voice was firm. "One of these days, you'll see that your life is better without me."

I leaned back in the phone booth. It was Saturday night at Al's Tap. The place was filling up with men, shouting, laughter, but all of that felt miles away. I said, "You're not ever coming back home, are you?"

"That's to be determined, Revie. I—"

"We're never going to be together again," I said to myself as much as to her.

"I'm not in a position right now to make a commitment one way or—"

"*Don't.*" My voice cracked. "Don't talk to me like a lawyer. Tell me the truth."

She sounded sorry to say it—her voice got small like she was wincing on the other end of the line—but for once in her life, she gave me the truth. Not a story, not a joke, not a prediction. Just the truth, in all its naked ugliness.

"Revie," she said. "I'm *happy.*"

I waited for my father to take me home. I waited for him to go to bed. Then I waited another half-hour or so, to make sure he was entirely asleep. After that, I was all done waiting.

I went into the kitchen, unwrapped a stick of butter, and slipped it into his soup.

The butter bobbed up in the crockpot, slick and shiny. The phrase *burial at sea* came to mind. Miss Dupay was right, I thought: staples were good to have on hand. But Pastor Mike? Pastor Mike was full of shit. As far as I could tell, the universe was an old snarl of Christmas lights.

"Blub blub blub," I whispered, poking the butter down into the soup. Then I closed the lid so the butter would melt quickly, blending into the broth, to begin its work of undoing.

# Chapter 18

The next morning, my father ate his soup without mentioning an especially buttery taste. That night, I added another stick and a handful of sugar. When he still didn't say anything, I grew bolder. In addition to the nightly submarine of butter, I began adding a little oil or sugar every chance I got.

But you can only sabotage a man's soup for so long before he notices. It took more than a week, but finally my father sat up straight and blinked at his spoon.

"This stuff tastes better all the time," he said, developing a theory on the spot about how his taste buds must have been blown out from years of abuse with refined sugars and processed foods, but now—now!—his rehabilitated tongue was picking up all these subtle flavors. "The natural sweetness of the cabbage leaf. The richness of the broth. If I had a Pepsi right now, my head would explode!"

Miss Dupay came by regularly with staples, unwittingly fueling my campaign. My sabotage had all the makings of a science experiment as I knew it from her class: liquids, heat, and of course the chart on the fridge where my father tracked his weight. I took notes on my discoveries. Crisco took a long time to melt, but didn't leave as much of a grease slick as cooking oil. If I put in too much sugar, the sweetness could be masked with an extra bay leaf or two.

In science class itself, what we did seemed to depend on Miss Dupay's mood. If she was up, she lectured, referencing her notebook of unifying theories instead of our textbook. When she was down, she'd announce Lab Day, meaning we could choose from any prefab lab in the textbook, which always set off a run on Bunsen burners. On Lab Days, she sat still, leaning on her elbows, staring vaguely at the murky frog tank.

She wasn't down often, but when she was, there was no cheering her up. Lunch was less fun on those days, but I had long since stopped going to the cafeteria, so I'd come and sit with her anyway. "What's wrong?" I asked her one day, but she just laughed mirthlessly. "Troubles at home. You know how it is."

I did and I didn't. When I asked her what she meant, she only shrugged and kneaded her sandwich baggie, slowly crushing her wafers to powder.

Penelope had her loom; I had my father's soup. The weight chart on the fridge told me that my campaign was working. The numbers, after holding steady for a while, were starting to rise. The last numbers were in darker ink, as though he'd etched them angrily.

"Whoa!" I said one morning when we were both in the kitchen. I was eating handfuls of Apple Jacks straight from the box; my father, of course, was having his morning soup, though he didn't seem to be enjoying it as much as he had before. "Putting on a few, huh?"

"It's the damnedest thing," he said. "I'm not doing anything different from when I was losing. If anything, I'm eating less."

"Probably just a fluctuation in gravity."

He shot me a look. He'd gotten more irritable since his weight loss had stopped. "Gravity's a constant. Don't they teach you anything at school?"

"Then explain tides," I said, parroting Miss Dupay. "Or gravity waves."

He grabbed one of his love handles and shook it like the scruff of a dog. "Explain *this*. My new clothes look ridiculous on me now."

Somehow, I managed not to mention that they had *always* looked ridiculous on him. Somehow I managed not to ask if I could pinch an inch. Instead, I merely nodded in sympathy.

That's when I should have walked away. Shut down the experiment. Let my father give up the diet in frustration and float back up to his starting weight in a couple of weeks. But I got greedy.

"Did you say you were eating *less*?" I said. "No wonder you're gaining weight. Your body thinks you're starving. It's packing away every spare calorie."

I'd gotten this from my mother, who was battling her own diet plateau by eating five stalks of celery before every meal to "trick her metabolism."

"You know what you need to do?" I said. "Eat *more* soup."

Still rubbing his thumb against a love handle, my father

looked at me. Me, a mere boy, the same boy who, just moments earlier, had suggested that his nine-pound weight gain was the result of a fluctuation in gravity. Then, in what can only be seen as a mark of pure desperation, he said, "You know what? You might be onto something."

It came to an end on a Sunday afternoon in December. My father and I were watching a Bears game when he clutched his stomach—"Oof."—and walked briskly to the bathroom. I waited until I heard the fan before tiptoeing into the kitchen, careful as a cat burglar, to lift the glass lid of the crockpot. Recently, I'd taken to sabotaging his soup at least three times a day, adding a little something special between each meal, whether he was in the house or not. Maybe I wanted to see how high I could push his weight; maybe a part of me wanted the game to come to an end.

As soon as I tipped the bottle of vegetable oil, I heard his voice.

"You."

I stiffened. The oil went *glub, glub.*

"Have a seat," he said, pulling out a chair roughly. I sat, afraid. He got down a bowl and ladled out some soup. "I bet this tastes great," he said, setting the bowl in front of me and narrowing his eyes. "But you tell me."

Oil glistened on the surface. Cabbage leaves fanned through the dark broth like the fins of a carp. "That's okay," I said.

He pulled off his rings and dropped them, one by one, on

the table. "We can do this the easy way," he said, "or the hard way. Your choice."

I grabbed the spoon. How bad could it be? I'd been tasting the broth for weeks. It was sweet and oily, but nothing I couldn't handle. But on that first bite, a fin of cabbage swirled in my mouth and I started to gag. "Don't you spit it out," he said.

God, it was awful. Apparently the cabbage leaves had trapped all the shit I'd been dumping in the soup for weeks; it was like eating a soggy oil filter. I took another look at my father's rings and forced myself to swallow. "I think I'm going to be sick."

"Later. First, tell me why you did this."

"I don't know," I moaned, and he motioned for me to eat another spoonful. I said, "Please, Dad, no."

He leaned close. "Tell me *why*."

I'm not sure how to explain what I said next. All I can say is, giving him an answer seemed like the only way to get out of eating a pound of toxic cabbage.

"Mom," I croaked. "Mom told me to do it."

His face twisted. He took the bowl of soup, dumped it in the sink, then flipped on the disposal and stood over the sink for a long time, even after the disposal stopped grinding up cabbage leaves.

He switched it off. "I should have known," he said, shooting me a dark look. "She pretended to be supportive about the diet, but of course she wasn't. Of *course* she doesn't want good things for me. It's not enough for her to leave—no—she wants total wreckage in her wake. She's like a *bulldozer.* Sherman through Atlanta!"

He'd forgotten his claim that he wasn't on a diet, but right then, I knew, wasn't the best time to remind him. Instead, I said, "Do you need her phone number?"

"Just another of her little games without a single thought for anyone else; the whole world is here for her amusement, that's what she thinks. Selfish! I know it's hard to hear these things about your own mother, Revie, but it's better that you find out now what kind of person she is—"

He picked up the cordless phone, but instead of dialing right away, he brandished it as he told me how selfish she was, sick really, she might even be a sociopath, I mean, who uses her son like this? His hands were shaking so bad that he had to dial three times before he got the right number. All that misdialing took a little steam out of him, and the rest of it dissipated as soon as she was able to interrupt him.

"Ah," he said, looking at me. "I see."

He shook his head, and I knew the jig was up. "I'm going to have to whip him," he told my mother. "Nothing else works. He won't listen, he—"

She interrupted him again, probably to plead for leniency. After listening for a moment, he said, "No, I know. I know. It's just—I hope you understand it's a little hard to take your advice on child-raising, considering." He rubbed the back of his neck, hard. "Considering *everything*, Rosalyn. For heaven's sake, don't make me go over that old territory again. Now, if you could please hang on for a goddamn second." He cupped a hand over the mouthpiece and looked at me. "You don't need to hear this."

"It's okay," I said, maybe a little too eagerly.

"Get out of here. Go to your room. Take a walk, I don't care. If I were you, I'd enjoy my last moments of freedom, because when I get done with this call, something's going to happen. I don't know what yet, but you'll see."

As I walked out of the kitchen, I heard my father say, "With all due respect, Rosalyn, you're not the one whose soup it was."

Whatever the punishment, it would be worth it. They were fighting, which meant that something was alive between them.

Winter in Paris: snow falls from a gray sky and in the morning the ground is pretty. Then the snow melts in the afternoon and freezes again at night, and this happens again and again until what remains is no longer snow but a kind of gruel. Some might call it slush, but that's not quite right: slush isn't made from road salt, leaf gunk, cigarette butts, bottle caps, and frozen dog turds. Slush doesn't slowly eat cars.

That evening I walked through the gruelscape until I came near the school. When I saw Miss Dupay on a chaise lounge under her porch light, I thought, *This is fate*, but now I think the odds were pretty good that she'd be out there, as they are with any heavy smoker who is not allowed to light up in the house.

She was caterpillared in her quilted parka, her hair loose around her shoulders. With a cigarette in one hand and a steaming coffee cup in the other, she looked vaguely volcanic.

Across the street, I raised my hand like I was hoping she would call on me. She looked a long time before beckoning me over with her cigarette.

I stomped over, knocking gruel off my shoes and getting the circulation going in my feet. They ached from the cold, though the rest of my body was warm from walking and the thought of my mother and father on the phone. Maybe they were still fighting, or maybe they'd moved onto some kind of reconciliation. Either way was fine with me. My lies and sabotage had generated a heat that could meld them back together again. So what if I hadn't planned for it to happen in quite this way? Miss Dupay had taught us the scientific word for this kind of happy accident: serendipity. Right then, I felt like one serendipitous bastard.

"Hey," I said playfully when I reached Miss Dupay's porch, but she wasn't looking at me. Her eyes were trained on the rippled snowfields behind the school. From inside her house came a crashing noise. "Daddy's on a rampage," she said in a flat voice.

"Yours too?"

I said this with eye-rolling camaraderie, but again Miss Dupay failed to respond in kind. I shouldn't have bothered: when she was in one of her moods, there was no lifting her out of it. Still, I couldn't help but try. "Things will get better," I told her. I raised my finger to quote Pastor Mike. "The universe is built on a circular track. Everything orbits."

Her coffee cup shattered against the porch column. A dark web of liquid ate through the film of snow on the porch. "That didn't," she said.

I took a step back. I wasn't going to cheer her up—that much was obvious—but she might drag me down. Already my serendipitous feeling was bleeding away as quickly as my body heat.

She turned toward me, but her eyes were blank, almost blind-looking. The wind stirred her hair across her face and she didn't brush it away. "You want to talk about the universe?" she said. "The universe is buckshot with vacuums, and so are we."

I nodded and took another step back. Usually her theories gave me a thrill, but now I felt spooked.

Inside the house, some delicate glass exploded, a light bulb, maybe, or a champagne flute. Miss Dupay didn't appear to notice. She said, "Every pain, every loss creates a new vacuum. Sex is just an attempt to fill a vacuum. And when that attempt fails, as it always does, it creates another vacuum."

Sex? Is that what we were talking about here? How did we get on that topic? All of a sudden I felt cold. I couldn't have been colder if all the blood had left my body.

Her eyes focused on me. "Come here."

I shuddered. "School night," I said through numb lips.

She flicked her cigarette into the darkness and beckoned me impatiently—"Come on, come on"—and I obeyed, coming toward her until my face was only inches from hers. My right heel chattered against the porch, and I had to put my hands on my knees to keep them from buckling. She placed her cold hands on my cheeks. "Black holes give off energy," she said. "But so do dying stars, right before they explode."

Her breath smelled like wet earth from the forest. I felt like

I might pass out. "I did not know that," I whispered.

"You're a supernova," she said. "The angel of death doesn't put off this much radiation."

I stumbled back, shards from her coffee cup cracking under my heels. She was wrong, I thought. My life was on an upswing. Even at that moment, my parents were rounding the corner, heading into the home stretch toward a reunion. I would be fine; we all would be fine.

"You're no psychic," I said. Her mouth opened, but I turned and ran before she could wreck me with another answer, and I did not stop running until I was home.

# Chapter 19

January's a bad time to mess with someone, especially in the region. It's cold and dark and full of gruel, and spring is nowhere in sight. The spirit becomes brittle, and it doesn't take much to snap it.

By the end of the month, half the men in Al's Tap looked like they were suffering from snapped-off spirits. The bar was busier, but also *quieter* than ever before. Around dinnertime, every table was filled with men, many of whom I'd never seen before, tucking into their meals and watching the television bolted to the corner, half-heartedly signaling for drinks during commercials. Who were these new guys? Steelworkers from LTV, Mish told me, a mill in East Chicago that had just declared bankruptcy.

Unemployed mill workers were nothing new for Al's Tap, but these men were different. Guys who'd been laid off were bitter, sure, but with an edge of dark comedy, harboring a hope that they might be called back to work. But bankruptcy—well, the LTV guys looked like their spirits had filed Chapter 11. They looked stunned, eyes like dead smelt's. *There's no coming back from this one*, they seemed to be thinking.

My father wasn't quite this bad, but he was pretty worn down. He talked little, slumped much, and ate like it was his job, but one of drudgery. It had been a month since the soup incident, and, remarkably, very little had changed between him and my mother. He still talked to her on the phone occasionally—no more and no less than before—though now he took his plate over to the phone booth.

The only real fallout from the cabbotage was that I had strict orders to come to the Tap directly after school. Once again, my father had decided he wanted to "keep a closer eye on me," though this time, he assured me, it would be a permanent state.

I groaned, I fussed, but the truth was that I didn't mind all that much. I liked the Tap, and I wanted to keep an eye on him, too, especially if he decided to go back to offering group lessons. He'd canceled that group, I found out from Rick. Whether he felt guilty about flirting, or he just couldn't face those ladies in the baggy pants and tent-like shirts he'd taken to wearing since abandoning his diet, I'll never know.

Night after night, my father and I sat at the bar like a couple of refugees on stools, watching re-runs, then the news, game shows, prime time shows, then the news again—until one night, the television went out with a flash of white light. Everyone cried out *Whoa!*

"Picture tube," said Mish, and everyone agreed, except for the TV repair guy who came the next afternoon, who said the problem was everything.

"Picture tube caused a short, scorched out the guts," said the repair guy. He turned the TV around on the bar so we could see how the insides looked bombed-out. "Chain reaction."

"So what you're saying," said Mish, who couldn't stand to be wrong, "is that the problem *started* with the picture tube. That the picture tube, in fact, was the catalyst that—"

"The problem is everything," said the repair guy flatly. "Your TV is trash."

For the next day or two, the Tap was awkward. No one knew where to look or how to act without the television. Most claimed to be glad it was gone—they didn't watch it anyway, they said, so good riddance to all that noise and distraction—but even these guys continued to position themselves toward the empty TV bracket like flowers to the sun. Shirley was the only one I believed when she said she was relieved. "Thirteen hours a day that thing's on. It was probably giving me brain tumors."

Shirley liked the new silence so much that she put an OUT OF ORDER sign on the jukebox, even though, to my knowledge, it worked perfectly well. Though, Shirley being Shirley, she might have sabotaged the jukebox in case anyone decided to test it out during that string of quiet evenings, which ended anyway when Momo brought in an accordion.

"My God, no," said Mish. He slapped his wallet on the bar and pushed it toward Shirley. "I will buy you a new television."

Patrons groaned, Shirley claimed that polka gave her hives, but no one actually left the bar when Momo warmed up, squeezing and expanding the bellows, the instrument giving off the smell of an old suitcase. "Oh, here we go," said Mish. "Roll out the goddamn barrel. Slap me with a kielbasa, what the hell."

When Momo started playing, his music wasn't like any polka I had ever heard, nor did it sound like the reedy tunes I knew from *Pepe Le Pew* cartoons. As he rocked gently on his barstool, hugging the instrument with his huge, cracked hands, the sound that came out was sweet and full of little, wheezing hops like the humming of an asthmatic baritone. Leaning against the bar, Shirley swayed on her thick forearms. "I can't believe it," she said. "Who would have thought that a fat guy with an accordion could sound so nice?"

After a few songs, Mish was the only one who continued to protest, which he did by buying Momo drink after drink in the logic that the big man couldn't play while he was lifting a glass.

"Can I have some quarters?" I asked my father. I'd blown through my weekly allotment, but he seemed to be captivated by the music, and I thought he might pay me off so I wouldn't pester him out of his reverie. I was right. He dug into his pockets without taking his eyes off Momo, who was now singing along with the accordion in rumbling, wordless tones like the idle of a diesel truck.

My mother answered on the first ring, a rarity. "Hello," she said in a strange, distant voice. She sounded like she was trying to hold her breath and speak at the same time. I said, "Are you... crying?"

"Oh, I'm fine." She blew her nose. "I just had the worst audition of my life, that's all. These people out here, they're unbelievable. After I read my lines, the director went, 'Tell me one reason why you should get this job.'"

At the bar, Momo raised his voice, singing in made-up

Latin. *Vita de stabile, esta de milo, simper fidelis, mamma zabelis...*
The words were wrong, but the feeling was right, and since
Momo was huge and drunk, no one made fun of him.

"So I told this guy, 'I've been playing this part for years!'"
For a second, my mother's voice lifted. Then she blew her nose
again, a tromboney blat that harmonized with Momo's song.
When she spoke again, she sounded as miserable as I'd ever
heard her. "But apparently that wasn't a good enough reason.
On the way out, he told me I had a real classy look, and he just
wished this role called for someone classy like me."

January had not been kind to my mother, either. Her
happiness had waned from the moment she announced it,
though her misery couldn't be explained by road salt or freezing
rain. Hollywood was sunny, or so she'd heard, anyway. Her
days were now spent behind the cosmetics counter at May's
department store, a job she'd taken because head shots and
fencing lessons had burned through her savings faster than
she'd anticipated ("Fencing lessons?" I'd said. "Hey," she said,
"a girl's got to set herself apart somehow."). Now she found
herself in a catch-22, because the more she worked, the less
time she had to practice her craft or to audition. Not that it
mattered: half the auditions were scams, and the other half
were looking for chesty bimbos.

"Except for this audition," she said, her breath catching.
"This one was a soup commercial. They were looking for a
mother."

That hit my heart like a spear. I nearly clucked in
sympathy—but I stopped myself.

If the novelty of Hollywood was wearing thin: great. If

she was totally miserable: even better. She could grow bitter, my father could grow bigger, and my job would be to keep pushing them down these dark roads until one of them broke down, and the other would have to come to the rescue.

Her bad news could become our good news. Ruination could be a path to reunion. As long as I held onto this dark hope, I could count myself among the laid-off, not the bankrupt.

My mother said, "What on earth is on the jukebox?"

"That's Momo," I said, and held the phone out toward the bar so she could listen. The big man's voice swelled with tenderness. *Bella finocchio, grazi de fol-de-rol...*

My father, watching with an aggrieved smile, looked like he might cry.

Despite the fact that the words were nonsense, the meaning of the song was clear. I could have translated on the spot. Momo was yearning for the company of a woman. He was crying out to God to send him a wife, to make him one, take one of his ribs, take a leg bone, go ahead, what good was it doing him, anyway?

Everything he was singing about, my parents once had. And now their love was a tape ball stuck to their hands that they kept trying to throw away. But they could fail at that, just as they were failing at everything else. Another couple of weeks, I thought, that's all it would take. Then we could turn the corner on our circular track, and start arcing back toward one another.

Momo stopped and wiped his eyes with a bar towel. I set the phone down and joined my father and everyone else in loud applause, but I could still hear my mother cry out from the receiver, *Bene, bravo, bravissimo!*

# Chapter 20

When Miss Dupay showed up at Al's Tap, it seemed like a coincidence, and a small one at that. Paris was not a big town. There were a couple of dozen places to eat, and everyone was bound to run into everyone else sooner or later. The Tap wasn't exactly frequented by young, single women, but how was Miss Dupay supposed to know that? She was still new in town.

It was a Friday evening. Lake perch, all you can eat, served with lemon and white bread. If a little bone stuck in your throat, the white bread was supposed to pull the bone out on its way down to your stomach. I've always liked a meal that comes with an edible emergency kit.

Momo's accordion rested by his feet while he packed away the perch, so the bar was already quiet when Miss Dupay opened the door, but it fell to silence when she stepped inside. Everyone looked at her, and she froze in the entryway. Shirley said, "Need directions, Miss?"

Clutching her handbag to her chest, Miss Dupay squinted through the dim, smoky light until she spotted me. She waved, and seemed deeply relieved when I waved back. My father gave me a curious look. "My teacher," I explained.

She took a seat down the bar and whispered her drink order—"Sloe gin fizz, please"—which I heard clearly because all the men in the place were quietly pretending not to watch her. Rick manually tucked his dead hand into his pocket to strike a casual pose.

Shirley banged around for several agonizing moments in search of superfine sugar before mixing a drink the color of a persimmon. Miss Dupay took a long, surprisingly hearty drink, then slipped off her coat. She still had on her school clothes: a black cardigan over rumpled jeans with dry-rotted penny loafers. The whitish swipe near her shoulder, I realized with a sinking feeling, was probably frosting, and if she noticed it later, there was a good chance she would pull her sweater to her mouth and suck on it. Would it have killed her to put on a little lipstick? Touch up her eyes a bit? Wear something *clean*? Seeing her through the eyes of the other patrons, I felt embarrassed for her.

I shouldn't have been. She didn't care what they thought, and besides, these guys were not exactly picky.

Miss Dupay took another drink and wiped her mouth with the back of her sleeve. "TV's out," she noted, sounding more like her usual, confident self. "Jukebox is out of order. What do you chatterboxes do for entertainment around here?"

Momo picked up the accordion with a hopeful look on his face.

"You know the difference between an onion and an accordion?" said Miss Dupay. "No one cries when you chop up an accordion."

A rumble of laughter went through the bar. Mish clapped in admiration. Miss Dupay pointed at him. "Okay, smart guy, you tell the next joke. Let's hear what you've got."

Mish stumbled through a joke, starting over twice. "Oh, did I forget to mention that the guy was a worrywart? He's a worrywart." I'd never seen him so discombobulated before. Above his dark glasses, his forehead was radiant with sweat.

When at last he finished, Miss Dupay turned back to Momo. "I can see why you brought out the accordion now. It was like a mercy killing."

"Here's a joke for you," said Momo. "Guy goes to a bar, where he meets this lady. They get to talking, and one thing leads to another—"

"Don't it always," said Mish. "I wish I lived in a joke."

Shirley patted his hand. "You do, honey."

"One thing leads to another," repeated Momo, "and before you know it, she's inviting him back to her place. 'Great!' says the guy, 'but I have to tell you, I'm pretty kinky.'"

I laughed with the rest of the bar, but nervously. Little eels swam through my veins. This was the joke he was going to tell a lady? A lady he didn't even know? I glanced over at Miss Dupay to find her looking at me, as if she were worried about my reaction. *Oh, I'm fine,* I wanted to assure her. *Nothing new to these ears!* I rolled my eyes, meaning to apologize for these lummoxes. She grinned and shrugged. I didn't know what this meant, but it couldn't be bad.

"When they get to her place," said Momo, "the girl excuses herself to go to the bathroom. The old pardon-me-while-I-slip-into-something-more-comfortable number. When she comes out, the guy's walking out the door. 'Where are you going?' says the girl. 'I thought we were going to have a good kinky time together.'

"'I did,' the guy says. 'I just fucked your dog and shit in your purse. I'm outta here!'"

The bar roared. Rick pulled out his dead hand and slapped it against his knee. No one laughed harder than Momo himself, who had to lay his head down on his arms, though he kept his head tilted toward Miss Dupay to see if she was laughing, too. She was! It didn't look like she was faking it, either. A lady teacher who liked dirty jokes? I was shocked. Shocked and thrilled.

"Tell the truth," she said to Momo when the laughter died down. "That was your last date, wasn't it?" She turned to Shirley and spoke out of the side of her mouth. "Remind me to keep an eye on my purse." Then she picked up her purse and gave it an exaggerated sniff, setting off a fresh round of howls. Oh, man, this was great. My gut was cramping up, I was laughing so hard.

It went on like this, joke after joke. Men were shouting over each other, trying to get a joke in edgewise, except for my father, the born audience, who seemed content to lean back and chuckle. Miss Dupay kept cutting them low, but they loved it. When had she gotten so sharp?

"I got one!" I shouted after Rick finished with his Moonwalking Jellyfish/Bad Toupee/Carol-Burnett-mopping-the-spotlight triptych. The bar got quiet. Everyone turned to me.

This was the first time in my life that I'd captured the

attention of an entire room full of adults. A buzz went through my system, a low and pleasant electrical current.

"Three guys are walking," I said, "and they come across a farm. They're pretty tired, so they ask the farmer if they can spend the night."

"Watch yourself," said my father. He put his fist over his mouth.

I couldn't have stopped if I'd wanted to. And I did not want to. In fact, I wanted this moment to go on forever. I could see why performing was so appealing to my mother: all these people, hanging on my every word, waiting to hear what came next, bathing me with the warm glow of their attention—in a way, this was the heart of every fantasy I'd ever had.

And then I blew it.

"'Sure,' said the farmer. 'Just don't fuck my daughter.'"

The room recoiled. My father's head dropped. Just like that, the magic was gone. "What?" I said. I pointed at Momo. "But he—and you guys—"

My father eased off his barstool. "Excuse us for a second, everybody."

After leading me back by the phone booth, he said, "Look. Either bring yourself down a notch, or we'll have to go home. Understand?"

I didn't understand why my joke was so much worse than everyone else's, but I did not want to go home. Apparently, my father didn't want to leave, either. He was already leaning back toward the bar before I could even nod my apology.

"Can I trust you to make better decisions?" he said,

backing toward his seat.

"You can trust me," I said.

In a joke, this part is known as the set-up.

Because this was a Friday night, the crowd swelled. I kept expecting the joke-telling group to break up, or to get overwhelmed by the crowd, but it held together through some combination of gravity and like aggregation. Miss Dupay moved to a table in the middle of the room, along with Mish, and Rick, and my father, too. The jokes got louder, pitchers went back and forth, and Miss Dupay kept it all going, like a wisecracking m.c.

I listened from the bar, and did not attempt any more jokes. My father glanced at me occasionally, and so did Miss Dupay. My father's looks were simple checks—*Did he stay where I put him? Good.*—but Miss Dupay seemed concerned about my well-being, so each time I responded to her with a thumbs-up. She winked and smiled.

When Mish took another run at his worrywart joke, Miss Dupay came up to the bar, ordered another sloe gin fizz, then ducked her head toward me. "Way past your bedtime, huh?"

"It's not a school night."

"You look wiped out."

"I'm okay."

"Seriously," she said. "You look like you're circling around, looking for a place to crash land."

I tried to look at myself in the mirror behind the bar, but all I saw was the calendar, the yawning tabby with $X$'d out eyes. "Well, I guess I'm a little tired, but—"

She grabbed my wrist and towed me over to my father.

Mish was saying, "So all the other fellas, they finally ask the happy guy, *What gives? You were the biggest worrywart in life. Why are you so happy in hell?* The guy turns to them with a huge smile and says, *Now I know it can't get no worse!*"

Miss Dupay leaned in. "Hey fellas, sorry fellas, just wanted to say goodbye and thanks for showing this girl a good time, etcetera, etcetera."

Everyone protested, but she held up a hand. Her other hand held my wrist behind her back. "Revie here is pretty bushed," she told my father. "If you want, I can run him home."

My father frowned. "Oh, no. That's not your job."

"It's no problem, really," she said. "Your house is totally on my way. I'll just drop him off, make sure he gets inside all right, then cruise on home, lickety-split! It'll take me all of an extra twenty seconds."

I could see my father struggling. "Well—"

She ruffled his hair. He grimaced, but he also blushed. "It's fine," she said. "You just finish that pitcher. Take your time. Hey, it's Friday night!"

She dropped my wrist and started for the door. The bar groaned with goodbyes, don't go-s, come-back-soons, but in another second that shifted into the general wash of sound common to Friday nights, as though we were already gone.

I looked at my father, who was turning back toward Mish and signaling him to keep the jokes coming. At the bar was Miss Dupay's forgotten drink, radiant in the low light, glowing like a heart in a zombie glass.

Then I looked at the door, where she stood, waiting for me.

# Chapter 21

The vinyl interior of Miss Dupay's battered sub-compact smelled like body odor. A crack snaked through the windshield like lightning caught in ice. Through the floorboard, I felt gruel flailing up from the road. Everything about the car was tiny and cheap, except for the stereo system, which took up half the dashboard and was l-o-u-d loud. It was so loud that she didn't seem to hear my directions. "Turn left!" I shouted. "LEFT!" In case she still hadn't heard me, I pointed. Miss Dupay pointed back at me, then continued straight down old 77th, out toward the country.

The music was a kind I'd never heard before. The beat was disco-like, but more insistent, and layered over with synthesizers. Under it all, someone was murmuring the same line over and over. I could almost make out what they were saying, but not quite. Maybe the bass was too high.

Miss Dupay slapped my hand away from the equalizer. Then she grabbed my wrist and guided my hand to the back of my own skull. "Feel those vibrations?" she shouted. "Down by your neck? House music goes straight to your amygdala!"

At this volume, her music was going straight to all the

amygdalas in a two-mile radius. We stopped at a red light and the plastic door panels buzzed from all the bass.

"Don't *think* about it," she said into a sudden canyon of silence. She'd punched out one tape and was slotting in another. "Amygdala is your lizard brain. Fear, appetite, memory. When those three come together, it's the cosmic jackpot."

The music started up again. *UN-chk, UN-chk, UN-chk.* It was like being inside God's angry heart. The light turned green. I pointed left. Miss Dupay shifted into first gear like she was throwing a punch, and went straight. *UN-chk, UN-chk.* I drew an upside-down *U* in the air. Miss Dupay shook her head, grinning.

Down 77th, a few miles south of town, was an old gravel driveway shrouded over with trash pines and bramble bushes. A bigger car might not have been able to scrape through the keyhole bower, but her sub-compact slid right through and pulled up to a house that had been empty for a long time. That's what I guessed, anyway, from the tree growing up through the chimney.

She put the car in park, shut off the lights, and turned down the music.

I looked straight ahead at the house and its tree. "It's like the tree's revenge on the chimney," I said. "*All those years burning wood, why, I'll*—"

"You don't have to joke," she said.

"I've heard of tree-houses, but this is ridiculous!"

"You don't even have to talk."

Her fingers nestled into my hair, tickling my amygdala. Little eels ran through my veins again, this time swarming around my crotch. Miss Dupay didn't know it, I was sure, but she was accidentally being very sexy.

Her fingers traced letters into my skull until I had to slide a forearm over my lap. *Get down*, I ordered my curious penis, which was beginning to nose around. I was in danger of making a fool of myself. Teachers did not drive students to condemned houses to have sex with them. Well, a male teacher might, particularly a band teacher or a swimming coach—the high school had lost a couple of teachers that way—but a lady teacher? With a middle-school boy? Ha. No chance.

What was happening here was something else entirely, something much more innocent. Just a perfectly innocent head massage that I was about to ruin with an erection that was burning like a rod of uranium.

Though, why was she untucking my shirt? What did that have to do with a head massage? If she wasn't careful, she was going to give me the impression that all of this was leading somewhere sexual. The last time I'd had that kind of thought, though, I'd ended up feeding grass to a bunch of camels. Maybe Miss Dupay was teaching me a lesson, trying to help me through my troubles like Lissy had. Maybe Miss Dupay thought that unbuckling my belt would help me relax. Well, she'd almost just relaxed me into ejaculating in my pants there—but she couldn't be held responsible for that. She couldn't have known that my penis was having a real bad misunderstanding.

"Boy, are we both going to be embarrassed in a minute!"

is what I meant to say just then, but my mouth was too dry to form any words. God, was my prick stiff! I could have broken a brick with it. I could have done a Bruce Lee number on a whole pile of bricks. There was just no reasoning with it when it got like this, so I gave up and stopped hiding it.

Still looking at the abandoned house, I whispered, "Sorry."

The next thing I saw was her shadow coming over me, her hair like a tree sudden with leaves.

When she drove me home, I kept touching my tender crotch as if to confirm that I had not imagined the whole thing. Pulling into my driveway, she said, "You're a smart guy, so I probably don't have to tell you what we did was a secret."

"Okay," I said. Tremors ran through my body like little aftershocks.

"You can't tell your friends, even. Anyone finds out, there will be no end of trouble. People wouldn't understand." She gave a little eye-roll, as if to say *Morons*. "Is this something you want to do again?"

In truth, all I wanted at that moment was to get inside my house before I fell apart. I was shaking pretty bad and I was afraid my teeth would start chattering or I'd start blubbering, though I didn't know why. Agreeing with her seemed the fastest way out of the car, so again I said, "Okay."

"Then play it cool."

I got out of the car with the slow, intentional movements of a drunk. When I went to close the door, she leaned across the seat and her face was illuminated by our porch light. Her eyes were wide and her skin was pulled tight so that, in a trick of the light, she looked like a terrified little girl. "Especially around Daddy."

I must have looked frightened myself, because suddenly she smiled and wagged her finger, becoming the jokester I'd seen at Al's Tap. "And that's an order, mister!"

# Section 3
## Descent

Resurrection Bender

-a Rosalyn Bryson story-

Jesus never meant to hurt his pet turtle. *They were just playing a game,* Flying Saucer, *which involved zooming the turtle around the room, and I suppose you could call this dangerous, but they had played this game a million times before without any problems, Jesus and his turtle, Hiawatha.*

*The best part of* Flying Saucer *was when Jesus would bring the turtle in for a landing on the bookshelf, or the end-table, or his mother's desk—never when she was there; Jesus knew he'd get in trouble for zooming his turtle—bringing Hiawatha down slow, pretending to activate his reverse thrusters, making rumbly noises with his, Jesus', mouth, and pausing right before touchdown to say in a robotic voice, "Deploy... landing gear." If Jesus held still long enough, Hiawatha would extend his scaly legs. It was the turtle's only trick.*

*The day of the accident, Jesus wasn't being careless or going extra fast. Hiawatha wasn't slimy. It just* happened, *like things sometimes do, the kind of situation where no one is really to blame, which is hard for some people to understand.*

*One second Jesus was zooming his turtle through the living room, and the next second Hiawatha was sailing through the air like a little discus, hitting the shelf of World Book Encyclopedias with a surprising thunk, then the wooden floor with an even bigger thunk.*

*Jesus rushed to pick the turtle up, and he felt the underside of the shell give, like a cracked egg. "Deploy landing gear," he whispered. Hiawatha's head lolled out like a tongue. The turtle blinked once, and Jesus felt the life go out of him.*

*"No," Jesus moaned. "No, no, no." His stomach felt like a rotten mushroom. He remembered the way the turtle's claws felt, fine as fish bones, when they would scrabble against his palm. He remembered lying down beside the terrarium and imitating the turtle's slow blinking. A boy and his turtle, you know how close they get.*

*Jesus squeezed the turtle as if he could meld the shell back together, though, at that point, what good would that have done for Hiawatha? The turtle was dead. A cracked shell was the least of its problems. Still, Jesus squeezed and squeezed, saying* Pleeeease—*and out came the legs.*

*At first Jesus thought it was just pressure: squeeze anything hard enough and something's bound to pop out. But then the legs started paddling air. The turtle raised its head and gave Jesus a slow blink. Jesus hoisted it up to the light of the picture window. The crack was gone, the shell was whole, Hiawatha was healed.*

*Jesus felt amazed. Also ashamed. Amazement and shame swirled in his gut like a baby tornado. What an incredible power—and he'd used it in a cover-up. A cover-up involving a pet.*

*Still, could you misuse a power you didn't even know you had?*

*That night, Jesus forgave himself for what he'd done to Hiawatha. Killing the turtle and bringing it back to life were both accidents, and he doubted Hiawatha remembered any of it, so as long as Jesus didn't do either of those things again, he'd be okay.*

*The second resurrection, a roadkill possum on old 77th, was just to make sure Jesus had an actual power, in case the incident with the turtle had been some kind of misunderstanding. The third (gull, window) was to see if squeezing had anything to do with it. He brought a raccoon back to life by whispering the words* Come alive *into its flea-boiling ears. When he re-animated the frog in the window well, he was in the middle of the laundry room, ten feet away, at least. He made finger-guns, said* Shazam, *and the frog twitched and started clawing at the glass.*

*He needed the practice, he told himself. One day he would use this power for something big and important, and he didn't want to be rusty. When that moment came, he didn't want to be like,* Well, let's see, I think I put my hand here, and—no, okay, that didn't work. Can someone help me roll this guy over?

*All the same, he figured, it was probably best not to tell anyone. Especially his parents. They didn't have powers. They wouldn't understand.*

*Well, that wasn't true, and Jesus knew it. His parents would have understood all too well. They would have told Jesus to stop using his power in such a vainglorious way. In the quiet moments that followed a resurrection, after the thrill wore off, Jesus often imagined his mother's look of disappointment and he knew she'd be in the right.*

*So he stopped. Sometimes for days at a time. But then he'd find himself walking to school, and there would be a flattened tabby, looking all dead and inviting...*

*Each time he swore would be the last time.* That's it, *he promised* God. No more. *God wasn't talking back to him yet, but Jesus could tell He was listening.*

*One time, only minutes after such a promise, Jesus found himself reviving a cricket—almost accidentally, that's how automatic it had become—and, distraught, he said,* I'll make you a deal, God: if I do it again, you can make me blind in one eye.

*This was followed by a secret thought:* I can just heal that eye, anyway.

*Part of Jesus hoped that God would intervene in some terrible way, like causing one of the resurrected animals to attack Jesus, but that didn't happen. Nor did Holyghost come by to suspend his powers, or even give him a stern lecture. Jesus was baffled and resentful. What were they waiting for, an engraved invitation?*

*Each resurrection brought less wonder and more guilt, but did Jesus stop? Did he even slow down? If anything, he picked up his pace. If he brought something to life before breakfast, he'd think,* Well, I guess I blew it for the day, *and go on a resurrection bender. Walking beside Bingo Lake, he would pass his hand over the water so that life bubbled up from the muck. People still remember that spring for how loud the nights were with animal cries.*

*On weekends, he'd check the mousetrap downstairs, then hit the street on his bike, trolling for roadkill. That year, one possum got run over on Cline Avenue eighteen different times.*

*One night his father served trout for dinner. Jesus snuck a filet down to Bingo Lake, but he couldn't bring it back to life. He swished it back and forth in the water. Breading floated away in clumps. He tried squeezing the filet, and got a small bone stuck in the web between his fingers.*

*Maybe you had to have the whole animal, Jesus thought. Or maybe it couldn't be cooked.*

*That's when he paused, suddenly disgusted with himself. He flung the filet into the pond. A caiman that had been frozen the previous winter scrambled in after it. Jesus buried his face in his hands, thinking* stop, just stop, please help me stop.

*I don't care who you are: when you catch yourself trying to resurrect dinner, you know you have a problem.*

# Chapter 22

Every year, the Broadmoor opened its executive course on the last Saturday in March. At dawn, after firing a shotgun to signal the start of the season, my father played the first round of the year in an Elmer Fudd hunter's cap. This year, he also brought along a thermos of Irish coffee, a canister of whipped cream, and a bag of bear claws. His diet was a distant memory, but he seemed to be making up for every deprivation he'd ever felt. Maybe that's what we were all doing.

By afternoon, the day was unseasonably warm, and my father was half-lit when he sauntered into the Pro Shop, where I was helping Rick workshop a new move. His tricks didn't creep me out anymore, for some reason. Maybe I'd gotten used to them, or maybe I was becoming a bit of a creep, myself. Rick had his hand on the countertop, and was lifting it about an inch and letting it drop again, so that it would collapse and expand, collapse and expand. *Polka squid*, he called this one, and upon my suggestion he sang, "Oom-pah, oom-pah, oom—"

"Hooky time," my father declared, throwing a mock-punch to my gut, but following through too much and making me gasp. He wanted to grill out at home, which he announced, for some reason, in a cartoonish Italian accent. "You make-a the steaks, I'll make-a the margaritas."

How much whiskey had he put in his coffee? I tried to beg off, but he hooked me around the shoulders, and I saw a headlock in my near future if I kept resisting, so I went with him. On my way out the door I looked at the clock, and saw, to my annoyance, that it was ten minutes to four.

Four o'clock was when Miss Dupay's Daddy went to the VFW for drinks. Four o'clock was when I usually gave my own father some excuse—"Science club" was a recent favorite— and sprinted off on my bike, stashing it in the scraggly privets of the children's park, then trotting along the sidewalk, unzipping my coat before I even got to Miss Dupay's door.

Ten minutes from the promised land, only to get shanghaied by my drunken father. Either he had the best timing in the universe, or the worst.

That spring, if I wasn't having sex with Miss Dupay, I was thinking about it. When I could get it. Where we would do it. The only thing I didn't think about was how, because that part was always the same: Miss Dupay pushing me over and climbing on top.

Basically, my only job was to get naked and lie back; she did the rest. Which was fine by me. She seemed to like it, and, to me, it felt like being worshipped.

But on that Saturday, my father's escape interrupted my regularly scheduled programming. That's how I ended up in the kitchen with a jar of cayenne pepper in my hand, considering whether to pound it into his steak, when the phone rang.

My mother was screaming.

High and ragged as a train whistle, loud enough to make my vision wobble. I had to hold the phone away from my head. Then I heard her talking, so I put it back to my ear.

"This is happening!" she said. "It's really happening!"

She screamed again.

She had landed a part. In a movie, an actual movie. Without—get this—even auditioning. She'd gotten a call asking if she was the girl who knew how to handle a sword. "The casting guy said to come on down, so I borrowed a saber from class, got on the bus, and rode across town with the sword between my legs like an umbrella." She cackled. "Only in Hollywood, right?"

I tried to laugh, but my face was numb. This was happening? Finally, when I'd understood that she was destined to fail in Hollywood, that the idea of cinematic success, no matter how modest, for an untrained Midwestern mother who was almost thirty years old was laughably naive—*now* this was happening?

"So I walk into the studio and everyone starts laughing. Turns out they had swords there, plenty of them. But I'll tell you what—walk into a room with your own sword, and you make an impression."

She crowed a laugh, and a door closed inside of me. *That's it*, I thought. *It's over. She's really not coming home. Ever.*

And what I felt was relief.

After living so long under the sword of Damocles—it had been over six months since Madame had said *You're going to lose her*—this moment felt like a mercy killing. No more worrying and waiting. No chance now that I would turn into a sad case like Rick, who was still waiting for his dead hand to come back to life. At that moment I understood the worrywart from Mish's joke, the one who smiled when he got to hell, because *now it couldn't get no worse!*

"Congratulations," I said, surprised to find that I meant it.

"Oh, I knew you'd be happy for me," she gushed. "That's why I told you first. Now put your father on the phone."

Pulling aside the curtain, I saw my father hosing off the patio furniture. On top of the grill sat a pitcher of margaritas. The day was barely sixty degrees, but the sun was out, and compared to the bone-scraping cold of February, it felt warm. Under a pair of baggy shorts, his plump calves gleamed like fish bellies. His face was burnished with wind and sun and tequila, and more than at any time in recent memory, he looked almost happy.

For weeks I'd been looking for opportunities to get them on the phone with each other, especially if I thought it might lead toward an argument. But this call wouldn't lead to a fight, or at least not a fair one. My mother was a starlet—Hollywood had anointed her, that's how I saw it—and my father had become a shlub who wore pants with drawstrings. This news would crush him.

"Tell you what," I told her. "I'll do it."


In the back yard, I broke the news to him as gently as I could. When I finished, he picked up the pitcher of margaritas and walked with heavy steps toward my mother's planters at the edge of the patio. They were just pots of dirt now. He stood with his back to me, looking up, watching a jet draw a chalk line across the sky. At last he said, "What kind of movie is it?"

It was called *Return to Zombie Island*, I told him. The director, a man my mother had referred to only as Corman, planned to shoot the entire film in six days. "Black and white," she'd said. "Classic. Romantic. Blondes look better in black and white, don't you think? Smoke looks better, zombies, too, everything."

My father dumped the margaritas into a clay pot, then turned around. "Good for her," he said. "I mean it. Good. For. Her. We're not going to spend a single instant begrudging her. You know what we're going to do instead of wishing that her movie deal would fall through?"

I was afraid to guess.

"Accept it," he said. "The other day, Shirley was telling me about the stages of grief." He ticked them off on his fingers. "Denial, anger, some other bad stage or two, and finally acceptance. We've done all the other stages in spades, pal, acceptance is the only option we have left!"

His laugh sounded like a yelp. Though I couldn't see beyond our fence, I imagined neighbors on their back decks, craning to eavesdrop. "Maybe we should go inside," I said.

He grabbed his stomach with both hands. "Right here, this is what I'm talking about. Before, with those tiny clothes, when I was trying to turn back the clock and change myself, what happened? Terrible shit. But now that I've accepted a little pot-belly, look at me. Comfortable. *Happy.*"

He kind of rasped this last word at me, which made it difficult to believe him. But it seemed like the wrong time to argue, so I nodded.

"We accept, we move on." He set the empty pitcher on the grill and came toward me. I forced myself to stand still, though everything inside of me was pulling away. "We could learn something from your mother on that count. She's an expert at moving on."

He cleared his throat as if to dredge out the bitterness, then took my face in his hands. "It's just you and me now, pal."

I squirmed, afraid he might kiss me, but he held me tight behind the ears and I couldn't get away. His breath was metallic with liquor and lime. The sun was setting behind him; I could not see his face, so his voice seemed to come out of a dark hole. "You and me for the duration."

*For the duration.* That was the term used by Mrs. Jankovic's doctor when he'd ordered her on bed rest. When my father said it, though, it sounded like a life sentence.

I sympathized with my father, but I had other plans for the duration.

Sunday morning, I told him I was going to late church with Woz, then I biked through a cold mist to Miss Dupay's house. Ten minutes later I was lying on her bed, naked and cooling, and she was trying to talk me out of feeling guilty about sex. "If anyone should feel bad, it's me. And I don't. I do *not*. Every day I ask Jesus to keep me from temptation. I can't help it if he's bad at his job."

I had no idea what she was talking about. I felt sleepy and warm and kind of like I was floating, suspended in a thick fluid like the answer block in the magic eight-ball I had just picked off her cluttered nightstand. I'd been up half the night before, worried about my father, wondering what would happen to us, but sex had lifted all of those concerns away. The first few moments afterward always felt like a reprieve from everything, including thinking about more sex.

A question floated into my brain. "Does she love me?" I asked the magic eight-ball.

"Time to go," she said, tugging the sheets out from under me to throw into the wash.

Maybe she hadn't heard me. Or maybe she was just nervous. She always got like this just before Daddy was due back home. The eight-ball said *Better Not Tell You Now*. I tried a different approach. Looking at her, I said, "Tell me that you love me."

My clothes landed on me, all cold buttons and zippers. "Don't tell Daddy."

"What? Don't tell him that you love me, or—"

"Just don't. Don't anything. We've got a delicate balance here. Anyone saying anything to anyone else could ruin it."

She pulled on a stretched-out sweatshirt. Moments like this—her hair sweaty and snarled, skinny legs sticking out under the bell of her sweatshirt—she looked like a kid. Or maybe that's just how I wanted to see her.

"Love isn't going to ruin anything," I said. "It'll make everything better, won't it?"

She stopped pulling on her jeans to give me a look of disbelief. "Love," she said, "is the root of all evil."

She tugged up her jeans, hopping and twisting until she

got them all the way up. Miss Dupay wore her jeans high, which gave her a little pooch. Now she didn't look like a kid anymore. "Look," she said, softening a bit. "I know why you're bringing up this love stuff."

"You do?"

"Sure. You're like Adam. That guy had everything he could ever want or need in the garden. Fat City. Set for life, right? So why did he eat the apple?"

"Eve made him?"

She rolled her eyes. "Uch. Typical. Blame the woman. No. Nothing—*nothing*—makes people as uncomfortable as bliss. We tell ourselves that we're having a good time, that we just want to make it the tiniest bit better, when really we're setting out to tear apart any bit of happiness we've been lucky enough to stumble upon."

She put on her glasses and her transformation into a teacher was complete. Maybe that's why I didn't question her, though plenty of questions come to mind now. Like why she thought God had created that troublesome tree in the first place. Or why, knowing human nature like He did, God went out of his way to tell Adam not to eat from it. Or why, if Miss Dupay was so all-fired comfortable with bliss, she kept bringing up Daddy.

But even if I'd thought of those questions, I wouldn't have had time to ask them before the phone rang.

Whatever good feeling was left in my body dissipated. I didn't know who it was, but I sensed that my life wasn't going to get any better after she took this call.

Miss Dupay put a finger to her lips, picked up the receiver

and said a cool hello. I heard a man's voice come through the receiver. *Please be a telemarketer*, I prayed.

"Uh-huh," she said, twining the curlicue cord around a finger. "Sure, yeah, me too."

She laughed politely, and my stomach tightened. It was just a courtesy laugh, but it made me realize that she never laughed around me. "That sounds like a fine idea," she said. "What night works for you?"

I reached over and tugged on one of her belt loops, but she swatted my hand away. I reached again and pulled her down to the bed, kissing the side of her neck, snaking my arms under her sweatshirt. She clamped her elbows down on my hands like a bear trap. "I'm sorry—I hear my teakettle on the stove. Yep—no, that's fine—okay, see you Saturday!"

She pulled away from me and hung up the phone, then looked at it as though she was afraid it might ring again. I was afraid, too, but not of the phone. For the first time, I was afraid I might lose her. Was it possible? A moment earlier I'd been trying to coax a confession of love out of her—and now I was worried that she might slip away from me entirely. Was love really so slippery? And why did my guts feel like they were on a hard boil?

I tried to keep my voice light, but it came out snarly. "Got a date lined up after me?"

She looked up with the same spooked look she got whenever she warned me about Daddy. "That was your father," she said. "I'm coming over for dinner."

# Chapter 23

"This isn't a date," my father told me on the night Miss Dupay was coming over, though I hadn't asked him if it was. "Just so you know."

We were both in the kitchen, though I was the only one working on the marinara. He'd tried to help, but had been so clumsy and distracted that I told him I would take care of it. Now he was sitting at the table, drinking brandy from a foggy liqueur glass to calm his nerves.

I gave him a dark look, then chopped an onion. My hands were shaky—my father wasn't the only one feeling jangled that night—and when I wedged the knife into my thumbnail, I gave up and scraped the rough chop into a pot already simmering with oil. My father took a sip of brandy, then cleared his throat roughly. "Hello," he said. "Hello! Hello. Say, do you have any homework tonight?"

I shook my head.

"I'm sure you can find some. After you finish eating, work in your room for a while. Okay, buddy?"

I dumped a can of stewed tomatoes into a bowl. They looked like little hearts. I crushed them with my hands. "I thought you said this wasn't a date," I said. "Buddy."

"Adults like privacy sometimes. To talk."

To talk, sure. My ass. I might have bought that line a few months earlier, but not anymore. I knew what was on his mind because it was on my mind, too. One of the things on my mind, anyway. Tonight was the night my mother was supposed to finish shooting her movie. I glanced at the clock, subtracting three hours to get California time. Did movie studios operate on regular business hours?

My father poured himself another little glass. "What does your teacher like to talk about?"

"The unifying theories of the universe," I said. "Know any?"

He scratched his jaw, blinking at the corner of the room. "Naw," he admitted. "Got any you can spare?"

I brought the bowl of tomato glop over to the stove, where the onions were brown and sizzling at the bottom of the pan in a way that told me they were already stuck. *Oh well*, I thought as I dumped the tomatoes on top without scraping up the onions. I cooked; my father could clean.

"The universe works like a toilet," I said. "Things start off far apart, but everything swirls together faster and faster in the end."

He grimaced. "Thanks, but I probably won't be bringing up any toilet theories during dinner."

I glanced at the clock, then the phone. Would my mother call? We hadn't made any plans the last time we'd talked, a week earlier. Her silence was no surprise—Corman wanted to film day and night, she'd told me—but now I was itching to hear her stories about what it was like to be on a set, if she'd met any famous people, if anyone had asked for her autograph. I was curious, too, if she'd sound any different now that she was a starlet.

Filming a movie could change a person, I suspected. Especially someone like my mother, who was looking to be changed.

The marinara was popping. Little blobs of sauce shot out like solar flares, hitting the cabinets, the microwave, the coffeemaker. I should have turned it down, but I just retreated to the kitchen island and let the pot spatter while I busied myself with a salad.

When the doorbell rang, my father stopped using his thumb to wipe brandy from his mustache, and pushed himself up from the table. To my surprise, he stepped toward me. "Do I look okay?"

I looked him over, hoping to point out something to undermine his confidence—but what I saw only withered my own. His shirt was crisp. His jeans were as dark as a starry night. He'd just gotten his hair cut short, like an act of good faith toward spring. He might have been pudgy, but that only made me realize how sick and worn he'd looked during the winter.

How good did he look? So good that the speck of marinara that had just spotted his white oxford looked as pretty and intentional as a pocket square.

I gave him a thumbs-up, feeling sick in my gut.

If this was a date, I thought, I didn't stand a chance.

Miss Dupay entered in a funny, high mood. "Now, which one of you's my date?" she asked when she came into the kitchen, putting her hands on her hips and feigning confusion. When my father pretended to be confused, too, she threw her head back and laughed so hard that I could see the silver in her molars and for a moment it seemed like she couldn't stop laughing and would go crazy before our eyes.

At the table she twirled up big, comical bites of spaghetti like tiny cotton candies. "Mm-*mmm*. Mamma-mia! Bela Lugosi! That's-a what I call-a spaghetti!"

Glancing at the hallway, she said, "I keep expecting your big friend with the accordion to come strolling out." She dropped her fork with a clatter, put one hand to her chest, and swayed back and forth, singing, *"Are you lonely tonight? Are you… something tonight?* Come on, boys, you know how it goes! Sing along!"

It didn't occur to me that she might be nervous; I thought she was just excited to be in front of a new audience. But unlike her performance at Al's Tap, this little show irritated me. Why wasn't she like this when we were together? And why had she gotten so dressed up?

Her hair was pinned back with a couple of chopsticks. Split ends floated around her face like cilia. On her green blouse was a brooch so large it looked like a police shield. Every time she bent toward her plate, it sagged dangerously low, threatening to skim her spaghetti. Was this outfit for me or for him? No way to know. No way to ask her later, either, because of course she'd say, *For you, Revie,* but how could I believe her? She'd never dressed up for me before. Although, to be fair, we'd never gone out on an actual date. Maybe this was her way of dressing up for me without drawing suspicion. Though she was drawing plenty of mine. I was starting to get the idea that she saved her best moods and material for other people. Sure, I got to have sex with her, but was that enough? It was not, I decided. Not anymore. I wanted all of her. It was the only way to be sure I wouldn't lose her.

Miss Dupay might have gotten talkative when she was nervous, but my father and I went the other direction. Neither of us laughed much, but my father did smile and say, "Now, that's funny," after almost everything she said. She plied my father with prompts, but each of her questions—*So, you're a golf pro?* or *You grew up around here?*—was met with little more than a nod. "Yep," said my father, turning the liqueur glass around on the tabletop. "Guilty as charged."

At last there came a moment when everyone was silent. We all looked at our plates, piled with cold spaghetti. No one had taken more than three bites. The salad bowl was a wet mess in the middle of the table. Putting down my fork, I glanced at the phone, which felt like a fourth person in the room. My father picked up the bottle of brandy and poured two drinks with such slow, deliberate care that I knew he was lit up like a switchboard. When he tipped his head back to drink, Miss Dupay looked at me directly for the first time all night. Her eyes widened slightly. *Help me.*

I cleared my throat. I said, "The universe is a toilet."

But I forgot the rest of it, and they both drew back, like *Huh?* Still, my idiotic remark must have been enough to break the logjam of silence, because the next thing I knew, Miss

Dupay was giving my father another prompt, the last one any of us would need all night. "So," she said. "I hear your—I hear someone's making a movie!"

My father blinked. "Boy, that news gets around fast. How did you find out?"

Her face froze for a second, like someone had paused her brain. "I guess," she said slowly, "that Revie must have mentioned it."

"Mentioned it?" Now my father looked really confused. "Back up a second. I feel like I'm missing a piece here. When would he—I mean, was there a class discussion about mothers or something?"

Nodding furiously, I said, "I'm pretty sure that's what it was. Yep. I can see it in my head right now. It was a whole big thing at school. We all talked about our mothers. They called it… Mother Day."

My father swung his head around to me, screwing up his face. "But Mother's Day isn't until May."

"*Mother* Day," I said. "It's different. No cards or gifts. You just sit around and talk about—"

Miss Dupay leaned toward my father and I was glad to shut up. She might have been caught off guard for a moment, but that moment was over and now she oozed certainty and something else, besides. Not sexiness, exactly, but the kind of warm comfort that women can emit, the sense that she'd make everything better. *Succor.* That's the word. The one that sounds a lot like *sucker.*

"Sometimes," she said, "Revie comes by during lunch for extra help with his science homework. He must have told me then."

I said, "That was a joke, what I said before. *Mother Day.* Ha."

Miss Dupay shot me a look. *Play it cool,* she seemed to be saying, just as she'd told me in the car after our first time. But playing it cool had never been my strength, and being with Miss Dupay hadn't exactly helped me in that regard. Every time she walked past me in science class, I felt like my organs were being pulled around by magnets. I'd get flashbacks of the small trail of moles below her breast like a spattering of mud. In the middle of class one day, my teeth had started chattering. "Don't breathe on me, dude," said Woz, the first words he'd spoken to me in weeks. He scooted his chair away. "Whatever you got, I don't want."

In the kitchen, my father frowned at a glob of marinara on the table. "It's just that—please pardon me, I don't mean to be rude, but I have to ask—do you get into personal business with all your students?"

I said, "The door is open the whole time. The *whole time.*"

Miss Dupay put her heel on my foot and pressed down. "I'm available to all my students, but Revie here is pretty much the only one who's taken me up on my offer."

My father sat back with his old look of calculation, like he was working out algorithms in his head. My heart kicked like it was trying to break out of my chest. *The jig is up,* I thought. He was going to figure out that the missing piece was sex. It was all I could do to keep from leaping up and shouting that *YES, it was TRUE, and she was MINE, he couldn't ever have her,* before running out into the street to throw myself in front of a speeding Oldsmobile.

The only thing that kept me still was Miss Dupay's heel, pressing harder and harder into my foot until at last my father lowered his eyes. "Talk about your extra mile. Talk about giving until it hurts." He lifted his drink to her. "I wish we had more teachers like you."

"Me, too," I said, and got a sharp kick in the shin.


After dinner my father reminded me about my "homework," then escorted Miss Dupay into the living room. I took the cordless phone into my room. Though I didn't trust my father with Miss Dupay, I doubted he could make much headway in just a few minutes. My father might have been handsome, but he was no smooth operator.

It was around six o' clock California time when I dialed my mother's number. "Pick up," I muttered, but the phone rang until the recorded lady came on to say *If you would like to make a call, please hang up and dial again.* I hung up. I dialed again. Could they still be filming? Or was she at some kind of cast party? Imagining my mother dancing poolside with some guy in a zombie costume gave me a sharp pain near my liver. Couldn't she tell the other actors to hold on one second, turn down the music, I just have to make this one very important call to my son? After six days of silence, she couldn't do that one little thing?

I guessed not. I guessed that doing the lambada with a zombie was more important than letting her son know that she, Miss Big Time Movie Star, was alive.

Oh, I would let her have it when I got her on the phone. I didn't care how hungover she'd be, or how repentant, I would make her cry.

I dialed Woz. He answered in a thick voice, sounding like he'd been sleeping. I said, "I just wanted to make sure my phone worked."

"Well, it does. Wait, why do you need to know if your phone—"

Then I surprised myself. "Hey, how long are you going to be mad at me?"

"I don't know." He sighed. "Just now, I kind of forgot that I was. What you did was really an asshole move, though."

"So was the thing you did, saying how great it was that my mom was gone."

A pause. "I guess I did, huh? I'm sorry, man. I didn't really mean to—"

"We're both assholes," I said before we edged any closer to sentimentality.

Woz agreed. "I'm a gaping one, and you're a flaming one."

"*You're* the flaming one," I insisted, then hung up so I could check on my father. I opened my door slowly so it wouldn't squeak, got down on my belly, and swam up the wooden hallway toward the living room where he sat with Miss Dupay on the couch.

I couldn't see their hands—the couch faced away from me—but, to my relief, their heads didn't seem all that close together. I slid up to the meniscus of light in time to hear my father say, "But how did he seem?"

"Seem?" she said.

*He?* I thought.

My father said, "If one is okay, and ten is out of his mind, where would his needle fall on that scale?"

Were they talking about me? Was this was why he'd invited her over? Was it possible that this actually *wasn't* a date? Scales fell from my heart, soft as petals.

She said, "Sanity cannot be quantified. Trust me—I've tried."

"My own needle," he said, "is on one. Good luck and Godspeed, that's what I would tell Rosalyn if she called up right now. Break a leg. Hell, break two. I'll even go see her movie. I will buy a ticket and see it, that's how well I wish her."

My father picked up the bottle of Christian Brothers from the end table to pour them both another dose. After taking a drink, he wiped his mustache for a long time; either he'd gotten sloppy with the liquor or his lips were going numb. "No need to worry about me, nossir. And the Reever will be fine, too. Sure, he's a swoony kid, sensitive as a bird, and, okay, he's a little light on common sense, and he's a bad follower—or, I should say, a real good follower of bad leaders—"

The scales stopped falling off my heart. *We get your point,* I thought. *Move on.*

"Tell me," he said. "Does he have a hard time at school? Does he get picked on?"

Heat stole up my neck. A moment earlier, I'd been touched that he was asking about me, but this was too much. This was just invasive.

My father leaned toward Miss Dupay, as though, full of concern for his child, he didn't want to miss her answer, but his face kept sinking toward hers and all of a sudden—I saw it, though I couldn't believe it—his lips puckered.

Miss Dupay stood from the couch, briskly smoothing the wrinkles from her pants.

Well. I'd never seen that gesture from her before. In fact, I'd never seen her make any kind of tidying gesture. She kept brushing herself, running her hands down her sleeves next. She must have been as jarred as I was. "How about I help you with the dishes?"

My father struggled up from the couch, holding out one arm for balance as he swayed in place, laughing softly. *Whoa, Nelly.* He didn't look nearly as handsome as he had earlier. His white oxford was wrinkled and nearly untucked on one side, and his face was streaked red from drinking. "Naw," he said. "Let's dance."

Lurching forward, he looked like he might fall on her, but in a surprisingly graceful move he slipped one arm around her waist and clasped her other hand in a dance frame straight out of an old movie. When had my father learned to dance? I sat up like a prairie dog, ready to break up this romantic scene, but Miss Dupay spotted me over his shoulder and made a shooing motion.

My father closed his eyes and mumbled a bar or two of Little Walter.

*My babe don't stand no cheatin', my babe.*

*Oh yeah, she don't stand no cheatin', my babe,*

*Oh yeah, she don't stand no cheatin',*

*She don't stand none of that midnight creepin',*
*My babe, true little baby, my babe.*

He was putting the make on a woman with a song about how his own woman couldn't stand cheating. It's possible, I guess, that he was being ironic, but I doubt it. My father wasn't big on irony, even when he was in full and sober possession of his wits. I can only guess that cheating was on his mind, and this just happened to be the song called up to his mental jukebox—but still: unbelievable.

Miss Dupay broke the dance frame with a badly faked sneeze. My father took a step back, nearly fell over the end table, then landed on the couch. "No," he said, picking up a conversational thread long since dropped. "The one I worry about is Rosalyn herself."

"Uh-huh," said Miss Dupay, picking up the bottle of brandy and putting it on top of the television, out of my father's reach. "It's a tough world for a woman to be alone in, that's for sure."

"That's not what I mean." He threw out his hand in some kind of plea, either to understand him, or to pull him back on his feet. But Miss Dupay stayed back by the television, and eventually he dropped his hand. "Alone is what she *wants.* I'm talking about those B-movies. You seen them? Half the women end up topless."

Miss Dupay glanced at me in the hallway. "Maybe she'll be in the other half."

"You wouldn't say that if you saw her breasts." He stifled

a belch. "That director will have her topless in no time. And poor Rosalyn—I love her, but man, can she have her head in the clouds sometimes—she probably thinks she's making *art*."

He said this last word with heavy disgust. Whether it was for art, B movies, or my mother, I wasn't sure. Maybe all three.

"There she is, thinking she's like one of those classy statues with nude breasts that Michelangelo used to make, and meanwhile the director is thinking, *what a rack!*" He cleared his throat. "Pardon my French."

Miss Dupay raised her eyebrows at me, like *What am I supposed to do here?* I shook my head tightly. *Nothing.* This was hard to listen to, but I wanted to hear where it was all going.

"So there you are in Hollywood," he said, kicking his legs up on the couch and laying his head down on the armrest, "thinking you have everything you ever wanted… but now what? You just started your career half-naked with a zombie— my God, where do you go from there?"

"Home," said Miss Dupay firmly, sticking out her hand. "I've had a wonderful time, but I've got to get to church in the morning, so—"

"Videotape," my father groaned. "That's the worst part. It's one thing for her to be up there on the big screen with her blouse ripped open for half the world to see, but now, thanks to videotape, her breasts will go into people's *homes*, and not just once, either, but over and over, pause, rewind, slow motion, play, *re*play, and from now to eternity men will get an eyeful—boys, *boys* as young and innocent as Revie will get their first glimpse of womanhood on the TV, and it will be burned into their minds forever! When one of those boys dies, the breasts that flash before his eyes will be the breasts of my wife!"

He threw his hands up in another plea—but for what? I don't think he could have answered that question even if I had shouted it from the shadows. He held this pose for a moment, his hands floating, his mouth open like he might go on, but then, slowly, like a flower closing its petals for the night, his hands sank, his mouth closed, his eyelids shut.

In the hallway, I shuddered so hard that my knees rattled on the floor.

Nothing my mother had ever done could top that performance. It was the bravest, most humiliating thing I had ever seen. My father could have taken off all his clothes and still not been more naked. I wanted to jump into the light of the living room and tell him that I loved him; the words were a big, aching bubble in my throat. I wanted to shout *bravo, bravissimo!*—but that's the downside of eavesdropping: you can't applaud.

All you can do is slink away, which I did as soon as Miss Dupay let herself out.

# Chapter 24

This time, when my mother didn't call, my father and I didn't make excuses to each other. We didn't say that the film had probably run over schedule, or that she must have unplugged the phone to get some much-needed sleep. We just exchanged grim looks after each failed attempt to reach her, as it dawned on us that worry could outlive hope.

"You know what we should do when she calls?" my father said. "Not answer. Give her a taste of her own medicine. Let *her* worry, for once."

We nodded at each other, like that could possibly happen.

By the middle of the week, my father was stationed on the couch with the phone in his lap like a sick pet. The television stayed on day and night, filling the air with noise so we wouldn't have to. He'd stopped going to work, so I skipped school, too, ostensibly to make food runs so my father could keep up his phone vigil. He didn't seem to notice that I left to pick up dinner at 3:45, and didn't return until around 6:00. He also didn't seem to notice that I came home smelling like a sea urchin after my afternoon rendezvous with Miss Dupay.

One evening, late that week, I was biking home with styrofoam containers of lake perch in my backpack when I got the idea, as sudden and urgent as a stomach cramp, to go back to Miss Dupay's house for a second round.

No sooner did I have that thought than it became a need. It didn't matter that I'd just left her house a few minutes before; just then, the only thing that mattered was the twenty-three long hours I would have to endure before I could be with her again. Going back was a bad idea. Miss Dupay had told me many times that Daddy came home from the VFW in time for dinner. And then there was my own father to consider: an extra-long absence might spark his suspicion.

Turning back toward her house, I thought, *I'd better hurry, then.*

I was too late. Daddy's white Mercury was already in the driveway. "Shit," I breathed, and looked up at the sky, which never got entirely dark over the region. Clouds stretched over the night like an old undershirt. My ribcage filled with pain and want, and I thought of the sacred heart of Jesus, the old picture of Christ looking dreamy and mild while his heart goes supernova through his chest. I used to think of that picture as glorious: how fantastic to have a heart like a disco ball! But maybe Jesus was thinking, *This hurts like hell*, or *I can't make it stop, not even for a moment's peace.*

Not that I harbored any more illusions about being like Jesus. His heart radiated light; I was pretty sure mine ate it.

I glanced at my watch. Over twenty-two hours. A desert of time. I'd die before I made it across.

Before I knew what I was doing, I found myself walking up the drive, stepping through the mangy boxwoods to the window, and cupping my hands around my face to peer through a gap in the curtains.

Against the far wall was a big television, playing a college basketball game so loudly I could hear it through the glass. No lamps were on, though, and it took me a moment to spot the mound in the corner, and another moment to understand that it must be Daddy, cranked back to a nearly horizontal position in a lay-z-boy. The way his chest rose and fell told me he was sleeping, so I kept on looking.

When a bright flash from the TV illuminated the room, I got a good look at him. Jesus, he was big. Not as big as Madame, but then, who was? Burly, I guess was the word. *Big enough to eat a tree and shit two-by-fours*, Shirley might have said. His short, wavy, white hair reminded me of a cow's forehead.

The television flashed again like sheet lightning, and I saw him looking at me.

I stumbled back, knocking my head against a bird-feeder attached to a shepherd's crook. Seeds poured over my hair and down my shirt. I stopped brushing at myself when I heard the jangle of springs. That was the sound of the lay-z-boy coming down, followed by the sound of Daddy tromping to the door, which was the sound, for all I knew, of the end of my bliss.

If Miss Dupay ever wants evidence for her theories about humans exerting gravity, she need look no further than this moment, when I had every reason to run, but could not bring myself to leave her orbit. If it wasn't gravity that made me step up and ring her doorbell just then, I don't know what it was.

The next thing I heard, thank God, was Miss Dupay's voice. "I'll get it!"

The door opened. Her eyes went hard, but her voice came out artificially bright. "Well, hello."

"I'm raising funds for the band," I said. "Care to make a donation?"

"I already gave." She crossed her arms. "A lot."

"The band needs more. We're nowhere near our goal."

"Teachers have limited resources. Especially subs."

We stared at each other until Daddy, who was back in his lay-z-boy, roared, "Lord Christ! Are you trying to heat the whole neighborhood?" Miss Dupay glanced into the living room—"Sorry, Daddy"—then stepped onto the porch and closed the door behind her. Before she could speak, I said, "My mother is missing." But even as those words left my mouth, I knew they wouldn't be enough to coerce her, so I heard myself add, "We think—we think she might have killed herself."

Miss Dupay lifted a hand to her mouth. I coughed, and, to my surprise, started crying. I couldn't tell if I was pretending, and, if I was, if I'd ever be able to stop.

She blinked at the porch light, shaking her head. I couldn't tell if she was trying to keep back her own tears, or if she was exasperated. "Oh, Revie," she said, and I feared she would cut me loose right then, tell me that whatever she got from me wasn't worth all this trouble, but she did not. "I can't talk here," she said, though I think we both knew it wasn't a conversation I was after. "Give me twenty minutes, okay? I'll meet you at the treehouse."

"Thank you." I sniffed, sounding pitiful even to my own ears, but still I couldn't stop crying. As I biked to the treehouse, tears streamed across my temples. I managed to quiet down when she pulled up in her Rabbit, but my hands were shaking too badly to undo my own belt buckle, so I fell back against the seat, pointed to my jeans and said, "Please."

"Lord Christ," she snapped. "Do I have to do everything?" She yanked open my belt and tugged up my shirt. Seeds flew everywhere, raining all over the seats and floor, like I had dried and burst open.

# Chapter 25

When I came home, my father was waiting for me on the porch steps. I stopped on the driveway, downwind.

He rose, shaking his head. Then he started toward me.

I said, "Traffic was... And then Shirley made me..."

Halfway down the drive, he stopped. The streetlamp lit his face, and I saw that he wasn't angry, but shaken. "She called," he said.

The way he said it, I knew this wasn't good news.

She'd been nearly hysterical, he told me, saying all kinds of crazy stuff. "That she was like Lucifer, cast down from heaven, all the other angels erasing his permanent record. That she had her own lost episodes now."

She'd been cut from the movie. Every line, every last frame. My father tried to console her, and she did calm down, but that's when she claimed it was a sign.

"I told her no," he said. "I said, Rosalyn, God did not cut you from that movie."

She wouldn't listen to him. It would have been one thing,

she insisted, to struggle and struggle out there, but to get a part so quickly and then to get cut—it was definitely a sign.

At this point in the telling, my father paused. If my mother had been the one telling the story, this would have seemed like a dramatic pause, but my father just seemed afraid to go on. We were sitting on the porch steps, and he was bent over, huddling his knees like a kid trying to make himself small enough to escape notice.

I nudged my father with my elbow. "Then what?"

"That's basically what I asked. I said, Well, Rosalyn, what do you intend to do?"

It was a turn on my mother's trademark question, the one she loved to ask, the one she loved to hear from her audience. *What happens next?* And when my father told me her answer, one that I had never heard from her before, I understood why he was spooked.

"I don't know," she'd said, and then hung up.

# Chapter 26

That night a cold wind began to blow. Cirrus clouds moved at the speed of time-lapse photography. The wind carried the smell of Lake Michigan—dead smelt and wet newspaper and turned-over earth—that usually meant a storm was coming, but the wind just blew and blew, unaccompanied by rain or snow or sleet. "I wish it would open up," said my father, opening the front door to check on the sky. "Open up or blow over, instead of just threatening us like this."

His main worry was that his morning flight to LAX would be cancelled. He'd booked a ticket right after calling the police in California, who'd flatly told him there was nothing they could do for him. "You can't even go check on her?" my father asked. "Keep an eye on her, just until I get out there?" They couldn't, they told him. That's what made them police, not chaperones.

He didn't admit that he was scared she might do something foolish, maybe even hurt herself or disappear forever, but of course he was, and so was I. I tried not to think about what I'd told Miss Dupay to get her out of her house. Call it a lie, a prediction, or a hoax—Madame would say that these were just different rags on the same body.

My father wrote out a list of emergency numbers for me and taped it next to the phone. Eyeing the list, he seemed to imagine the troubles that would necessitate the dialing of these numbers. "You know what?" he said, "Why don't I just call Shirley? I bet she'd let you stay over at her—"

"Dad, it's just one night."

"It might be two."

"Don't worry about me," I said, half-hoping that he wouldn't listen to me. "I'll be *fine*."

In the morning the clouds were pouchy and ringed with violet, like bags under the eyes of God. I drank instant coffee by the picture window, watching my father leave with a single carry-on, watching the school bus come and go, watching naked trees quake in the wind.

I turned on the television, but my mind was too flitty to pay attention to anything so demanding as a rerun of *Fantasy Island*, so I ended up wandering around the house, checking each phone in turn to make sure they all had dial tones. Around lunch time, I picked up a phone and dialed the school. "Miss Dupay's room, please," I told the secretary in the deepest voice I could manage. "I am a concerned parent."

The secretary wasn't suspicious, but Miss Dupay was. She sounded tired and half-exasperated even before I told her to take the rest of the day off and come over to my house.

She exhaled into the receiver. "You ever hear the one about the golden goose? You're about to squeeze me to death."

"My mother—" I was afraid to finish that sentence, so I started over. "I really need you right now. I don't know. . . I don't know what I'm liable to do if I'm alone all day."

Silence on the line. I held my breath. Outside the picture window, trees bowed to the east. At that moment, my father was flying into a headwind, going to California to find his wife. Meanwhile, his son was implying that he might kill himself if he had to wait three hours to have sex with his substitute teacher.

"Hang on until two," she said in a tight voice. "My last class is a prep, so I'll leave early. But I'm not skipping anything else."

If there was a point of no return, we'd passed it long ago. By this time, we couldn't say no to ourselves, much less to each other.


The wind blew straight through into the evening. Trees groaned like nails being pulled from a board. Windows chattered in their frames. On the patio, an empty planter butted against the back door. I could hear all of this because Miss Dupay, for once, was quiet.

She hadn't said a word when she came into the house, or when I undressed her, or when I laid her down on the pallet I'd made on the living room floor. "You okay?" I asked her. She lifted her eyebrows slightly—*I've been better*—but didn't say anything. I kissed her neck, waiting for her to push me over and straddle me like she always did, but she just yawned in my ear.

I could have stopped then—I should have—but instead, for the first time, I pried her legs apart and pressed myself into her. She wasn't ready. The feeling was rough, rough as a cat's tongue. Her mouth opened a bit and I thought she might wince or whimper, but she didn't. Just smacked her lips in seeming boredom. I pressed harder, moving inside her in little budges, like the plates of the earth grinding past each other.

When I finished, she pushed me off and turned away to button up her shirt.

If Holyghost had appeared to me back on my birthday to let me know that soon I would be having regular sex with a real woman, I would have pictured myself as one happy boy. And if Holyghost had gone on to tell me that my mother would film a movie, I'd have imagined her as happy, too. Yet here we were, anything but. In my chest was a struggling feeling, like a moth trapped inside a light fixture.

The phone rang. I looked at Miss Dupay. Before I could say anything, she rolled her eyes. "I know, I know… I'm not here. But I bet you'll want me here when you hang up."

I ignored that remark and answered the phone. It was my father. "You made it," I said.

"Oh, I'm here, all right." He'd actually landed a couple of hours earlier, but he hadn't called because he wanted to start his search right away. So why was he calling now? "I found her car."

He'd been talking to Mrs. Melendez, one of my mother's neighbors, when he saw the station wagon swing into the parking lot. He rushed down the stairs, expecting to see his wife, only to find a stranger behind the wheel. "Some skinny, old Mexican fella. I say, 'Where's my wife?' and he's all *no habla, no habla* until I threaten to call the police. Well, he knows *that* word."

I tried to imagine my father, a man who had never yelled at me in public, threatening a stranger. I couldn't begin to picture it.

"So Mrs. Melendez comes hustling down the stairs—she's a real busybody, I could tell right away—offering to translate. After a lot of back and forth, the guy pulls a piece of paper out of his back pocket. Little slip of paper, says *One Ford Fairmont: $130. From: Rosalyn Bryson. To: Ramon Gonzales.* Like a goddamn gift tag."

"Was it her handwriting?"

"Yeah, it was her handwriting. And that's exactly the kind of thing your mother would do, too—never mind that we still owe four thousand on that car—so I knew this Ramon wasn't lying."

"What did you do?"

"I repossessed the car."

I nearly dropped the phone. I know that desperate times can bring out strange aspects of a person's character, but none of this stuff—recklessness, combativeness—was in my father to begin with. He had flipped.

"This is good news," my father said. "It means she has no transportation, and I do. Advantage us."

I wasn't so sure that giving away her possessions was a good sign. To me, it seemed like she was lightening her load, getting ready to fly again, only this time she wouldn't need a car where she was going. But I didn't say anything for the same reason I didn't tell anyone about me and Miss Dupay: no one wanted to hear it, because who would it help?

"Everything okay on your end?" my father asked.

Across the room, Miss Dupay pulled on her shoes. I snapped my fingers at her. She gave me a withering look, but sat back down. "A-okay," I said.

"Just so you know," Miss Dupay said when I got off the phone, "I wasn't going to leave in the middle of your call. My feet were cold."

"Stay."

There's no good way to say that word. Either you sound like a beggar or a master. This one sounded like a plea.

"I'll come back tomorrow," she offered. "Maybe even check on you before school. I can't promise anything, but—"

"Stay."

My voice was rougher this time, on account of the growing knot in my throat. My father wasn't the only one who had flipped.

"Now, Revie," she said slowly, sounding like a teacher. "You know that can't happen."

When I didn't answer, she slipped on her jacket and started buttoning it. She was seconds away from picking up her purse and walking out the door. Now was the time to say that I didn't know what I might do if I was left alone, but I'd already spent that currency. I'd heard the one about the boy who cried wolf, and I knew the moral: once you started repeating yourself, you got devoured.

So I turned over the only card I had left to play.

"Stay," I said again. "Or I'll tell Daddy."

She stopped buttoning. Her face went slack. "That's not funny."

I picked up the phone.

"You wouldn't," she said, though she didn't seem real sure about that.

I started to dial and she flew across the room and fell on me, covering me with dry kisses while pulling the phone out of my hand and stuffing it under a throw pillow. Then she set her forehead against mine, her hair falling around my face, filtering light like the branches of a willow, until our breathing slowed, together.

She pulled back and cradled my face, looking like she might cry.

"Give me a half-hour," she said. "I just need to rush home to get some things."

I nodded and she walked to the door, where she stalled with her hand on the knob. When she looked back, her eyes were bright with tears. "I love you," she said.

She slipped out before I could respond, and that was the last I saw of Miss Dupay.


The picture window in our front room was framed by red, velvety curtains tied back with soft, golden rope. At night, it didn't take much imagination to see the dark window as a movie screen in the moments before a film flickers to life. My mother used to dim the lights by throwing an afghan over the lamp so we could play a game she called *Home Movies*.

The whole idea of the game was to describe what you saw

on the screen. "Easy-peasy, right?"

Maybe for her. While she conjured up images of flying devils, forlorn lovers, a man crouching behind a door with a single round left in his revolver, I struggled to make up the sketchiest of scenes. *Uh, there's a guy? He has this long, black cane. He walks into a room and all the people jump up, scared, and—wait, did I mention he's a skeleton? He's a skeleton.*

When I was very young, I thought she could see actual movies on the picture window, like they were playing in a dimension only she could access, but soon enough I figured out that she was making her scenes up, the same as I was, only she was much, much better at it. She was so good, in fact, that once she got going and I let my mind go drifty, I could see her movies on the picture window, and it became real enough for me.

That night, while waiting for Miss Dupay to return, I dreamed my mother onto the picture window.

*A woman*, I told myself. *She has a sword. She's running, her long blonde hair trailing behind her, but then she comes to a cliff. She stops and turns, holding up her sword, to make a stand.*

You'd think I would dream of Miss Dupay. But now that I knew she loved me, I didn't worry about losing her; my mind was free to drift to other things.

*The zombies come out of the forest. The woman takes a step back. Pebbles skitter off the cliff into the angry sea below. When the first zombie reaches for her, she lops off his arm with a two-handed slice. Same with the second zombie, and the third, but they keep pressing toward her. More pebbles kick off into the surf, and now the camera pans out to show a dozen zombies ringed around her with more coming*

*out of the forest, a legion of zombies, and it becomes clear that she is*
*not going to fight her way out of this one.*

I could see my mother. At that moment, I could not have
seen her more clearly if she'd been projected onto an actual
movie screen—the tiny crook in her nose, sweat along her
hairline, the lamp of panic in her eyes—but a knock at the
door brought me back to myself, dry-mouthed and confused.
Who was there? And why was I naked? Then I remembered
the answer to both questions: Miss Dupay.

"Coming!" I shouted. On my way, I wrapped a bedsheet
around my waist, then almost dropped it when I opened the
door.

Standing on my doorstep was a man in a quilted flannel
jacket. The wind made his hair riffle like short feathers. He
looked familiar, but I couldn't place him. Did I know him
from Al's Tap? Was he a member at the Broadmoor? Whoever
he was, was he going to tell my father that I had answered the
door in a toga?

Winching the sheet tighter around myself, I said, "Do I
know you?"

He smiled, tight-lipped. The way he was standing with
his hands jammed in his pockets made him look as thick as
a pillar. Behind him, particles of snow traced through the
gray night like tiny meteors. When he answered with a slight
southern accent—"Mind if we have a word, son?"—I knew I
was looking at Daddy.

# Chapter 27

Daddy invited me to take a load off at the kitchen table while he poked through the cabinets, looking for a can of coffee. He whistled a lighthearted tune through his teeth, which did nothing to put me at ease. "Stewart's!" he said when he found the plaid can. "I see that I am in the company of a gourmand." He winked at me. "This is what we drink at our house, too."

Of course it was. Stewart's was one of the staples brought over by Miss Dupay, but I did not mention this. "My dad's on his way home," I said. "He could walk through that door any minute."

Daddy laughed softly, as though we were sharing an old joke. "That'd be one hell of a trick, son. Is he taking the Concorde home from California?"

My face must have gone rigid, because Daddy made a soft, clucking sound. "Relax, relax. We're just going to drink some coffee and come clean with each other about all these, ah, recent events. All of this will go just as easy as you let it, I promise."

Whistling again, he turned his back to me and measured out coffee grounds with a scuffed yellow scoop. I glanced at the hallway, wondering if I could make it out of the kitchen before he grabbed me. He looked old and slow, but Jesus, he was big. If he caught me, he'd crush my windpipe as easily as crumpling a ball of paper. Daddy turned around. "Do you happen to have any condensed milk? It would be in a little can with a cow's face on it, real sweet-looking cow, goofy smile, curly hair. Do you recall seeing anything like that around the house?"

My finger shook as I pointed to the pantry. Quickly, I tucked my hand back into the bed sheets so he wouldn't see my fear. As though it wasn't written all over my face; as though I had a chance at hiding anything from him anymore.

When the coffee finished brewing, he brought everything to the table on a serving platter: two cups, the carafe, a tin of condensed milk. He filled the cups halfway with coffee, then added a generous pour of milk, holding the can high over the cups with a ceremonial air, his eyebrows raised and his mouth slightly open as though he were about to say *Ahhhh*.

"Sweet coffee," he said, sliding a cup toward me. "I practically raised Winsome on it."

It took me a moment to understand that Winsome must be Miss Dupay's first name. I had been having sex with a woman without bothering to learn her first name. I said, "I'm sorry for what I did to your daughter."

That line struck me as oddly familiar, but I didn't remember that it was straight from the joke I'd tried to tell at Al's Tap, the one about the three guys and the farmer's daughter. It's probably good that I didn't recall what had happened to those three guys; I was scared enough.

Daddy laughed again, but this time he didn't smile, and the sound came out in soft thuds. *Huh huh.* "Oh, son. You can't help but get ahead of yourself, can you? That might even be the root of your problem, if I may be so bold."

"Love is the root of all evil," I said reflexively.

Daddy's fist came down on the table so hard that spoons jumped and his coffee slopped over its brim. "Do *not* quote my daughter's theories at me. Especially that one. That little girl knows shit about love, and even less about evil. Why, she's got those two thing so confused that she thinks—"

He caught himself. A grin spread across his face. He wagged his finger, like *You almost got me there!* "Oh, you're good. Very good. You had me getting ahead of *my*self. But you see what happens when you jump ahead?"

I glanced at the hallway again. Daddy rapped his knuckles against the tabletop. "I know what'll help us relax."

He went to the cabinet above the refrigerator and took down the brandy. Had he seen it earlier when he was looking for coffee, or had his daughter told him where to find the liquor? Whatever the case, the certainty of his movements only reinforced my sense that Daddy knew everything, that there was no point in trying to hide or lie. He took a drink from both cups, winced at the heat, then re-filled them to the brims with liquor.

He lifted his cup like he was making a toast. When I didn't follow, his face turned dark with disgust. "You've got to be kidding me," he said. "Here I am, reaching out to you with kindness instead of anger, and you won't even accept my hospitality? Well, goddamn. That'll teach me to—"

"No!" I cried. I tried to explain that the liquor was the problem, that I didn't drink, no snub intended, but this only made him more incredulous.

"O-oh," he sing-songed. "So you can get ahead of yourself in every other way, act like a big man, screw my daughter, but when it comes to a little drink, you—"

I took a drink. Boy, it was sweet. Sweet and fiery. Lava running down my throat. That first drink made me thirsty, somehow, so I took another.

Daddy leaned back and cradled his cup to his chest, looking like a contented monk. "You're a smart boy, I hear. So you've probably figured out by now that the, ah, affair between you and my daughter is over. You do know that, right? We can take that as our starting point?"

Worried as I was about my own life, that thought had actually not occurred to me. But when I nodded—mostly so he wouldn't get angry again—I felt a wave of relief, as though I'd let go of a burden. I blew out a long breath, feeling lighter and better already.

"So what we're talking about here," he said, "is what happens next. The wind-down. The mop-up." He took off his flannel jacket and pulled the sleeves of his dingy thermal shirt up to his elbows, exposing forearms as thick and nicked up as the exposed roots of an oak. "Winsome and I, we have a big job ahead of us. We have to pick up and move. Find a new place. Start over again. It's a big undertaking, especially at my age, I won't kid you. Your job, on the other hand,"—he nodded at me—"your job is a lot smaller."

I took another drink, as much as I could stand, and felt its warmth crawl through my veins. One small job to put all this bad business behind me. I liked the sound of that. Maybe Daddy had been right: maybe this *would* be just as easy as I let it be. "What is it?"

I had a choice, Daddy explained as he topped off my cup with a little more milk and brandy. I could ask forgiveness from the world, or from Jesus. "Not both," he said. "No man can serve two masters, etcetera." He raised a cautionary finger. "Don't answer right away. A decision like this, you want to be sure."

He warmed my cup after nearly every drink, a courtesy that made it hard to tell how much I was drinking. When the last threads of condensed milk ran out of the can, he said, "I'm so glad you had this. No house should be without, of course, but still, I didn't figure you'd have any here, what with your current, ah, situation. This must be left over from when your mother was still here, right?"

I said, "If I pick Jesus, that means no one else has to know, right?"

He grinned. "Winsome was right: when you concentrate, boy, you really concentrate. Your mind doesn't wander a bit. Like a bulldog, it clamps right on. Obsessive, you might say. But that's okay—most of the old saints were the same way." He nodded a long time in appreciation, then seemed to remember that I had asked him a question. "Oh, right, the Jesus choice. No one else has to know, that's right. And if you pick the world, we'll come clean with everyone around here."

I stared at him. Was I missing something? Was this a trick question? Who on earth would pick the second option? Daddy, apparently.

"Me, I'd take my chances with the world," Daddy said, digging in his pocket to pull out a pen and a little pad. "Not as easy, but then, you seem to like doing things the hard way. Can't say I blame you. That's the path I chose as a young man, myself."

"Actually," I said, my voice a little smeary from the liquor, "I'm leaning toward Jesus."

Daddy grimaced. "I don't know, that's kind of the coward's way out, isn't it?"

"Jesus," I said firmly. "That's my choice."

"But then you couldn't tell anyone else, even when it's burning like a coal in your mouth." He frowned, appearing to feel sorry for me. Then he waved his hand. "Forget it. Forget the choices. You don't have enough discipline to keep something like this between you and Jesus, so we might as well get it out in the open right now." He opened his notepad, clicked the pen. "I'll help you get started. *Dear Father—*"

I grabbed for the pen, but he swatted my arm away. It was just a casual flip, but he nearly knocked me out of my chair.

"*I am sorry to tell you*—or no, that's not right. *I screwed up, Dad. In our worst moment as a family, I did the most awful and selfish—*"

I slapped the table. "Jesus! I pick Jesus!"

"*Who knows what would have happened if I had been a better son to Mom instead of coming on to my teacher—*"

I screamed. Not even a word. An animal sound so loud it made my ears ring.

Daddy looked up from the notebook as though surprised

to find me upset. "You'd rather write it yourself?"

"*My* choice." I jabbed my chest. "You said!"

Daddy pressed his lips together, as if to concede that I

Bryan Furuness 247

had him there; he wished he hadn't said that, but he had, and try as he might, he couldn't think of a way to wriggle out of it now. "I've always said that a man is only as good as his word. I guess I'll have to keep mine, provided you'll keep yours. You will? You *do* understand that if you choose Jesus, you forfeit your right to tell anyone else, right? And that there are no loopholes or limitations to this, ah, covenant?"

Once, a lifetime ago, I had sworn Woz to secrecy. Not quite like this, but I, too, had used Jesus as my accomplice. Now I nodded, wondering why my eyes were welling up when Daddy was giving me exactly what I had asked for.

"You're man enough to handle it?" Daddy asked.

"I'm man enough," I croaked, wiping my eyes with the heels of my hands. Daddy caught me around my neck and pulled me in to his shoulder. He smelled like hay, like moldering hay soaked in Old Spice. I struggled a bit, but he rocked me—"Hush, hush"—and thumped me on the back, knocking loose a few barking sobs. I stopped trying to hold back my tears and just burrowed my wet face into his shoulder. Lord help me, it felt good to be held in a rough embrace.

He squeezed the back of my neck with his tusky palm, waiting until I got it all out, waiting until I was ready to hear what would happen next.

Daddy kneeled before the tub, adjusting the faucets. "It signifies your fresh start," he said. "Plus it won't hurt to clean you up some. You *are* a mess."

I glanced at myself in the bathroom mirror. My face was ruined with tears and sweet coffee; my cheeks glowed with two bright spots like Raggedy Ann. I ducked my head, embarassed.

Daddy struggled to his feet and nodded at the tub. "In you go."

I looked down at the sheet wrapped around my waist. Was I supposed to get naked in front of him? I was about to protest when I imagined the argument that would follow. Daddy was going to get his way eventually, so why fight him? It would just be easier to drop the sheet and step into the tub, so that's what I did.

Daddy nodded, satisfied, then left the bathroom, whistling through his teeth. I heard cabinet doors opening and closing. When he reappeared, he was carrying a serving platter with a dinner roll, a bread knife, and a large tumbler of brandy. "It's not exactly bread and wine," he said, letting himself down on the toilet seat with a grunt, "but it'll do."

He cut the dinner roll in half with the serrated knife. "Body," he said, holding up the bread like a piece of evidence, "given for you." He dunked the roll in the brandy—"Blood, shed for you"—and popped it into my mouth. I tried to chew, but the brandy burned my tongue, so I gave up and swallowed hard, feeling the soggy mess go down my throat like a comet.

Daddy handed me the tumbler, and wiped his face as though he'd just finished a hard day of work. "Life," he said, "is an escalator of pain. It goes from bad to worse, you can trust me on that one, it's a universal truth. Jesus knew it. That's why he went so willingly to the cross. His death, you could call it an assisted suicide. Think about it: he could have easily avoided it. Ran. Hid out. Used his powers. Instead, he walked right into it. When his disciples tried to stop it, he rebuked them. The Romans might have been the ones carrying it out, but Jesus practically forced their hand. How was his crucifixion any different than stepping out in front of an eighteen-wheeler?"

I had a nagging sense that Daddy was wrong about Jesus, but the combination of hot bath water and brandy moving through my veins like slow lightning was really hampering my thought process. *I'll think about it later,* I promised myself. *Maybe ask Pastor Mike.*

Daddy went on. "Your mother knew about pain, didn't she? Her life was one bad surprise after another, each one bigger than the last. She thought she could change her fortune out in Hollywood, but all she got was more disappointment until she realized that every change she'd ever make would be for the worse, no matter where she was. That's why she killed herself, Revie. No mystery about it, no mystery at all."

The matter of fact way that Daddy spoke made this sound like news that was old to everyone but me. Pain branched through my chest slowly, like it was taking root. My tears started up again, but this time I didn't bark or sniffle. I just breathed and let them go.

"The trick," he said, "is to end clean. If you end clean, you fly to heaven on the wings of a dove. My wife figured that out, bless her heart, and now she's in heaven. And you—right now, you're as clean as a whistle, because I've forgiven you."

I must have looked surprised, because Daddy repeated himself. "I forgive you. What you did was wrong, but I understand. You and I—we have a lot in common. More than you might think. For one thing, we both know what it's like to lose a loved one, and what it's like to try and fill that hole."

What was that business about his wife? When had we started talking about her? And why were these Dupays always bringing up holes? I finned my arms through the bath water, trying to recall what Miss Dupay had said about that subject.

"For another thing," Daddy continued, "you and I both know more about love than most people, certainly more than my daughter."

*The universe is buckshot with vacuums*, she had said the night I found her sitting on her porch. *So are we.*

"Love doesn't know limits," he said. "You can't stick it in neat, tidy compartments. You can't give it a list of arbitrary rules and say, *Here, follow these.* You might as well tell a crocodile to chew with its mouth closed. It's asinine, is what I'm saying."

*Every pain, every loss creates a new vacuum. Sex is just an attempt to fill a vacuum.*

Daddy said, "Love doesn't know you're not supposed to love old people, or cousins, or children. All those rules are made up by people, and they don't mean a single thing to the heart."

*And when that attempt fails, as it always does, it creates another vacuum.*

Daddy chuckled, shaking his head. "But why am I telling you this? You know it as well as I do. You're a smart boy."

Then it hit me. Everything clicked into place, and I understood that Daddy and I both loved his daughter in the most awful way.

My hand felt heavy as I raised it from the water. I was tired, tired to the bone. I felt like I could sleep for a thousand years and still not wake up feeling right. My voice sounded like it came from ten feet away when I said, "I forgive you, too."

Daddy nodded, long and slow. "Now you're as clean as you'll ever be, you know that? As blameless as the noon sun. But for how long? Only until you get out of the tub. Then all the sin and pain will start piling up again."

He picked up the knife, turned it over in his hands. "Jesus said *no, thanks* to the pain. So did my wife. So did your mother." He tested the knife with his thumb, then looked at me. "So can you. You can be with her in heaven tonight, you know."

Then I understood what he was talking about, and my weariness lifted enough for me to struggle upright in the tub. "I think I'll get out now—"

"Easy," said Daddy, putting a hand on my shoulder to press me, gently but insistently, back down. "It's nothing to be scared of."

"I'm not scared," I said, "I just don't think—"

"Was my daughter a good teacher?"

"What?" I was having a hard time following this conversation. Were we or were we not just talking about killing myself? Maybe we weren't. Maybe that was just a thought inside my own head. How much brandy had I drunk, anyway?

"My daughter, Winsome," Daddy said. "Was she a good teacher?"

Because I didn't know what else to do, I nodded.

"Good. An honorable profession, teaching. Without education, no one would ever improve their station in life." He scratched his jaw, as if deciding something. "We'll try one more time, I guess."

I said, "Where are you going to go?"

He smiled at me. "Don't worry about that. You need to take stock of your own situation. Winsome's gone. Your mother, too. And your father—well, he'd understand if you decided to check out. Oh, he'd feel bad for a while, but in time he'd see that you actually set him free, too. More brandy?"

I said no, I didn't want any more, and Daddy ran some hot water and got me a washcloth to lay over myself so I could lay all the way back in the tub without feeling too embarrassed. "Hell," he said, "even Adam wore a fig leaf." Gesturing toward the skylight, he told me that the Holy Ghost was smiling down on me. "Your mother, too. She's telling him, *This is my son, whom I love.* She's saying, *Tonight I will see him in Paradise.*" He asked me if I'd ever seen the magic trick where the magician pulled silk scarves out of his sleeves. "All these beautiful scarves, one after another. *Where are all the scarves coming from?* you might wonder. They just keep blooming and blooming."

Like his daughter's monologues, Daddy's speeches bounced all over the place, making their own logic. Then he offered me more brandy, and either I forgot that I'd said no, or maybe I thought it was rude to keep refusing such hospitality, so I said maybe a little, and he came back with a full tumbler. Then he started singing, in a high, sweet voice.

*My Bonnie lies over the ocean,*
*My Bonnie lies over the sea,*
*My Bonnie lies over the ocean,*
*Bring back my Bonnie to me.*

After a few verses, and a few more sips, I got the easy feeling I always got near the end of a movie, when the flash and noise of the climax had faded, and all the big decisions had been made, and all that remained was to see how the characters would turn out. It's the part of the movie when I'd start fading from the world of make-believe back into my own, the part when I'd start letting go.

Daddy held the last note, letting it resonate in the small bathroom. Then he picked up my wrist and softly drew a vertical line with his thumbnail. I shivered. "All you have to do is open up a zipper," he said. "One arm, then the other. Just slip it back under the water, and watch those scarves fly out until you feel good and sleepy. Then lay your head back and go to sleep, pray the Lord your soul to keep."

I tried to say something, but my mouth wasn't working anymore, so I blinked, once, which is how people in the movies say *okay* when they're in the hospital. Daddy must have understood, because he drummed a little rhythm on his knees and said, "I'll let myself out."

He placed the bread knife on the wall of the tub, pressed his hands together to make a short bow, and then, just like that, Daddy was gone.

# Chapter 28

Snow fell onto the bathroom skylight, filling it up from the slanted bottom. When I was a child, I liked to lie on my back in the snowy front yard and look up into the soft, brown night. I did this to scare myself.

Tightening my hood so I couldn't see any of the surrounding houses or streetlights—nothing but the sky, the falling snow, and the sawtooth tops of a few ragged pines—I'd pretend I was lost in the wilderness. Sometimes I told myself that my parents had died in a plane crash; other times I pretended I'd been kidnapped, but had managed to escape my captors—in any case I'd ended up alone on a wintry plain, and if I fell asleep, I would freeze to death.

This kind of scenario was always happening in the "Drama in Real Life" section of the *Reader's Digest*s that my mother stacked on the back of the toilet.

The game took a long time to get going. I would look at the falling snow, waiting for my imagination to convince the rest of my brain that I was not just lying in the yard like an idiot who couldn't figure out how to make a snow angel, but was, instead, an idiot stranded in the Yukon.

Eventually, if I stuck it out long enough, my eyes would unfocus, my breathing would slow, my mind would slip out of gear, and the Yukon daydream would float up like the answer in a magic eight ball. My eyelids would get heavier and heavier until, at last, they'd shut. Then I'd snap back awake with a gasp and a thrilling thought: *I could have died!*

This is how it went every time I played the game, except for the last time.

That night was soft, windless, almost warm. The snow sifted down as fine and gray as fallout. The hood of my parka was warm and dry. Whenever I moved, the fake fur tickled my ears and the snow squeaked beneath me.

I don't remember falling asleep. Nor do I know how long I was out. All I know is that I woke up coated with a thin layer of snow, except for my face, which blazed with wet heat. Snowflakes were tangled in my eyelashes, pricking my eyes and filling the world with broken light.

*I could have died*, I thought, but this time I was more shaken than thrilled. *I could be dead right now.*

I scrambled to my feet and slapped at myself with numb hands, the snow coming off my parka in little explosions. By the time I finished, I was trembling with fury. Was I angry at my own stupidity for leaving a warm house to lay down in a frozen yard? I was not. I was furious at my mother.

The fact that she didn't even know I was outside—I'd snuck out my window after she'd put me to bed—did nothing to cool my anger. She should have known, I thought.

An irrational thought, sure, but what kid doesn't think of his mother as omniscient? Hasn't every child gotten hurt and turned on his mother, screaming, *How could you let this happen to me?*

I barged in the front door. My mother flinched away from the typewriter, her hands coming up like bird claws. I took a few, heavy steps into the room, shedding snow all over the carpet. "It's *me*," I said, as if it was an accusation. Without taking her eyes off me, she blindly pressed buttons on the VCR remote. She probably meant to pause the movie she was transcribing, but instead she hit fast-forward. On the screen, a fight scene turned comical with speed. "How did you...?" she said. "How long have you been...?"

What kept her from finishing her sentences, I thought, was remorse. And no wonder she felt bad: on the coffee table, next to her typewriter, was a lipstick-stained glass of amaretto. While her only son was being sucked into a black hole of hypothermia, she'd been living it up in the warm house, drinking away.

I only wondered whether she felt bad *enough*. To make sure, I said, "Long enough to fall asleep."

She covered her mouth with her hand. Then she shook her head, thinking, no doubt, of how she might redeem herself in my very disappointed eyes. Finally she dropped her hand and looked at me. "Come here."

Here come the tears, I thought. Here comes the too-tight hug and the *my baby, my baby.* Well, let her try it. I would push her away. The first time, anyway. The second time, I would submit, reluctantly, but I wouldn't hug her back.

"Closer," she said.

Her hand came up so fast I didn't even see it. One second

I was looking at her, and the next second I was looking at the kitchen and my cheek was stinging. I didn't even make a sound, that's how surprised I was by her slap.

She grabbed my face with one hand, right across the mouth, and made me look into her furious eyes. What she said next surprised me nearly as much as the slap.

"How could you be so *careless*?"

Not such a strange thing for most mothers to say, I suppose, but *my* mother? She wasn't exactly a paragon of caution, after all.

Little children aren't the only ones who believe in the all-knowing, all-powerful mother. What new mother hasn't believed she could protect her child from harm? What new mother hasn't had the secret, magical thought, *Nothing terrible can happen if I'm watching over him*?

Most mothers shed this belief about the same time that their children begin to fall headlong into coffee tables—but not my mother. Like any other boy, I had my share of scrapes and scars, but I never came close to any real danger, and her belief survived into my adolescence, no doubt aided by my own strong belief in her. When did that belief fall apart?

The car accident was the shattering blow, but the first hairline crack might have appeared the night I fell asleep in the snow. When she slapped me, was she furious that she couldn't protect me?

Of course, this idea is something I've only come up with now. I had no such thoughts when she slapped me, or on the night Daddy came by. In the bathtub, I was only wondering how my mother could be so careless with herself. How I would love to see her again. How I would slap her face so hard.

The snow banked in the skylight. The bath water cooled. I picked up the bread knife and dipped it into the water to make it shine. Water dripped from its teeth. I was clean, clean. *Open up the zipper*, Daddy had said. *Lay your head back, and go to sleep.* Easy as anything.

I shivered, maybe from the cold, so I ran more hot water. I wanted it up around my chin before I started. Somehow the knife ended up near the drain, where it winked under the falling water like something from a fairy tale. Oh, well. I'd get it when I needed it. I'd dive down, swimming under the thundering falls in big frog-strokes, slip the knife between my teeth, and swim back up toward the rippling light. Or maybe the knife would rise up from the water in the hand of a secret maiden, a maiden who would float to the edge of the lake where I stood in my chain mail. She'd kiss me, press the knife into my hand, then kiss me again, while my disciple, disciple number one, Sir Woz, held our restless horses and pretended to avert his eyes, and the soundtrack would swell with the sound of accordions and a boy's choir crying out Latin words of wonder.

I don't know when I fell asleep, or for how long. Neither do I know what kept me from slipping under the water that rose to my chin before spilling over to the bathroom floor, running under the door, down the hallway, into bedrooms. Asleep, I did not hear the front door open, or the frantic steps down the hallway; I did not see the expression on the face that found me naked in the tub with a knife.

I came awake when the thundering faucet shut off.

Nothing seemed real in that first moment of waking: not the lake on the floor, not the snowy ceiling, and certainly not my mother, standing before me, holding out a towel like a blank scroll.

# Section 4
## Resurrection

*Parable of the Lost Finger*
*-a Rosalyn Bryson story-*

*Jesus was a good kid, but he could drive his mother crazy. Especially in the summertime.* She *couldn't get a single thing done around the house with him tagging after her, leaving a trail of dirty socks and used cereal bowls, mooing* I'm booooooooored.

*She tried giving him suggestions. Would he like to fold the laundry? Learn to make chicken chip bake? Run five laps around the house? She would time him...*

*Jesus met every suggestion with a flat look. To his mind, the only thing worse than boredom was an assignment.*

*Shooing him outside didn't really work, either. She'd hardly get the screen door shut before she'd hear it slide open again, and behold, there was Jesus, drinking iced tea at the kitchen island, leafing through the Sears catalog, the screen door wide open behind him.*

*That's why she took to locking Jesus out on summer days. Before you cluck your tongue, remember that this was the nineteen-eighties, and Jesus was far from the only kid exiled from his house on warm days. In fact, his mother got the idea from Lucifer's mother down the block, who'd told her, "Honey, there's a reason that mama birds have to kick their babies out of the nest."*

*Summer mornings, Lucifer would wander over to Jesus's garage, and most of the time he brought along his neighbor Becky. They were all twelve years old, but that summer Becky looked like she'd skipped ahead a few years.*

*She still had the same old Becky face—snub nose, spray of freckles—and the same old blonde Becky hair pulled back in a banana clip, but everything below the neck had gone weird. Breasts, to be specific, had entered the picture. Not that it was a particularly clear picture. She'd taken to wearing her father's t-shirts, which made it hard to keep track of developments, but sometimes the wind would flatten the cloth against her chest, and the boys would get an idea of what was under the shirt. But they wanted a better idea.*

*"Let's go to the pool," Lucifer said day after day, as if the idea had just occurred to him. "That's a great idea," Jesus would say. "It is so hot." But when Becky said, "You guys go ahead if you want to, I'll just go back home," the boys lost interest in the pool idea.*

*Jesus and Lucifer were both small for their age—"Late bloomers," their mothers assured each other—but at least they hadn't gotten gawky and clumsy like everyone else. In gym class, Lucifer could wing a dodgeball with such speed and accuracy that only Jesus could dodge it. But who wanted to be nimble? Nimble counted for nothing in middle school. During the day, Jesus and Lucifer made fun of their pimply classmates who tripped over their own feet, but each night both boys drank a gallon of milk and hung from the shower curtain rod, hoping to kick-start a growth spurt, or at least to stretch themselves an extra half-inch.*

*All this, and they didn't grow an inch. Becky blossomed, and tried to hide it with huge shirts and bad posture. The universe is cruel and hilarious.*

*That summer began as so many summers had before. They rode bikes over ketchup packets, chased each other with bottle rockets, attempted* yo mama *jokes, mutilated worms in the name of science, and argued about which one of the members in Duran Duran was gay ("It's a trick question," Lucifer protested. "They're all gay."). They invented games like* Firing Squad, *in which one person stood blindfolded against a garage door and attempted to catch the tennis balls the others rocketed at him. They held mock funerals, taking turns lying in a meadow of milkweed and scratchy Queen Anne's Lace while the other two looked at the body mournfully. When it was Becky's turn to be dead, they mourned her body a good, long time.*

*All of this made for a full and exciting first week of summer. By the second week, they were bored. One muggy morning they laid down on the garage floor, soaking in the coolness of the smooth concrete. Lucifer asked Becky if she had any questions about the male body, seriously, he would answer them.*

*"Knock it off, or I will leave," she said. "I will leave so fast."*

*"Let's scream our heads off," said Lucifer, turning toward Jesus. "I bet your mom will come running out if we scream."*

*They did, and she flung open the door. In her other hand, she held an unplugged iron like she might brain somebody with it. "What are you* doing?" *she said as soon as she realized that no one was hurt.*

*"It's a play," said Jesus. "We're practicing a play."*

*"Well, don't," she said. When the door closed, they heard her lock it.*

*Lucifer walked around the garage, touching the tools that dangled from the pegboard walls. Jesus said, "Don't touch that, don't touch that, that one's gonna fall, just don't," but he was too distracted by the sight of Becky making concrete angels to sound like he really meant it.*

*Then Lucifer came to the Radio Flyer wagon, and touched the handle hanging down.*

*What happened next wasn't Lucifer's fault. Nobody blamed him, even after it came out that the whole thing had been his idea. That was the thing about Lucifer: you could always count on him for an idea.*


*Like most neighborhoods around Paris, their block was filled with small ranch houses amid tall trees, mostly oaks and maples. Unlike the rest of the region, which had been scraped flat by glaciers a million years ago, their neighborhood had a big hill. And Jesus's house was at the top.*

*Lucifer wheeled the wagon to the sidewalk and pointed it down the hill. He got in front and folded the long black handle back to himself. "I'll steer."*

*Becky got in behind him and grabbed two handfuls of his shirt. "Don't think I'm going to put my arms around you, because I'm not," she said. But she did wrap her legs around his waist, Jesus noticed.*

*This left Jesus to push the wagon from behind, like a tobogganer. Which was harder than you might think—the top of the hill was flat, and the other two were not light—but after a few slow steps, the wagon started picking up speed. He jumped in the back, kneeing Becky's spine. "Sorry," he said. He put his hands on her shoulders, but she gave him a black look. "Sorry," he said again, and wrapped his fingers around the curved edge of the wagonbed.*

*The wagon dropped down the hill like a roller coaster car, running over sidewalk squares like clacketa-clacketa-clacketa. All three of them leaned forward, squinting into the wind—until Becky leaned back into Jesus and he felt her warm weight all over his front like a lead apron, and that's when the steering went just the slightest bit wobbly.*

*Lucifer had just enough time to say, "Whoa, now," before the front wheels turned and locked, slamming the wagon over onto its side. Becky and Lucifer spilled out like dice from a cup. Jesus hung on, clenching harder as the wagon scraped along the concrete with a sound like the end of the universe, finally coming to rest on some guy's lawn.*

*Becky sat up to touch a raw spot on her knee. "Nice driving, shithead."*

*"You're the one who leaned back," said Lucifer. "Threw off the balance."*

*Jesus rolled out of the wagon. His skull felt like it was packed with cotton.*

*Becky said, "How could you tell I leaned back?"*

*"Well, you did," said Lucifer. "You just admitted it."*

*Jesus held up his hand and waved it in front of his face.*

*Becky wiped blood from her knee and flicked it at Lucifer. "Glad you were paying attention to the road."*

*"Something happened," Jesus said in a thick voice.*

*They turned to see him holding up his hand. At first, because there wasn't much blood, they didn't know what they were seeing. Was this some kind of sign language? Was Jesus making a joke? A bad joke, like when old bachelor uncles pretend to pull their thumb into two pieces?*

*Becky's tongue fell with a clucking sound when she realized that the first joint of his index finger was gone.*

*Lucifer bolted up the hill. Becky took off after him, her t-shirt billowing like a ghost costume. It didn't look like they were going for help.*

*Stay calm, Jesus told himself as he walked up the hill, holding up his stump like a little torch. He rang the doorbell at his house, but got no answer. Then he tried the door inside the garage: still locked, and his mother didn't answer, even when he pounded. Now his finger was bleeding, and it looked like it was making up for lost time. Calm was a luxury he could no longer afford. If he didn't get help soon, he thought, he was going to calmly bleed to death.*

*Jesus kicked the door and screamed so loud it brought tears to his eyes, but still, no answer. Where the hell was his mother? Her station wagon was right there in the driveway! Was she in the bathroom? Was she ironing downstairs with the record player turned up loud? Or was she in the kitchen, thinking* I'm not falling for that play nonsense again? *Jesus headbutted the door, then spat on it. That didn't make any sense, but that's how angry he was.*

*In the end, it took a call from Mrs. Ray, the neighbor lady, to bring his mother out. "Your son's doing laps around your house," said Mrs. Ray. "And it looks like he's bleeding pretty good."*

*Nothing makes an Indiana mother move faster than humiliation in front of the neighbors. She burst out of the front door with a box of band-aids and a bottle of peroxide, both of which she dropped as soon as she saw her son's hand. "Car! Hospital!" she shouted. "Hustle, hurry, vamoose!" But here came Mr. Ray with a box of sandwich baggies, calling out, "We have to find the finger! They can sew it back on!"*

*Jesus's mother hesitated. She didn't want her boy to lose his finger, but she really didn't want to prolong this spectacle. But Mr. Ray was already grabbing her arm, and what was she supposed to do? Shake free? Say,* forget the finger, I just want this to be over? *She joined the search.*

*They dragged the hill. Mr. Ray, a former lifeguard at Lake Shafer, made them link arms and walk slowly down the sidewalk, three steps forward, two steps back. Jesus was at one end of the line, his hand swaddled in a towel, mainly so none of them would have to look at it. He had finally stopped screaming, but he couldn't keep from snuffling as he thought* my finger, my finger, my finger, *the thought like a new pulse. When his mother asked why they didn't just search around the wrecked wagon, Mr. Ray said that body parts never turned up where you expected them. The finger might have been thrown clear, or tumbled down the rest of the hill. It might have been carried off by a squirrel.*

*She said, "I am usually not a bad mother, I swear."*

*Mrs. Ray said, "Honestly, Hal, a squirrel?"*

*Mr. Ray led them down the hill, arm-in-arm, like the world's saddest folk dance.*

*In the end, Jesus was the one who found the finger. It was just where his mother had predicted, in the grass a few feet away from the crashed wagon. Poking straight up, it looked like a little stake pounded into the ground.*

*This should have been a happy moment, the moment when everyone felt huge relief, as in the stories of the lost sheep, or the lost coin—but Jesus didn't feel happy. What he felt, when he found his finger, was wobbly.*

*His knees buckled, his mother screamed, and for the second time that day, he hit the sidewalk.*

*The doctor sewed the finger back on, just like Mr. Ray had said he would. The nerves even grew back, mostly. After a year or so, Jesus hardly even thought about it. But when the fingertip got tingly on cold days, or someone noticed that one index finger was just a skosh shorter than the other one, Jesus would think about the day of the crash. And what he remembered first wasn't the crash itself, or his mother locking him out, or his friends running away when he needed them most. What he remembered was the finger on the lawn.*

*Death was coming for Jesus. He knew that back then, just as he knew that death wasn't going to be the end for him. But when he saw his finger—bolt upright on the grass, as if Jesus had been buried and was crawling up through the soil—he knew for the first time that death wasn't going to be the hard part.*

# Chapter 29

For months, whenever I had dreamed of my mother's homecoming, it played like a reunion scene from the movies: hard hugs, teary smiles, all put to a triumphant soundtrack.

What I found out over the next several weeks is that Hollywood doesn't know shit about homecomings. With all the bad blood, recriminations, suspicion, power struggles, and stand-offs, reunions are just break-ups in reverse.

After driving the station wagon home, my father promptly moved downstairs. He busied himself with private lessons, though his real occupation seemed to be avoiding contact with us. Though he was only ten feet beneath my room, in some ways he seemed further away than my mother had ever been.

She took a job, too, behind the cosmetics counter at Carson Pirie Scott. Hollywood had burned away her baby fat, and she looked even thinner when she got her hair bobbed, and deepened the color to ash blonde. She started wearing silk scarves. She smelled like a rich lady.

For the first couple of weeks, we stayed in our separate corners. My mother didn't ask me what I was doing in the tub with a knife, I didn't ask why she'd left Hollywood the way she had, and my father said nothing to either of us. No one, it seemed, wanted to fire the first question. Mutually assured destruction, I suppose.

My mother was back home; I kept telling myself that was the most important thing. So why did I miss her more than ever?

In science class, Mrs. Jankovic came back, though she looked terrible. Heavy and lumpy, with swollen hands. The rumor was that she'd lost the baby.

I wasn't sure if I believed that. If you lost a baby, your whole life would be derailed, right? Wouldn't you be too damaged to go back to work? Besides, how does someone lose a baby, anyhow?

"Too much sex," said Bettina Raymer one morning in front of the school. Bettina had recently discovered make-up and hairspray, and her exuberant use of both products gave her a perpetually surprised and blasted look, as though a box of crayons had exploded in her face. "All that poking. Irritates the womb."

A small group of us stood under the flagpole, considering the idea that sex could both make a baby and kill it. The flag, stiff with wind, clanged against the pole like an idiot blacksmith.

"Cigarettes?" someone else suggested. Woz said that Mrs. Jankovic didn't smoke, but Bettina said it didn't have to be cigarettes, exactly, it could be cigars, nicotine gum, chewing tobacco, though Woz said that he had a hard time picturing

Mrs. Jankovic with a dip in her mouth.

I looked at Woz. When had he gotten so reasonable? Maybe it was his new contacts, or his spiky haircut, but just then he seemed thinner, taller, *older* than I remembered. This made me sad for some reason, like I'd lost something.

"Liquor?" said Carly, curling her hair around a finger. "I'm thinking whiskey?"

"*Cocaine*," said Bettina, sending a murmur of shock and excitement through the group.

Being present at the birth of a rumor made me feel privileged and awful at once—and not just for Mrs. Jankovic, either. It didn't take much to imagine this group talking about me. How long until someone like Bettina started wondering why Miss Dupay had suddenly disappeared, and why I seemed so distracted?

In the schoolyard, the rumors kept coming—womb cancer, a tumble down the stairs, spicy food, too much jogging, sleeping on her stomach—until Woz spoke up again. "Maybe," he said, "she didn't exactly *lose* the baby."

He glanced over both shoulders before mouthing the word: *abortion.*

Carly shuddered. "That poor fetus." Bettina blamed the father, saying he must have put her up to it.

A minute earlier, it had been a baby; now it was a fetus. That marked the end of speculation. The debate was over, a rumor was born: the idea of abortion was so horrible it had to be right.

That evening I went downstairs to visit my father. As I came through the door, I saw him squatting in a makeshift campsite at the far end of the basement. A thin steak sizzled on an electric skillet as he fiddled with the portable TV, adjusting the antenna to get better reception on *Barney Miller*.

I looked at the sleeping bag on the floor. "Why aren't you sleeping on the couch?"

Without standing, he pivoted toward the skillet to flip the steak over with his fingers. "Hard floor's good for my back."

When he'd first come home, I'd given him his space. Like the rest of us, he needed some time to cool off, figure out his next move—but by this point my mother had been home nearly two weeks, and he only seemed to be hunkering down further. The mini-fridge in the corner was a bad sign. How long before he started cooking in the fireplace?

"This is nuts," I said. "Come upstairs."

He shook his head, grabbed the steak, and, after flopping it onto his plate, sucked the juice off his fingers. Upstairs, my mother was running water, probably washing her clothes in the sink. I'd offered to run a load of laundry for her so she wouldn't have to go down to the basement herself, but she'd refused, claiming that she had come to prefer hand-washed clothes. ("Less pilling," she said. "Tastes great," I'd answered, but she hadn't laughed.) Later, my father would probably take his dishes into the shower with him. Both of them were martyrs of inconvenience.

Next to a stack of folded pants lay a Bible with a pale circle on its cover. It was hard to tell whether he'd been reading it, or using it as a drink coaster. I nudged the Bible with my toe. "What about the parable of the lost son? At the end of that one, no one holds a grudge."

"You don't know that. The story cuts out right after the party. What about the next day? And the day after that?"

He *had* been reading the Bible. Which was less surprising than the fact that he was now imagining beyond the end of the story. Poking at the steak with a mangled fork, he said, "The way I figure it, the old man probably woke up, hungover, to a house trashed from the party. Questions started buzzing around his head. *How, exactly, did that kid manage to blow all his money so fast? And what is he still doing in bed while his brother is already out plowing the back forty?* Then you have your so-called good brother. You better believe he was hatching some special welcome-back plans for the lost son. The lost son's life was about to get a lot harder, I guarantee that."

I looked at the aluminum foil crunched around the TV antenna, the blood and fat drying in the skillet. The piles of clothing, like ruined columns. Add a cardboard lean-to, and it could have passed for a homeless guy's shelter on Lower Wacker Drive. Sadness filled my chest like water. "Dad, what are you going to do?"

He shook his head at the steak. "If I knew, would I be living like this?"


In science class, Mrs. Jankovic told us to keep our folders closed and to put away our textbooks; we were just going to talk for a minute or two. "I did not have an abortion," she said.

My book hit the floor with a smack. I don't know how anyone else reacted, because I kept my eyes on my lab table, mortified not only that she'd heard the rumor, but that she was *acknowledging* it. Didn't she know that the polite response to a rumor was to pretend it didn't exist? That whatever the rumor, whatever the truth—all that stuff was private and should be buried under a mountain like so much nuclear waste? I knew then that Mrs. Jankovic could not have grown up in Indiana.

She didn't sound embarrassed or upset in the least, merely worn-out. "I kept going into early labor," she said. "The doctors stopped it again and again, but then one day…"

When she paused, I couldn't help myself: I looked up. She was pressing her lips together, seeming to collect herself. When she went on, her voice was louder. "She was a girl. She lived for one night. But her lungs—" Mrs. Jankovic squinted at the back corner, shook her head. "They weren't strong enough."

The classroom was quiet. Quieter, even, than those lunches when Miss Dupay had been in a mood, emanating a fierce, sullen silence. I wished someone would say something to break this awful silence.

"Did she have a name?" asked Carly.

I wished it was quiet again.

"Leah," said Mrs. Jankovic. "After my mother."

"Why was she born so early?" asked Bettina.

"No one knows," said Mrs. Jankovic. "These things are a mystery."

I pressed my thumb into the knobs of gum under my table, wishing they were fast-forward buttons. Or pause buttons, so I could lie down and sleep until I forgot about all of this. But my desk was primitive, useless, a trap, and I had to sit there as this awfulness played out in front of me—girls raising their hands with more questions, and Mrs. Jankovic, inexplicably, answering them—and I couldn't decide which was worse, making a woman talk about her lost baby, or making us listen to her.

Woz raised his hand. *Oh God*, I thought. *He's going to ask to go to the bathroom.*

The old Woz might have asked that, but not this new guy, with his contacts, and combed hair, and an actual chin. What this new guy said was infinitely worse.

"Are you going to try again?" he asked her.

I scooted my chair away from him, I was so appalled. And I wasn't the only one—I heard a gasp or two around the room. Woz had crossed the line. He was asking about sex and death and faith, in *science class*, of all places. He might as well have asked Mrs. Jankovic where she thought she'd be spending eternity.

Mrs. Jankovic looked at the lab sink at her teacher's table. "Are we going to try again?" she said. She reached out absently and wiped a bit of white schmutz off the faucet, probably frosting left behind by Miss Dupay. "We haven't decided," she said. "But I think we will."

The first smacking sound caught me by surprise. Then there was another clap on the other side of the room, and all of a sudden everyone was clapping. It was the wrong response, perhaps, or maybe just absurd, but what else could we do?

For a moment it was the solemn applause that a crowd at a football game gives an injured player when he finally stands and limps toward the sideline, but then it became raucous, frenzied, almost *furious* clapping, and I got caught up in it, too, because I was so relieved that we were done talking about this business, though that didn't explain the lump in my throat.

Kids were stamping, drumming fists on lab tables, and the room was so loud that it mostly covered the sound that came out of me when I stood up along with everyone else. I meant to whoop, but what came out of me was a ragged bleat, the sound of an animal caught in barbed wire.

A few kids gave me a look—*what a weirdo*—but everyone else kept their eyes on Mrs. Jankovic as she templed her shaking hands in front of her mouth. She laughed, and tears jeweled her eyes. God, was she brave. God, was she beautiful.

# Chapter 30

The rest of the school day, I walked around feeling like I might burst out with laughter or a triumphant shout at any moment. I was carrying around this wild bird in my throat, and it would have to be released sometime, somewhere, so I thought, *I'll tell my mother.*

What would I tell her about the scene in science class? Something about how there was hope in the world, or how nothing was ever finished as long as you were alive—I would figure it out when I saw her. Truth could be struck on the anvil of the moment just as well as a lie; I was suddenly sure of it.

When I got home, I had a few hours to kill before she got off work. I tried to keep myself busy, but my mind wouldn't stick to the simplest thing. I thawed out a frozen burrito, forgot about it, only to discover it later when I put another burrito in the microwave. I turned on the television, but every time a commercial came on, I could not recall what I'd been watching. I turned everything off and sat down on the couch to wait. The crash, when it came, was hard and fast.

One second I was buzzing with a vague good feeling, and

the next I was hollow and shaky. I put my feet up on the couch, and the last thing I remember was thinking, *maybe I'll close my eyes.*

I don't know what time my mother shook me awake, but the front window was dark. "Do you feel all right?" she asked, frowning. "Did you have any dinner?"

I wanted to answer, but my head was filled with slag, and I couldn't make sense of these questions. She patted my shoulder. "I'll bring you some crackers. And Sprite. Do you want some Sprite?"

I nodded, then fell asleep before she came back.

The next morning I awoke in my bed with no idea how I'd gotten there, but relieved to find that I still had on all my clothes from the previous day. "Morning, sunshine," my mother said, laying a wet washcloth on my forehead. She filled a hot water bottle with ice cubes and put it behind my neck, then heaped an extra blanket on the bed when I complained that I was cold. She brought me a sleeve of Saltines and a bottle of Pepto, though I hadn't complained of a stomachache. None of her actions fit together, but I think she was trying every motherly thing she'd ever heard of.

I had the nagging feeling that I wanted to tell her something, but what was it? My head would not wake up. In a cracked voice, I said, "Hey—"

Just then my father walked in, nearly bumping into her. "Ah, geez," he said, touching his heart as though she'd scared him. He must have thought she'd already be at work. "I just came up to—I wouldn't have, but—"

"It's okay."

"I just wanted to see how he was doing. If I'd known that you—"

"It's *okay*, Tim."

He nodded, then they both tried to get out of the way at the same time and bumped into one another.

"Excuse me," he said.

"Pardon me."

"I'll go left."

"My left, or—oh, sorry."

"Stay put."

"Well, I'm *trying*," she said.

"I guess I shouldn't be surprised you can't stay in one place," he muttered.

I stopped chewing. The Saltines turned to quikrete in my mouth.

My mother crossed her arms. Staying put would not be a problem for her now. Quietly, she said, "You don't want to work anything out, do you?"

His voice came back, mocking. "Well, I'm *trying*."

"You son of a bitch," she whispered.

The phone rang. Both of them ignored it. "Phone," I said when it rang again, but they stayed where they were, blocking each other, and eventually the phone stopped ringing.


Everything about that sick time is hazy. What I remember, mainly, is the tip-of-the-tongue feeling I had as I tried to remember what I'd wanted to tell my mother. And it may never have come to me, if my mother hadn't eventually tapped into the source, as Madame might have said.

She was home, having called off work to take care of me. She must have been worried about losing her new job, but she was acting cheery. When she cranked open my window, a branch from the flowering crab tree brushed against the screen, filling my room with a sweet smell that made my throat itch. "Ah!" she said, taking an exaggerated sniff. "Fresh as an Irish spring!"

I tried to smile—this cheeriness was for my benefit, I knew—but I probably only grimaced. After pressing the back of her hand to my forehead to check my temperature, she ruffled my knotty hair, which hurt because I hadn't showered in days.

"You know what I think it is?" she said. "Mono." She wagged her finger, teasing me. "The kissing disease. Have you been kissing girls?"

I rolled my head toward the window.

"Oh, that's *it*, isn't it?" She sounded delighted, though she might have just been trying to raise my spirits with some silliness. "What's her name?"

My throat got tight, as though something solid was crawling up. I felt like the abandoned house with the tree growing up the chimney.

"Hmm," she said. "Maybe it's not mono, after all. Maybe you're just heartsick. I bet you're mooning about, thinking about some gal you've been smooching." She poked my ribs. "Who is it? Who's the lucky girl?"

Without looking away from the window, I shook my head.

Her voice swelled with mock indignation. "I want to

know who's taking Revie from his momma."

I felt the burning around my eyes before I knew I was crying. "Hey, what's the matter?" she said, sounding surprised. "I was just fooling around. Can't you take a joke anymore? Revie, come here. Come *here*." She was pulling on my shoulder, but I kept wrenching away to burrow my face into my pillow. But I was weak, and before long she hauled me over and was looking into my eyes. "Hey, I'm sorry. How was I supposed to know you'd be so sensitive about it? You don't have to be, though. Kissing girls is okay."

I shook my head.

"Well, now, sure it is. As long as it's only kissing." She dropped her chin and her voice. "Was it only kissing?"

I shook my head again. Tears spilled into the cups of my ears.

"You hugged her then. Is that what we're talking about here, a little kissing and hugging?"

I gave her a look.

"No. Okay. Huh." Her hands darted across my bedspread, straightening edges and smoothing little wrinkles. "You know—ha—when I showed you *The Joy of Sex*, I didn't mean, like, put this into practice right away. That was more for the future. You know that's what I meant, right?"

My throat ached. My throat was *constipated*. Now my stomach was getting a funny feeling, too, like something was on its way up, like my body was a ball return at the bowling lanes, which made me think of Pastor Mike and his circular tracks. That's what it felt like when I sat up, like a bowling ball was on its way up to my mouth.

"Miss Dupay," I said.

For a moment, my mother's face was all confusion, and then it was not.

That night, when she intercepted my father as he came in through the garage, there was no arguing or dancing in the hallway. Taking his hand, she led him to the front room and told him in a simple, clear way what his son had been up to.

I had told her everything—so much that, for once, she didn't ask *What happened next?*—but I could not imagine telling my father. My shame with him was doubled. Like Daddy had said, I betrayed him when he needed me most.

My father listened with a hand over his mouth, closing his eyes every once in a while. If someone had been watching through the picture window, he might have thought my parents were talking about a minor disappointment, some scrape, a rejected application of some kind.

I know all this because I was lying on the hallway floor, just outside the rim of light. My mother was sitting on the couch, which she had recently turned to face the window instead of the television. "Revie says he doesn't want us to call the police," she said.

"Do we listen to him?"

She shook her head, like *I don't know.* "This is serious." She lowered her voice. "This is rape."

A jolt of electricity went through my system. Rape? No, it wasn't. Boys did not get raped.

My father looked nearly as shocked as I felt. "Oh, Rosalyn,

no. This is serious, yes, but it's not—"

"What would you call it?"

My father went to the window, a dark mirror now that the sun had gone down. He cleared his throat several times, and I could tell he was crying and was angry about it. He pounded his chest. "Stupid frog in my throat."

My mother said, "If I had been around—"

"*Ach.*" He waved his hand at her. "At least you were gone. It happened right under my goddamned nose."

"Gone. That's a hell of an excuse. I abandoned my family, and for what? All so I could get cut from a stupid zombie movie."

"I practically handed him over to her. I said, *Sure, drive him home.* All so I could have another drink."

Sometimes, I thought, boys did get raped, but it was by other boys, and usually in juvie. What happened to me wasn't like that, but it wasn't like hitting the sexual lottery, either, which is how some people would have thought of the situation. Which brought me back to my mother's question: what would you call it?

My parents, however, didn't circle back. They were on a different trajectory.

My father said, "I invited her over to dinner, this Miss Dupay. If she had given me half a chance, I would have slept with her."

"I did a shower scene," my mother said. "A zombie came into the bathroom and I stabbed him right through the curtain. It didn't make any sense—I mean, why would I have a sword in the shower?—but I did it anyway. The water was cold, and they shot extra-long. It felt like I was soaping myself for ten minutes, at least."

You know the feeling you get when you touch your tongue to a battery, and your tongue goes tingly and rubbery-thick at once? That's how my whole body felt just then. I was beyond shock; my circuits were fried.

My father slumped down next to her on the couch. They looked like a couple of discarded dolls. In a tired voice, he said, "Did you wear panties in the shower, at least?"

She nodded. "But if they had asked me not to…"

My father shook his head at the ceiling.

"I'm telling you, nothing made sense out there," she said. "I stopped making sense to myself."

He reached over and turned off a lamp, dimming the room enough for the outside world to appear on the window. A misty night: the streets were wet and black, the branches of the crabapple bowed with heavy, wet flowers, the orange light of the streetlamp big and hairy in the mist.

"So what do we do about Revie?" he said.

"He wants us to forget about it. Not tell anyone. Pretend it never happened."

My father stroked his mustache for a long time. "Is that even possible? If you bury something, won't it just come back later on?"

*Please don't tell*, I prayed. *I won't let it come back.*

"I don't know," my mother said at last.

"Well, that's honest. I don't know, either."

I slid on my belly into the living room to be near them, even if they did not know it. Together we watched the picture window, the street that curved around our house, the passing cars on a warm spring night, the headlight ghosts on the wall that quickly rose and disappeared.

Eventually my father started to push himself up from the couch. "We'd better sleep on this, I guess. I'll be downstairs if—"

She must have grabbed his arm, because he stopped in mid-rise, and, after a moment, sank back down to the couch. My mother switched off the other lamp, and the picture window filled with the orange light of the streetlamp, like a star in the midst of bursting.

# Chapter 31

"It won't last," said Mish. He was leaning against the dumpster behind Al's Tap, arguing, as usual, with everyone. "I'll bet my ass it doesn't last another year."

"No one wants your ass," said Shirley, pouring another bottle of vodka into a galvanized tub of punch. "Besides, you said the same thing last year."

We were in the back lot, setting up for our farewell party. Over by the dry cleaners, a pig turned slowly on a spit. My father doodled dish soap all over the asphalt, especially around the dumpster, hosed it into suds, and set to work scrubbing the lot with a garage broom. The sun made rainbows on the soap bubbles, and the air smelled like lemons and meat. Bees swirled like chimney smoke over the dumpster. It was a beautiful day in the region.

Sitting on the concrete pad next to the dumpster, I felt like a piece of meat set out to thaw, but still, it was better than I'd felt in weeks. My mother had been right—I had mono—and I was getting better, but slowly. I lay back on the warm concrete, closed my eyes, and listened to Mish predict the demise of the mini-mills.

By this time, the big mills had been pretty well crippled—Wisconsin Steel was gone, South Works had been shut down, and Inland was shedding workers in waves—but recently, mini-mills had started cropping up to recycle scrap metal. They employed fewer workers than the hulking old mills, but they were supposed to be extremely efficient.

"I was right last year, and I'm still right now," Mish said.

"You and the guy with the sign that says *The End is Near,*" said Shirley. "Eventually, you'll both be right."

Mish said, "Tell me you think mini-mills are going to save the region. I want to hear you say it, little Miss Optimist."

Calling Shirley an optimist probably said less about her than it said about the deep level of pessimism in the region. Mish might have been a cynic, but he was in good company. Every year, betting pools were formed over when the Cubs would be eliminated from the playoffs. Homemade fallout shelters outnumbered backyard pools.

It hadn't always been this way. Gary had been founded in a spirit of wild optimism. At the turn of the twentieth century, the idea was to build the largest company town in American history, an industrial utopia. The town's first nickname was *Magic City.* By the time I came along, it was better known as *The Murder Capital of America.*

"Nothing's going to save the region," said Shirley, dumping a bottle of rum into the tub. "But nothing's going to kill it, either."

I would like to say that I agreed with Shirley, but when it came down to it, I was more like Mish: I had an easier time believing in invention than in reinvention. That's what I'd discovered about myself earlier that week, when my parents told me we were moving to Indianapolis. But that announcement wasn't even the most surprising part of the family meeting. The real shock came after my father told me to expect all kinds of questions once we got down there. "What brings you to town, where did you come from, that kind of thing."

He stopped and glanced at my mother. They were both on the couch, dressed up, for some reason: my mother in a simple, lemony dress, and my father in dark pants and his white oxford. The old pinprick of marinara on his chest had faded to a dusty rose, like a souvenir of an old wound. I was in the easy chair directly across from them. The TV tray by my side held a glass of 7 Up and a little bowl of oyster crackers. Before the meeting had started, they'd both fussed over me, making sure I was comfortable, wondering if there was anything else I needed—which tells me how worried they must have been about how I'd take their news, especially this second part. My mother nodded at my father, and he went on. "So let's get our stories straight," he said.

"Stories?" I said.

My mother said, "It wouldn't really be a fresh start if we dragged along all the garbage from our past, would it?"

I shook my head, confused. "You don't mean that we're going to, like, make *up* stories about ourselves..."

They looked at me. My God, that was exactly what they meant. "Well," I said, sitting back in my chair. "That is the most retarded thing I have ever heard in my life."

"Is it?" my father said. "Is the witness protection program retarded?"

My mother put her hand on his knee. "What we're saying here, Revie, is that it might be best to cut loose of our past. Certain parts of it, anyway. You were right about wanting to bury that business with the sub. In fact, everything that happened this past year is just..." She frowned, looking for the right word. "Too radioactive. It would burn holes in our future."

I shook my head in disbelief. Had my mother learned nothing from her trip to Hollywood? Like how you can't really escape anything? And my father—a year ago, he'd pointed to my mother's stories as a source of our problems. Now he wanted to live inside one?

The universe was shaped like a racetrack. Truth was an awful boomerang. I knew this, and I was twelve years old. How could they be so naive?

But what else could we do—stay here?

I imagined walking to school, passing Miss Dupay's old house, filing into the science classroom, day after day—and all at once, I knew I couldn't do it. Their plan might have sounded foolish, but staying was impossible.

"Oh, what the hell," I said, which was the strongest endorsement I could give. "I'll try it."

My father gripped an armrest and nodded hard. My mother grabbed me in a hug, elbowing the dish of oyster crackers onto the floor. And just like that, we had our own lost episodes.

At Al's Tap, guests arrived around dinnertime, bearing platters of three-bean salad, tubs of creamy coleslaw, corningware filled with mustardy potato salad. Momo showed up with the biggest crock of butter I have ever seen. "Good Lord!" shouted Mish, who was already into the punch. "Did you steal that off some Amish woman's porch?"

Woz biked past the lot several times until I came out and waved him inside. He pulled in, and stood astride his bike. I tipped up my chin to say *Hey*, but couldn't think of a single word to say to him.

Less than a year earlier, we'd been so close that I'd inflicted my worst secrets on him. He'd wanted to be my first disciple. That may as well have been a different lifetime for how awkward we were around each other now. We looked around the lot, desperate to avoid eye contact.

At last, he pointed to the hog on the spit and deadpanned, "Kill the pig. Cut his throat. Spill his blood." I snorted, and before the awkwardness could creep back, Woz said, "Is that a giant crock of *butter*?" and headed off to check it out.

Rick from the Broadmoor showed up with a date, a mousy blonde who kept covering her mouth with her hand every time she laughed, which was often. For once, Rick didn't do any hand tricks. He only bounced his bad hand in his good one lightly, like it was a fussy baby.

My father spent most of the afternoon introducing his Broadmoor friends to his Al's Tap friends. The Broadmoor people were all sunglasses and tans, while the bar crowd squinted in the sunshine like they'd just been expelled from a cave. They looked different out in the open, smaller somehow.

Even Momo, who Shirley put to work cutting up fruit for the punch bowl, looked almost human-sized, and this made me feel tender toward him, toward all of them.

By evening, the lot was packed, and my father sent me up the fire escape to take a picture of the crowd from the landing. "Say cheese!" he shouted, and the crowd showed me their teeth and emitted a long, droning sound. After taking the shot, I stayed on the landing to look at all these people who had turned out to send us off.

It's one of the sadder truths in life that you never realize how many friends you have until it's time to leave them.

But hell, it could have been worse. Most people don't get a crowd like this until their funeral. Though in a sense, that's exactly what this was: a funeral for our old lives.

Not that I realized this at the time. No, what I thought as I scanned the crowd from the landing, was that nearly every single person was a friend of my father's. All these people knew my mother; they all *loved* my mother, but who here belonged to her? No one. No one belonged to her alone.

Standing on the fire escape, I was amazed that she hadn't left earlier. Amazed, too, that my father would be able to leave now.

Then I noticed that one person was missing.

I came down the stairs and grabbed Woz's bike. He wouldn't mind, I thought. He was busy circulating through the crowd, sneaking drinks from abandoned cups. And if anyone else saw me leave, they'd probably think I was going to say goodbye to the town, or some other nonsense.

The strip mall was old, and set back from the highway. Mansard tiles lay on the sidewalk like dropped teeth. The sign at the entrance read *Your Des nation Shoppi g Loc tio !* but it seemed more like a retail graveyard than a spot for a church.

I'd gone to the Lutheran church in search of Pastor Mike, only to discover that the hedges were overgrown, the lawn knotted with crabgrass, and the windows covered with dust and pollen. A water-crinkled note on the door said that Pastor Mike had moved to this strip mall, but now that I was here, I was having a hard time believing that anyone, much less a pastor, would relocate to such a dump. I was about to head back to Al's Tap when I heard a voice behind me. "Kid Jesus."

I turned to see Pastor Mike. He looked younger than when I'd last seen him. His beard was gone, and he'd gained a few pounds, which gave him a cheery, laid-back look. He clapped me on the shoulder. "Come on in."

The interior of the retail space where he was "setting up shop" was either half-finished or half-destroyed, it was impossible to tell. Sheetrock hung on the walls, but wires dangled from the ceiling, and the concrete floor was webbed with massive cracks. In the back corner was a freezer and a hot plate. Flashing back to my father's campsite in the basement, I said, "You're not living in here, are you?"

"Just until I get things up and running."

"Get *what* up and running?"

He looked around, as though he, too, was having trouble imagining this hole as anything but a burned-out socket. "Not a church, I can tell you that much."

He went to the chest freezer, took out a casserole covered with tinfoil, and set it on the hotplate. Fiddling with the knobs, he said, "Can I offer you some chicken chip bake?"

I felt a twinge. Chicken chip bake was what Miss Dupay had brought over on her first visit. Sometimes, when I thought of her, the taste of salt and cream still came into my mouth. "I'm okay," I said.

Pastor Mike produced two camp chairs and we sat around the hotplate, watching steam come off the casserole. I told him I was sorry he'd lost his church, but he waved me off. "The church model constrained me. Old people didn't want to be confronted about their big cars or bigoted views. The young ones didn't want to hear what the Bible actually said, and they definitely didn't want to put any money in the collection plate. But all of them were alike when it came right down to it."

"Selfish?"

"Self-centered, maybe. But more than that. They all wanted to re-make Jesus in their own image." He peeled back a tinfoil corner and poked at the casserole with a fork. "Most of them don't take it as far as you did, of course, but still, you're not all that unique, my friend. Billions of people out there think that Jesus personally supports everything they do. Jesus is their toady. Their yes-man."

"So what are you going to do, tell them no?"

He gave me a look like *Someone should.* Then he grimaced. "I don't know what I'm going to do, to be real honest. I'm in full discernment mode right now. Doing a lot of waiting. Listening." He patted his stomach, half-grinning. "Eating."

Outside the window, two shabby robins fought over a scrap of wire. They alternated between beating each other furiously with their wings and stopping to look around, probably for predators.

"My mother came back," I said. Then I told him how we were going to move to Indy the next day, and how we were supposed to become new people. "This is dumb, right? There's no way this is going to work, is there?"

He nodded slowly, chewing on the question. "Remember the first time you came to the church? When you said that Jesus didn't find out he was Jesus until he was twelve? That really stuck with me. I've thought about it a lot."

"But that's not what I'm asking about now—"

"He knew way before. Maybe an angel told him, or maybe it was hard-wired into his brain, but he knew, probably as early as he could think. He just kept it to himself until he was twelve."

I shook my head at the hot plate. Why had I even come here? Pastor Mike always gave me the worst gifts, these white elephant stories. And now he wasn't even getting the Jesus stuff right. I may not have known much about the Bible, I told him, but keeping secrets didn't sound very Jesus-like.

"*Au contraire*," he said, then told me the one about the blind man who Jesus healed, then swore to secrecy. "And what about the crucifixion? Jesus saw it coming a mile away, but he didn't let his disciples in on it until the last minute. So the idea that Jesus kept his identity a secret for a long time fits his m.o. perfectly."

Pastor Mike peeked under the foil again. The casserole

was soft and bubbling. He stuck in his fork, pulled it out, and
held up a warm, goopy mass. "The real question is, why? Was
he waiting until he figured out how to tell people, or until
they were ready to hear it?"

He popped the fork into his mouth and made a noisy show
of how much he liked the casserole. He pointed the fork at
me. "You're asking yourself the wrong question, Revie. In
my experience, people aren't all that perceptive. You can fool
them just as long as you want to. The real question is, how
long do you want to hold onto those secrets? How long do you
want to cover up who you really are?"

"Forever," I said.

Pastor Mike laughed softly, then tucked into the casserole.

I did keep my secrets. Not well, but neither did I blow my
cover. In Indianapolis, I became a terrible liar, swapping out
one story for another, trying on persona after persona like so
many wigs. I cycled through haircuts—freak flag, skater cut,
preppie wave, straightedge buzz—though most of the time my
hair was stuck in some awkward in-between stage. At school,
I claimed to have been in a gang called the Homeslices, and
that my best friend, Jellohead, had been gunned down in a
drive-by in Gary. *Rest in peace, Jellohead!* I'd cry at the end of
this story, throwing up a gang sign that looked curiously like
the shadow puppet of a butterfly.

No one questioned any of this. Oh, a lot of people
dismissed me, or made savage fun of me, but no one asked for
the truth. As in the story of the boy who cried wolf, people
generally came to ignore me.

But they still paid attention to my mother, who started off

behind the perfume counter at Nordstrom's and quickly rose to management. The nature of her charisma changed, but it did not weaken. She became coy. She mastered a knowing smile. Like a jazz musician who knew what notes not to play, she revealed little and implied much.

Sometimes I missed my mother, the way she used to be. It seemed that Pastor Mike had been right about how the universe was built on a circular track: we had gotten her back after all. But I can't help but think that Madame had been right, too, when she'd predicted, *You're going to lose her.*

My mother's new friends and neighbors and co-workers didn't know what they were missing, though, and her new personality drove them wild with curiosity. The less she told them, the more they wanted to know. Meanwhile, I was flooding the market with shoddy lies that nobody wanted.

Here's a unifying theory: the law of supply and demand applies to everything, even stories.

One story, however, I never told. Even in my twenties, when I was at my worst, flipping characters whenever my shame hit critical mass—the comp lit snob, the beery wildman of Third Street, the failed B-movie screenwriter—I still did not tell anyone about Miss Dupay. Even when I turned twenty-eight, the same age my mother had been when she took off for Hollywood, and I was tired of treating life like a game of musical chairs, I kept that story to myself.

Did I keep quiet because I didn't know how to tell that story, or because I didn't think anyone was ready to hear it? Or both?

To this day, it's still hard to know what to call it. If it

wasn't rape, and it wasn't a sexual windfall, what was it?

Sometimes, I think of old Bible stories. When I imagine the one about Eve and the tree, I can picture the instant she bit into the fruit, a suspended moment when all the knowledge of good and evil broke into her mind, a moment that must have been exquisite and painful and thrilling and *too much*, too much all at once, like getting anointed by lightning.

That's as close as I can come to the truth of what happened with Miss Dupay. But that's not something you can say to someone without sounding crazy, so I never did.

Until now.

By the time I got back to the farewell party, an evening shadow was pushing across the back lot, and our friends from Al's Tap gravitated toward it, hunting relief from the sunlight.

Soon after the shadow flooded the lot, Momo emerged from the bar with his accordion, wheezing out romantic tunes and singing along in made-up Latin. The Broadmoor people left immediately. The rest of the crowd—all regulars from the Tap—smiled and swayed a little, like the music was an underwater current.

I watched from the concrete pad. When the sun set, I lay back to look at the sky. Strings of light criss-crossed the air between the Tap and the dry cleaners, simple white bulbs, just beautiful. Maybe they seemed that way because they reminded me of the town square in Fort Carsen and Lissy, the only girl in the past year who hadn't left me with a pack of terrible memories, or maybe it's always beautiful to see a night sky laced up with white lights.

My father brought me a rough blanket from the car. When he arranged it over me, I meant to say thank you, but instead I blurted out, "I love you, Dad." He gave me a queer look. "You feeling okay?"

I wasn't, but what was I supposed to say? *I'm worried, Dad. If Jesus couldn't keep a secret, how am I supposed to?*

That question would have been enough to ruin a whole month for my father, so I told him I was a little tired, that's all, and faked a yawn, which turned into a real yawn.

"You want to go home?" he said, though his eyes said *Please say no.* I shook my head and he grabbed my neck, affectionately but hard. He was a little drunk. "Okay, buddy. You just let me know when you want to go."

Momo sang, and someone clanged the ladle around the punch tub to chase down the last cupful, and Woz passed out on a folding chair with his head cranked back like a Pez dispenser. I didn't want him to get in trouble for drinking, so I slipped off the pad, hooked him under the arms and dragged him to a dark spot by the dumpster. His neck was shiny with drool, and he smelled sweet as a pineapple. I had a strange urge to hold him, maybe rock him a bit—but I just leaned him up against the brick wall and tried to arrange him in a way that wouldn't give him neck cramps when he woke.

That was the last I saw of Woz. When I went to check on him later, he was gone, along with his bike. He slipped out of my life in the same quiet way I'd slipped out of his when I'd fallen in with Miss Dupay. This wasn't payback on his part, I'm sure; this is just how young dorks take their leave.

Not that my father's friends were much better at saying goodbye. All night long I watched men come up to him, smiling in mock outrage. "Thanks for abandoning me, asshole," one of them said. "Who's supposed to fix my slice now? Rick?"

My father grinned back. "I probably should have told you this before I took all your money for those lessons, but your swing is hopeless."

"Any last bit of advice?" another man asked.

"Yeah," said my father. "Take up handball."

None of these men said goodbye, not in so many words. *See you in the funny pages*, they said, *good luck down south, don't do anything I wouldn't do.* If they said anything as heartfelt as *Take care*, they paired it with *you crazy bastard.*

Momo kept playing until the party dwindled down to a half dozen friends who didn't look like they planned on leaving anytime soon, but finally he ran out of songs.

"What about *Puff the Magic Dragon*?" suggested Mish. "I don't know that one," said Momo, and Mish looked insulted. "What are you, a communist? Who doesn't know *Puff the Magic Dragon*?" Momo shrugged. He didn't, for one. Mish said, "Well, that's a huge oversight on your part, pal. If I had an accordion, that would be one of the first songs I'd learn. I'd make it a priority." Momo said, "Sometimes I wish you'd shut the hell up." Mish opened his mouth in an *O*, as though he were shocked, speechless, but then a sound came out of his mouth, a tuneful noise, and he was singing, slowly, like a lullaby.

*Bear down, Chicago Bears,*
*Make every play clear the way to victory.*

Other voices joined in. Arms looped around waists. A rough circle formed.

*Bear down, Chicago Bears,*

*Put up a fight with a might so fearlessly.*

Was this the only song everyone knew? Or was this the only one that seemed right for this bittersweet occasion? All I knew was that this circle was filled with all the heat and light and love left in the world, and I wanted to be a part of it, but I couldn't bring myself to climb down from the pad. I was tired and heavy with worry; joining that circle and acting joyful would be too big a lie, even for me. But I could watch.

From the pad, I beheld the beauty of these people. Heads down, slurring, crowned by white lights, they were glorious. When they sang *We'll never forget the way you thrilled the nation, with your T-formation*, a fight song had never sounded so wistful, so much like a lover's promise, so much like a farewell.


Here's how it ended, our last night in Paris.

At some point I fell asleep; I don't know if it was on the concrete pad or on the drive home. I remember my father lifting me out of the car and carrying me toward our porch, where the tip of a cigarette glowed in the darkness. "Tim...?" my mother said.

The cigarette pinwheeled onto the lawn.

"What took you so long?" called a man from the porch. "I've been standing here with my thumb up my ass for an *hour.*"

"Tim," my mother said. "What's going on?"

"It's okay," my father said, apparently to both of them. He was breathing hard, but whether it was from excitement or because I was heavy, I don't know. "It's all okay. You need a hand carrying in those crates?"

The man glanced at the two crates of rough wood by his feet, then shot my father a wry look. "I got them up here just fine, didn't I?"

"What *is* this?" my mother said, but no one answered her. My father just opened the door and went down the stairs, still carrying me under the legs like a bride. She pestered him every step of the way, but he wouldn't say a word, just hummed and smiled. I don't know if he had ever been on this side of suspense before, but clearly he was enjoying it.

In the basement, he laid me on the couch, kissed my mother on the cheek, then ran over to the light switch. What on earth was going on? I struggled up to watch the man set down the crates with a deep grunt. He rose and took a few leisurely drags from his cigarette, looking like he planned to take his time, enjoy that smoke and maybe one or two others, and if we had to wait as long as he'd waited for us, well, that would just be too damn—

"What's in the boxes?" my mother and I said at the same time.

Shaking his head, the man fished a slim jim out of his back pocket. "Heaven forbid you people should have to wait for anything."

The first crate popped open to reveal a nest of shredded newspaper. Then—miracle of miracles—the man fished out a 16mm projector.

"You *didn't*," my mother said.

My father looked at the floor, smiling like a maniac.

From the second crate, the man pulled out a windowshade screen and a couple of film reels. "This is the rough cut," he said. "I mean real rough, so don't expect great quality, okay?" He didn't say what was on the reels, but he didn't have to. This was *Return to Zombie Island*, the version that included my mother.

"Oh, Tim," my mother said, her voice a little muddy. My skin prickled. "Lights," said the cameraman, and my father turned off the lights and joined us on the couch, down by my mother. A private screening, close to my mother and father, lumped together on an old couch: I'll never find a more perfect theater.

Behind us, the cameraman blew out a thoughtful breath, sending a living ghost of smoke rolling along the ceiling, backstroking toward the screen, before breaking apart in rococo swirls. Numbers appeared on the screen, counting down.

I snuggled in close to my mother, ready for the beginning. For once, I wasn't worried about what would happen next.